# Always a Suspect

## by

## Susan Vaughan

*Task Force Eagle, Book 1*

# Dedication

For all those patient people who answered my many
technical questions about the DEA, hypothermia,
bombs, winter trekking, seafood sales, and Maine
Acadian culture: DEA Special Agent Pamela Hay,
Sherry Hosford, Jim Moore, Neal Guyer, Stan and Pam
Elliot, author Sylvie Kurtz, and the generous writers of
RWA. Many thanks and hugs to my Harlequin editor,
Patricia Smith, who guided me through the publication
process and made this a better book. And for my
husband, who believed then and still does.

# Dedication

For all those patient people who answered my many
technical questions about the DEA, hypothermia,
bombs, winter trekking, seafood sales, and Maine
Acadian culture: DEA Special Agent Pamela Hay,
Sherry Hosford, Jim Moore, Neal Guyer, Stan and Pam
Elliot, author Sylvie Kurtz, and the generous writers of
RWA. Many thanks and hugs to my Harlequin editor,
Patricia Smith, who guided me through the publication
process and made this a better book. And for my
husband, who believed then and still does.

Chapter One

MARIE CLAIRE SAINT-ANGE didn't look like a woman who could murder three men.

None of the articles Michael Quinn had read prepared him for his first glimpse of the woman the Weymouth, Maine, newspaper called the Widow Spider.

Although she had an oversize black cardigan wrapped around her tall, slender form, his gaze browsed sweetly rounded curves. Her black pants and turtleneck looked expensive. Wing-like waves of dark brown hair framed a sensuous face with big doe eyes and full lips.

His breath lodged somewhere south of his throat and his blood, south of his belt. Even on this winter day, his blood burned.

A man would have to be dead not to react to her sultry beauty. Was hers a face from heaven, as her name suggested? Or of a siren?

Of course neither Lizzie Borden nor Ted Bundy had looked like butchers. If facial features could label killers, who would need cops like him?

He mentally kicked himself in the butt. He would keep as distant from that female as possible. He'd come on business. Anything else could be a hell of a lot more dangerous. For him.

Talking to a bearded old man in a tattered parka, Saint-Ange stood in a cleared space on her snow-covered side porch. Michael closed the door of his SUV, parked behind a new black luxury one. Sweet wheels. The widow was doing all right.

She sketched a wave of greeting. He gave a nod of acknowledgment, and she continued her conversation.

He scanned the two-story white Victorian. Simple green wreaths with crimson bows on the door. Classy but not ostentatious. Not unlike the decorations on all the other large frame houses on the quiet street.

How did they feel at the Weymouth town office about their sleepy little Portland suburb harboring a sexy serial killer?

Hoping to eavesdrop, he sauntered up the curving sidewalk to the porch. A gust of wind brushed the last clumps of new-fallen snow from tree branches and shrubs. The cold didn't bother him, but how could the woman stand it out here in just a sweater?

"Don't you fret none, Miz Claire," the old man said in his Down-East Maine accent. "Elisha Fogg's not too old for a few more years' shovelin'."

Unsmiling, she stared at him a long moment. Then she tilted her head in a uniquely French posture. "Certainly. But I won't pay you to shovel the porch. The wind will clear it soon enough. Go home, Elisha."

In contrast with her cold manner, her voice was throaty, with the musical lilt and pronunciation of her northern Maine Acadian background.

Old Elisha muttered what might have been "Yes, ma'am," then shuffled past Michael toward a decrepit old truck parked at the curb.

Odd that she'd cut corners on the snow shoveling when she'd spent big money on a new ride.

After watching the old truck chug away, Michael

frowned and turned, only to be struck dumb by eyes the color of dark chocolate. The intensity of her stare unnerved yet aroused him. Did she have any idea of the impact of that liquid gaze? Sure as hell, a woman like that was born knowing her power over men.

In the set of her shoulders he saw self-assurance and determination, and in her eyes intelligence and... vulnerability that woke the protective instincts he damn well thought he'd buried. The Widow Spider's confidence hung by a single strand.

"I assume you're the private investigator?"

He shook off his unwanted thoughts. "Yeah. Michael Quinn. Mr. Cunningham said you were expecting me."

"Come in, then. It's too cold to stand out here any longer." She opened the carved oak door. "Unless you're afraid. Did he tell you about me?"

Thinking of how she'd kept the old man out in the cold arguing and then stinting him on his pay, Michael scowled. "I know who you are. Cunningham gave me the newspaper clippings. After you."

Spine rigid as an icicle, she preceded him into the wide foyer. After setting two locks on the heavy door, she hung his coat and her sweater on a brass tree. To his left spread a gracious parlor bigger than his entire apartment, but she led him to a smaller living room on the right.

Close behind her, Michael inhaled a light herbal scent. Shampoo or lotion, not perfume, but just as arousing. He noted that her haughty rigidity didn't extend to her hips, which swayed with each step. Deliberate or she couldn't help it?

"Sit down, Mr. Quinn. This room will warm up in a

bit." She lifted a log from the wood box beside the hearth and fed it into the small high-tech wood stove set in the fireplace.

"Big house to heat that way." He regarded the camel-backed couch. Antique or a very expensive reproduction? An assessing glance at the other aspects of the room—gleaming dark wood, hand-carved paneling, marble-topped tables, Oriental rugs—convinced his inexpert eye the couch was an original.

The house wasn't merely renovated, as his sketchy file said. It ranked as a damn showplace ready for a magazine spread.

A partially decorated balsam fir that brushed the ceiling and neatly stacked boxes of ornaments filled the large front window. Unusual that a rich widow like her didn't have the Christmas decorations done professionally.

He eased into a green wing chair near the hearth.

"The furnace does its job, but I prefer the ambience of wood heat." She sat opposite him in a twin of his chair.

She wore little or no makeup, no adornments of any kind. He wouldn't mind tasting the natural red of her lips. In the warmth of the lamplight, her dewy skin, like that of a young girl, belied the thirty odd years he knew to be her age. Hands itching to touch her, he clasped his fingers on his knees.

He didn't want to be here, didn't like the feel of this case, didn't like coming into it less prepared than usual. From the onset, something about it had sent cold tingles to the base of his skull. He sure as hell didn't want a case about a woman whose mere presence stirred everything male in him. But he had no choice.

Saint-Ange consulted a manila folder she slid from an adjacent small table. Her direct gaze heated his blood as if she'd stoked a fire in him instead of in the wood stove.

"Fitz tells me that until eight months ago, you were an agent for the Drug Enforcement Administration, based in Boston. One of their best investigators. Why did you quit?"

He shrugged. "I'd had enough." Enough damned drug dealers, enough wallowing in greed and slime, enough misplaced emotional involvement. Enough failure.

This time he didn't have to care or feel responsible or protective. Didn't have to feel, didn't want to feel, period. His only stake in this case would be completing it and moving on.

She probably expected him to say more. Tough. "Why did you hire me?"

She clapped shut the folder. "I want you to clear me."

"Clear you." The tingling again. He rubbed his nape. He hoped to God she didn't need protection. Given his track record, no one should trust him to protect a snow cone. "But I understood you've never been charged with anything."

In a very feminine gesture, she tossed her hair back.

Damn, but she was beautiful. If she ever let herself smile, if she ever smiled at *him*, he'd erupt into a fireball. He was already having a hell of a time keeping cool.

"Officially, no. But by every other means—in the press and in everyone's eyes—I've been charged, convicted, and sentenced."

"You're innocent, of course." He couldn't prevent an accusatory tone.

Shoulders straight, she glared at him. "You can think whatever you want, Mr. Quinn. Few believe in my innocence. Though Fitz has been my financial adviser for years, sometimes I think even he doubts me. The police are chasing a cat with five paws trying to prove I killed those men. I've hired you to find the truth of how each died, so I can live in peace."

Her gaze held pride and strength, but underneath he detected a sadness that didn't jibe with what little he'd read about her. Innocent? Or acting?

The last death had occurred eleven months ago. A long time to wait before seeking help. Did she aim to make herself look good by hiring a P.I.?

He ran a hand across the back of his neck. "Seems to me you've held up okay under media and police pressure. What makes now any different?"

Abruptly, she shot to her feet and strode to the side window. Her dark hair fell in thick waves to the middle of her back. He waited while she searched for words.

Claire struggled against the burning in her eyes. This man challenged her control. The flinty cynicism and the brooding eyes, gray and implacable as the granite they resembled, sliced through her protective shield. That he might dislike or even fear her shouldn't bother her. Usually she cultivated that reaction. It shouldn't matter how shabby her treatment of poor old Elisha appeared, but for some reason, it did.

Aloofness and a prickly attitude served her well. It did double duty in protecting the old man's pride and his back at the same time.

Confronted by this scowling man, she drew from the strength of character instilled in her by the *tantes*.

Gazing anywhere but at him, she spoke with forced calm. "In their desperation to pin something—anything—on me, the police are questioning my aunts in Fort Kent, in northern Maine. I grew up there, in the St. John Valley, where the culture is Acadian French and Catholic. From birth, I spoke French and English interchangeably. Almost as a litany, my aunts have always told me that the tragedies in my life have been sent by *le bon Dieu*, by the good Lord, as a curse or a sort of trial by fire. I don't want them burned by the flames."

"A curse?" He cleared his throat. "Weren't they interrogated before?"

"You don't understand. *Tante* Odette and *Tante* Rolande raised me. They're very old now, in their late eighties, and fragile." She faced him again.

Like a block of New England bedrock, he sat quietly, awaiting her explanation. Under six feet tall, he appeared larger because of his stocky, muscular frame. He emanated banked power, the coiled force of a warrior.

She drew a deep breath. "That state detective, Pratt"—she spat the name with venom—"asked them about my parents. Bringing up their deaths will only distress them and serve no purpose."

"Your parents? How did they die?"

Would he suspect her for that as well? The bad seed. The idea left a taste as harsh as the ashes in the stove.

She sat again. With quivering fingers, she straightened the magazines on the end table, fanning them like playing cards. "I was ten. We all contracted a bacterial infection, E. coli, from some contaminated meat. By the time *Tante* Odette persuaded them to see a doctor, it was too late. I had eaten only a bite or two, so I lived."

His gaze ran over her with cool appraisal. "And you went to live with your aunts after that?"

"Until I finished high school. They lived nearby, together. Neither ever married. I was a chick with two mother hens." She left her chair and knelt to stir the fire, which had warmed the room, and glanced back at him as he cleared his throat.

"Two French hens." His lips twitched toward a smile.

The poker fell from her hand. Quinn caught it easily before it marred the hardwood floor. When he extended the fire tool to her, their hands brushed.

Claire started, seared as if by his body heat. But that was silly. Averting her gaze, she prodded the flaming logs.

He hesitated a moment, as if waiting for a reply to his jest, then continued, "Then you moved here to live with your cousin. Is that right?"

"No, I had money for two years of college. I came to live with Martine and her family after that."

"To help with the small children. You met Jonathan Farnsworth, your first husband, then. He was Martine's stepson."

She nodded. "You sound like a cop interrogating a suspect, Mr. Quinn. I thought I hired you to cross-examine others about my case, not me."

How could he sit there so impassively stripping her layers of protection with his questions? She went to stand at the mantel and lined up the five brass candlesticks from shortest to tallest.

For so long, she'd held in her feelings, kept herself strong and detached. It was the only way to survive the losses and the censure, the taunts and the threats. Revealing her main reason for hiring him would expose her fears, her weakness. She had to preserve her strong image.

No longer could she drift along, waiting for her waking nightmare to end. No longer could she hope it would all go away. So she'd telephoned Fitz about hiring an investigator.

"To find the truth, Ms. Saint-Ange, as you requested," he said, "I'll need to know everything, including your side of the story. The news clippings were lacking in anything but sensationalism and innuendo."

Quinn leaned forward, as if ready for combat. The layered sinews of his thighs strained the khaki fabric of his trousers. Muscles bulged beneath his collarless denim shirt. His imposing physique and harshly carved features must have instilled terror in drug dealers.

"Mr. Quinn—"

"Just Quinn. Or Michael," he said. "Mr. Quinn is my father."

Michael was too familiar. But Fitz had assured her he could be trusted. She had no one else. "Quinn, then. I need your help, but don't ask me to relive those memories in excruciating detail."

He levered himself from the deep confines of the wing chair and loomed above her more imposing than before, and more intimidating. His chestnut-brown hair brushed his collar and threatened to flop onto his forehead. His square face wasn't handsome, but was nevertheless compelling in its intense maleness and strength.

Disliking his imposing stance, she rose, but not without a warm flutter of reaction. *Mais non*, she couldn't allow herself to be attracted to him, to any man. It wasn't safe.

"If I don't have the facts," he said, "I'm no good to you. Detail the deaths for me, or find someone else."

His uncompromising tone set her back a pace. "You can get the whole story from the police files. Here's the detective's phone number and the address of his Portland office." Claire plucked a slip of paper from her folder.

For the first time, she noticed that the bronze cast to his skin left white crinkles around his eyes. A tan, not merely a swarthy complexion. Curious.

"Fine, if all you want me to know is their side of things. If I work for you, shouldn't I have yours?"

Slumping inwardly, she accepted his logic. "All right, Quinn. Sit down. I'll go through it for you." She lined up the folder with the magazines on the table. No need to consult it. She knew the events by heart.

From a pocket, he extracted a small notebook and pen. "Just the basic chronology for now," he said softly. "We can fill in the details later."

Had this blunt man with his strong, blunt face actually yielded because of her distress? In his gaze, she perceived a gleam that belied his obvious dislike of her. Not her distress, but her beauty influenced him.

Her beauty, her curse, one and the same, as if she needed a reminder. Attraction led to tragedy.

*The curse of your beauty is to be alone.*

"All I really know," he continued, "is that over the last seven years, three men connected to you died."

Steeling herself against the painful retrospection, she said, "Yes, the first two deaths were accidents, or at least appeared accidental. My first husband, Jonathan Farnsworth, died in an automobile accident on a narrow coastal road."

"Was there another vehicle involved?"

"No. He went over a cliff." She knew her voice sounded robotic, but recitation staved off an emotional onslaught.

"And the next?" He flipped to the next notebook page.

"My second husband, Paul Santerre. He drowned while out on his yacht. Again alone."

"But it wasn't until the third man died five years later that the cops stepped in?"

Drenched in memories, she nodded. "That was when Alan Worcester died in an avalanche at Caribou Peak Ski Resort. Avalanches are extremely rare in Maine, so they were suspicious." The state police, the entity charged with investigating homicides in the state of Maine, had accused her of murder. *Three murders.* She shuddered.

"But they didn't find enough solid evidence of foul play in any of the three deaths to incriminate you."

"No, nor anyone else. Jonathan's father is very influential with both the press and the authorities, so they continue trying, probing, prying." She lifted a shoulder in an attempt at dismissal. "The most damning link to me was that I'd been married to the first two men and engaged to the third."

"I'll go now." He got to his feet once more. "And

contact Pratt today. Once I've read the official reports, I'll come back."

She accompanied him to the hall, where she retrieved his bulky coat.

"Talk to Detective Lieutenant Pratt," she said. "Read their stacks of files. Fill in the gaps. Then we'll begin our investigation."

He pivoted at the open doorway. "What did you mean, *we'll* begin investigating?"

His powerful masculine presence unnerved her, but she wouldn't be cowed. She folded her arms. "I'm paying you well for this case, Quinn. I will accompany you on interviews. We share all information."

"No way, lady." He shook his big head, like a bull preparing to charge. "You've hired me to investigate. I'll do just that and report back. I work alone, not with a damn partner, especially a client."

Claire thrust out her chin and drilled him with a glare. "Over the past months, people have accused me of horrible things. The media sensationalized the case, vilified me. They called me many names, Widow Spider and Bloody Mary the *least* offensive. It's my life at stake. As long as you're working for me, I'm your damn partner."

Chapter Two

ONCE HIS EXPLORER rounded the corner out of sight of the widow's house, Michael pulled over to the curb. He managed to peel his fingers from the steering wheel, a stand-in for the woman's throat.

With that bitchy attitude, how did she ever get three men to fall for her?

Damn, he knew how. Even when she snarled at him, he wanted his hands on her. And not to strangle her. Before that, in spite of himself, he'd even attempted flirtation with that asinine remark about the French hens.

Hell. She would be in his face the whole time. And he had no one to watch his back. Maybe talking to the relatives of the men she'd murdered would shake her off. How much of that could she take? How tough was the Widow Spider?

He punched buttons on his phone and waited. When a familiar voice answered, he barked, "Yo, Cruz, couldn't you have found some other damn sucker for this job?"

" 'Come into my parlor,' " said the spider to the fly. "Did the lady put the moves on you, *mano*?" Ricardo Cruz often used the Cuban vernacular for brother.

"No, I wish to hell it was that simple. She wants to be my damn partner." Michael shoved his fingers through his hair, longer than usual. Between getting yanked off the mountain and showing up here, he'd had no time to get it cut.

"What do you mean? She believed your cover story about quitting the DEA and becoming a P.I., didn't she?"

"I did quit the DEA," Michael protested.

"Paperwork, buddy, red tape. Nothing's official without it. You were on leave. Boss called you back because we had no one else available for undercover."

Maybe. Their Group Supervisor might be delaying his resignation on purpose. "The GS could be getting back at me for my last... snafu."

"He's done some weird things lately, but it's more likely he doesn't want to lose a man of your talents."

His friend's unfailing optimism did nothing to erase Michael's cynicism. His response was a one-word epithet.

Cruz chuckled. "So, did she buy your undercover ploy or not?"

"No problem there. But after what she's been through, the widow's savvy and skeptical. She trusts no one to investigate for her. She wants in on every move."

"The lady's just made your job a hell of a lot more interesting." Cruz chuckled. "Unless you're afraid."

She'd asked him that too. Shit. "The file you gave me is thin enough to floss with. What's the DEA's stake in this?"

"Since your attention's likely to be as short as your temper, I'll condense," Cruz said cheerfully. "We had a team closing in on hubby number two, Santerre. He ran a cool smuggling operation for our old enemy El Águila. Picked up shipments of drugs offshore in his boat and drove them to Boston in his seafood truck."

"Stuffed lobster, huh?"

"Your weird sense of humor shows up at the oddest times, partner. Anyway, the team was about to pick him off when he conveniently died. Then after a few months' hiatus, drug traffic from this area rose again."

"So even though the bereaved widow sold the seafood company," Michael said, "you think she might be carrying on his other business."

"She still owns the powerboat. She must have known what hubby was up to, where all that money came from."

Michael still didn't like the setup. "Did she kill them or didn't she? Murder's not the DEA's business, and shadowing the widow's a piss-poor way to catch drug smugglers. How does she ship the stuff south if she doesn't own the damn seafood business anymore? Why the hell didn't the GS plant an agent there instead?"

"Yeah, well, he thinks your gig might work. Just do your job. You owe me."

Michael punched End Call, wishing for the luxury of slamming down a receiver.

He did sure as hell owe Cruz. Big time. Rick had saved his skin twice. Once literally in a darkened warehouse when a Mexican hit man, courtesy of El Águila, jumped him from behind. Later, Rick covered for him when his double failures sent him off the deep end.

Thank God the deal didn't include guarding the widow. He wasn't the person to rely on for protection. The last people who counted on him died.

He owed Cruz all right. So Michael would figure

out how to conduct an investigation while trying to keep his *partner* happy.

Was the Widow Spider a drug dealer as well as a murderer? A murderer whose languid walk and bedroom eyes had already mesmerized her next potential victim.

Cocaine and heroin brought in a hell of a lot more profit than scallops and clams. And the widow lived well.

Whether he liked it or not, he sat smack dab in the middle of the widow's web.

****

Claire stood a moment in the hallway. Her left foot tapped with the same rapid rhythm as her heartbeat. Quinn was supposed to be a good investigator. The best, Fitz had said. But she didn't know if she could tolerate working with him long enough to achieve her goal.

Arrogant *chameau*! No, not a camel, a bull, and bull-headed. But she didn't fear him. She held to her demand in spite of his outburst. If fear didn't cause her pulse to race, it must have been the excitement of finally taking action. Surely that was it.

He'd stomped away like a raging bull pawing the ground. "We'll see," he'd said, about her working with him.

"Yes, we'll see."

She checked the double locks on her front door before walking to the back of the house and through the swinging door to the kitchen. Dog claws clattered across the tile floor. "Alley, how are you, little one?" Claire checked the back door lock. Then she knelt to pet the wriggling mixed-breed. "You can come out now and help me decorate the tree."

Pointed ears alert, the little tan dog pranced ahead of her. A year after the amputation, Alley trotted around on three legs with the agility of most dogs with four. She sniffed the boxes of ornaments before settling on the hearth rug to supervise, a tongue-lolling grin on her whiskery muzzle.

Claire smiled at the dog's approval. The short winter afternoon having been transformed into evening, she pulled down the living room shades and checked the window locks. After plugging in the lights, she lined up the boxes. She lifted the lids and placed each one beside its box.

From the tissue paper in a large white box, she withdrew a small needlepoint Christmas tree, embroidered with "Jonathan & Claire." A lovingly crafted gift from *Tante* Rolande for their first—and only—Christmas together. Clutching it, she nearly sobbed. How could she bear to hang all these memories again?

Why should she? Resolved, she replaced the lids on the boxes.

"This year, Alley, we'll hang only new ones. Crimson balls and gold stars and silver snowflakes. What do you think, little one?"

The dog's tail thumped agreement.

She consulted the mantel clock. Five-thirty. If the Weymouth Hardware Store was still open, she could buy them now, and the snow blower she'd noticed in their ad. Then she wouldn't have time to change her mind and let the burden of her curse stop her from storing the mementos. From hiding them.

She whisked to the kitchen to telephone the store.

She'd just located the listing in the directory when the house phone rang.

Please, *mon Dieu*, no. She hesitated, her hand hovering within inches of the phone. She really ought to get rid of this landline. With trembling fingers, she snatched up the receiver.

Only silence answered her greeting.

****

Slogging through the state's Major Crime Unit files on Marie Claire Saint-Ange for the next few days ate up most of Michael's time.

Detective Sergeant Pratt sneered at the idea of cooperation, but MCU policy dictated that the state police had to give the feds anything they wanted. After his lieutenant insisted, Pratt slammed down the folders and left Michael alone in an interview room.

Finally, Michael closed the last folder and laid it on top of the rest. He didn't know how many pages of reports and computer printouts he'd read, but they stacked up twice as high as the large foam cup holding his coffee, now as cold as this case.

He stared at the opposite wall, a drab tan with not even a bulletin board for relief. MCU headquarters in Augusta was like any police offices—drab cubicles, drab metal desks surrounded by drably painted walls. A stimulating workplace, about like the DEA offices.

He stood and rolled the stiffness from his shoulders. Man, he wished himself back in the White Mountains. He didn't know how the hell the DEA found him in his wilderness camp.

"You done with my files, Quinn?" the detective said from the open doorway. A smirk on his lined face, he swaggered into the room.

"Your files, Pratt? Not official MCU files?"

"Mine more than anyone else's. Took a bucket loader to dig up all that info years after the fact." Pratt straightened his electric-blue tie over the matching shirt, cheap imitations of the clothes worn by last season's TV cops. He hiked up his pants and tried to tuck in his gut, but too much beer and fried clams made that impossible. Pratt was a competent, middle-aged, balding cop whose frustration with this case turned him nasty.

"Info, yes," Michael said, "evidence, maybe. You haven't got enough to pin on a gnat and you damn well know it."

"Maybe, but the DEA has a hell of a lot less, or you wouldn't be here raiding my files. Just why's the DEA snooping into this, anyway?"

Michael arched one eyebrow.

"Yeah, yeah, I get it. Official business." Pratt scooped up the folders and held them propped on his belly. "She did it, all right. She plotted it out like a damn movie script, murdered all three men in cold blood. And one day I'll prove it."

Michael snagged his parka from the back of his chair. "I'm finished for now, but I want a copy of those files. I need to study every angle and all the players."

Pratt wouldn't notice that one folder was missing a few sheets, now stowed carefully in an inside parka pocket. Michael would analyze them further before he returned to the widow.

The detective gaped at him. "The entire damn thing? That'll take some time. We're not exactly overstaffed here."

No sense butting heads. "I'd appreciate anything

you can do, Pratt. I see you've done a straight-up investigation." He headed for the door.

The detective sucked in his cheeks. "We try. If nothing else, by putting the bitch in the spotlight, we've prevented more deaths. 'Course, she hasn't been involved with another man. Until now."

At that, Michael turned back from the hallway. "Until now? That wasn't in the files. Who?"

Pratt spat into the metal wastebasket. "You."

Chapter Three

WHEN THE DOORBELL rang, Claire hoped it was Quinn. It better be. Who else would visit her this morning? Or any time? Old Elisha was her only caller, and only because of their business arrangement.

She saved her current desktop file. Concentration and inspiration eluded her, anyway. Since the phone calls began and even more since Quinn's interview three days ago, she found her thoughts focusing on her problems instead of the work that used to provide escape from them. With a sigh, she rose from the desk.

A quick glance told her everything lay in order—paper clips and pencils in their organizer, reference books side by side, evenly stacked printouts beside them. She gave cursory consideration to closing the program. No, Quinn had no reason to snoop in there.

Sliding closed the pocket door to the former dining room, she tucked a loose curl back into the single braid down her back and strode to the front door.

"Quinn. I expected you sooner."

He pantomimed tipping a hat. "Ms. Saint-Ange."

She wanted to maintain distance, reveal as little of herself as possible, but something about this man complicated that. He loomed as large as she recalled. Too imposing. Too male. Too attractive in a rugged sort of way. "Was the file on me that massive, or did Pratt keep you cooling your heels?"

"Detective Sergeant Pratt had no reason to cooperate with a private snoop. It took calling in a few favors and some time to gain access to the files." He draped his parka on the coat tree.

"Have you decided how to begin?"

"I'll check out Paul Santerre's boat—" he consulted his small notebook "—the *Rêve* something, but I want to talk to you first." His commanding tone rendered it more than a request.

"The *Rêve de coeur*. It means 'heart's dream' or 'heart's desire.' And I'll take you to the boatyard once we've talked."

"I said before that I work alone." A fierce scowl drawing his brows together, he spoke in a rumbling timbre that slid up her spine. "It's bad policy to take clients along on an investigation."

She cleared her throat, both to shake his strange effect on her and to ready herself for combat. She folded her arms. "I understand that, but I insist."

"In your case, I see why you're anxious, and there seems to be little danger."

"So why can't—"

He held up a hand. "Here's the deal. You can come along, but I'm in charge. I conduct the interviews, backgrounders, searches, whatever. You observe, take notes if you want, but keep your mouth shut."

Shocked that he didn't challenge her escort further, she found no words, merely inclined her head in acknowledgment. He didn't seem like a man who'd yield easily, who'd give in at all, but she wouldn't question his about-face now.

A glance took in his dark blue corduroys and knit shirt. The open collar revealed a smattering of tautly curled hairs, as crisp as the man himself.

She felt his gray eyes on her, and the warmth of unwanted awareness feathered through her. She gestured toward the living room. "You might as well call me Claire. Have a seat. If you like, I'll go make us some coffee."

"Coffee would be good." One side of his mouth quirked, but the flinty eyes showed no humor.

"We'll need wood for the stove. I haven't used the living room this morning."

Rather than question his attitude, Claire hurried from the room. In the refuge of her kitchen she could regroup her defenses against this man.

"I'll carry the wood," Quinn said from behind her.

She stifled a gasp.

His demeanor was pleasant, but his gaze surveyed every detail of the modern renovations—custom mahogany cabinets in a Victorian style, granite countertops, European appliances, her display of French tin dessert molds that replaced the original oil painting Paul had hung.

Did Quinn intend to snoop all through her house? And through her life? Is that why he consented to her working with him? She shook off the suspicions. Because of her problems, she saw bogeymen everywhere.

After a low whistle, he said, "Mighty fancy kitchen."

"Paul insisted." She fisted her hands at her side. How could she protect herself against his compelling presence if he invaded her space like this? "I believe I invited you into the living room, not my kitchen."

"Pull in your stinger… Claire. I'm not out to get

you. This is just a job. Since you insist on our working together, we might as well be cordial. Is the woodpile out here?" A grim set to his mouth, he stalked to the back door.

On a sigh, she nodded. "I'll show you." She stepped into her lined boots and led the way through the small covered back porch and down the steps into the snow-blanketed yard.

No new snow had fallen, but the leaden clouds and the cold remained. Unusual in southern Maine, snow this early in December, perhaps a harbinger of the winter. Plenty of snow for the ski areas.

A shiver skittered over Claire's arms. After last winter's tragedy, she wasn't sure she'd ever ski again.

A spate of happy yips greeted them. Bright-eyed and curious, Alley pranced up to her mistress. She diligently sniffed Quinn's shoes and trouser legs, then sat and offered him a canine smile.

The severe line of Quinn's mouth softened and he knelt. "Yo, pup, you're a friendly one. What's your name?"

Her small head seemed swallowed by the surprisingly gentle caress of his wide hand.

An image of that blunt-fingered hand on her breast flashed into Claire's mind. She blinked it away and wondered how his hands—along with all the rest of him—became so muscular. Not a question she could ask him.

Alley always barked and growled at newcomers, especially men. Claire counted on her pet's protective nature to intimidate Quinn, to distance him. *Quelle blague*, what a joke. She turned away so Quinn wouldn't see her shock.

"Her name's Alley." Claire willed indifference to Quinn's liking her dog, and vice versa. "I thought we were out here for firewood. It's over here."

Behind the porch, cordwood towered in three even rows, the first as high as Claire's head. Trying to ignore him, she grabbed two logs.

Inexplicably, he pounded on the middle of the first row. "This one's about to topple," he said. "It's way too high for such a narrow pile. I suppose that old man stacked these."

His critical tone rankled. She'd stacked them herself, even if Quinn thought she imposed on old Elisha. There weren't enough logs for a fourth stack, so she'd piled it high.

"It's not as precarious as you think." She slammed another log atop her load.

"Here." He relieved her of her burden, "I can carry a lot more than you. Heap me up."

She didn't want to hand him the logs, to be that close to him, to feel the heat of his body, to risk brushing against his hard form. But he was right. He could carry more.

When she complied, he continued, "Nice dog. What happened to her leg?"

"Someone took her to the animal shelter, her left hind leg badly mangled. I don't know where she'd come from, but they found her in a back alley. Must have nursed her wound for days, poor thing. The vet had to amputate." She deposited one final log atop the pyramid in his arms. "There, that's enough."

He followed her into the house. "They found her in an alley, so you named her that?"

"It seemed appropriate." He was the first person to

understand that fact. Others thought the name some French derivation.

Claire closed the door behind him, and then slipped out of her boots, leaving them in the boot tray beside the door.

"Do you still want coffee?" She didn't meet his gaze.

"I do. I'll build the fire." Quinn carried his load toward the living room.

Busying herself with the grinder and the drip coffeemaker, she fought to suppress her awareness—heat suffusing her blood, heart hammering. She'd buried all that, hadn't she?

But her insides softened to pudding at the sight of Quinn's broad shoulders and rugged face.

*Mon Dieu*, not him, of all people.

"Anything I can do to help?"

At the rumble of his deep voice close behind—*again*—she bobbled the two coffee mugs she was removing from a high shelf.

Instantly, his arms surrounded her. Quinn caught one mug, and she the other.

"You sure spook easy." Remaining with his arms caging her, he set the cup on the granite counter.

"I'm not accustomed to having people sneak up on me," she said between gritted teeth. She pivoted to face him.

His glower matching hers, his sandy brows beetled.

Glaring at him was both easy and difficult because he didn't budge. Arms as hard and thick as marble pillars still bracketed her. His wide torso, oozing heat and power from every pore, blocked her.

She smelled the fresh scent of his soap. If she

advanced a millimeter, her breasts would brush his chest. Before she was tempted to do that or more, she leaned against the counter's sharp edge.

"Did you really come out here to offer help?" she said. "Or did you think I'd dump arsenic in the cream?"

"Isn't it only husbands and fiancés you kill?"

In her overactive imagination, his hard arms closed in on her like walls. Her heart tripped on itself at the pure sexual current flowing through her.

*Eh bien*, nothing pure about it.

"No cream," he continued in that mesmerizing voice, "just sugar, but maybe you make coffee the French way. What is it—café something?"

"Café au lait."

His gray eyes gleamed with light, lasers that seemed to see inside her. If so, he knew how his nearness affected her.

"You're in my way. The coffee's ready." She tipped her head toward the coffeemaker.

With a mocking nod, Quinn sidestepped as if opening a door.

With what dignity she could muster, Claire swept across the room. She poured the steaming brew, and then placed the mugs on a silver tray aligned with the cream and sugar.

"Look," Quinn said, "scrap all the fuss. This is no tea party." Before she could lift the tray to carry it to the other room, he snatched a mug, dumped sugar in it and stirred it briskly. Risking a scalded mouth, he gulped a third of the steaming brew.

Three spoons of sugar. A sweet tooth in such a disciplined man surprised and amused her. Maybe for quick energy on those midnight stakeouts to catch philandering husbands. Or murderers.

She sipped her coffee halfheartedly. She didn't want to be cooped up with this man in a cozy living room. "Suppose we drive to the harbor while we talk?" she said.

"Suits me." He downed the remainder of his coffee. "I haven't lit the fire yet. Let's go."

Before she could reply, he marched to the hall for his parka.

He agreed so quickly; did he need space too? Not that a moving vehicle meant space. She donned her own coat and boots. When the telephone rang, she ignored it and locked the door behind her.

"You have an answering machine to get that?" Quinn asked from the walkway.

"Yes, or they'll call back if it's important. Probably a telemarketer." If it was *him*, he wouldn't leave a message. She wanted to know Quinn better before she told him about the calls, two more since his first visit.

## Chapter Four

ONCE OUTSIDE IN the crisp air, Michael wrested his control back into place. Waiting in the drive, he watched his *employer* stroll toward him. It wasn't the kitchen's roasted coffee aroma that had him salivating like a starving man outside a bakery shop window, but the languid sway of the widow's hips in the slinky black skirt that molded to every curve.

He'd used his offers of help as an excuse for scoping out more of this showplace house. Then when he'd snatched the falling coffee mug, he couldn't move away from her. From her herbal scent. From her soft curves outlined in a fluffy black sweater—close enough to touch. From her fathomless eyes, wide with awareness—or maybe fear.

Why the hell would she be afraid of him? Damn! Was it that easy? Is that how she sucked in those other men? Not him. It was only a fleeting impulse. What he'd needed was that coffee. Hot and strong.

His assignment was to learn as much about her as he could, but that compromised his personal goal of maintaining distance. Hell of a situation.

He tore his gaze from her. Decked in the reds and greens of the season, two-story Victorian and colonial homes sat solidly on both sides of the street in this well-to-do Portland suburb. Across street, a tan luxury sedan rolled into the driveway of a stately colonial. A fur-covered woman slid out, eyed Michael and Claire with tight-lipped disapproval, then dashed into the house without a backward glance.

Claire made her careful way toward him down the icy walk. A long black quilted coat hid her curves, to his relief and regret. Did she wear nothing but black? Black slacks, black sweater, black skirt.

Widow's weeds or camouflage?

Her gaze straight ahead, Claire revealed her tension at the woman's shunning only in the tight grip on her purse. Michael would bet the knuckles hidden beneath her leather gloves were bone white. A pariah in her own neighborhood.

He didn't like the twinge that idea gave him. No emotional involvement. He couldn't handle it or the tragedy it might lead to. His cop's brain called that faulty logic, but, damn, objectivity was necessary.

Besides interfering with his methods, having her accompany him every step of the investigation would damn near tie him in knots. Cruz said that, for some unfathomable reason, the boss insisted he comply with her request. Not only had he stepped into the widow's web, now he was going to wrap himself in its sticky strands.

After holding the door for Claire, he eased into his seat, started the ignition, and backed out of the driveway.

"The police reports said the wind came up while your second husband was out on the *Rêve de... de*, on the *Rêve*." Keeping the conversation on the case would maintain distance. "How savvy was Paul on the bay?"

His peripheral vision caught her nod.

"He grew up lobstering with his dad," she said.

"Once he bought the *Rêve*, he went fishing when he wasn't using it for business. Paul knew these waters as well as anyone."

"Did you ever go with him?" What he really wanted to ask was more intimate. Like if she'd loved him... or Jonathan. But was it a question for the case or for him? "Where were you that day?"

"What you mean is, what's my alibi." Acerbity tinged her voice. "I hardly ever went out with him. And that day in August, I was in South Portland, at the university library." Her laugh rang as bitter as her words. "No one can vouch for me. I spent the day in the reference room. Didn't check out a book or ask for help."

Before he could inquire why she was at the university, she said, "Here's the harbor. Drive down the hill and turn left. There, the red metal building to your left. That's Greavey's Boatyard. The *Rêve* is stored there."

He turned into a slush-covered gravel parking lot and stopped. The day's damp cold hung over Weymouth Cove in a veil of fine mist. No pleasure craft and only a few fishing boats sat at their moorings.

Claire led the way across the sloppy expanse to a door in the lower side of the massive storage shed. A man stood at the window of a small office wing attached to the larger building. She glanced toward the man, who nodded in acknowledgment.

Inside the metal building, the air seemed colder, damper, sharp to the nose. One wall contained open slots, like giant mailboxes, for smaller outboards. Larger sail and power craft, like the *Rêve*, stood around the cement floor propped up on metal stands or on boat

31

trailers. At the far end of the cavernous structure a power sander whined.

"They don't mind owners going in," Claire said. "Some are in here all winter working on their boats."

"Not you?"

He'd thought the boat was still in the water. If the widow were involved with the drug smuggling, she sure wasn't using the *Rêve* in that effort. There it sat, high and dry, propped securely on a framework.

"I hardly ever use it. In the spring, I'll probably sell her." Claire hugged herself against the cold.

Scanning its equipment and lines, Michael circled the sleek power yacht, which occupied one corner of the building. His only experience with boats came from Boston's commercial shipping, not luxury craft, yet he recognized quality when he saw it. The *Rêve* was forty feet of aerodynamic fiberglass, its superstructure bristling with electronics.

Was the sonar for locating fish or for skirting the Coast Guard to meet smugglers with bales of marijuana and bindles of crack cocaine?

"You can climb aboard," she said in a mechanical tone. "There's a ladder against the wall."

*Is it painful for you to be here? Did you love him?* Or was the strain in her voice because she'd killed him? But he said, "The file reported the prop was tangled in fishing line. His skiff must have overturned when he tried to free it."

"Yes." She came to stand beside him at the stern. "A scallop dragger found the boat farther out in Casco Bay than he usually went. Beyond the islands. Just drifting."

"And Santerre?"

"The skiff turned up a week later on the north shore of Great Chebeague Island. Paul's body, or what was left of him, was jammed beneath the wreckage." Her eyes looked as bleak as a winter sea, and just as mysterious.

"I'll wait outside." She headed to the exit.

Michael adjusted the ladder against the boat's hull and climbed up. A few minutes' superficial search turned up nothing except assorted compartments and bilge areas where contraband could have been stowed. He'd have to return with an evidence kit and without his *partner*.

Outside, he found Claire at the dock gazing at a lobster boat and its entourage of squabbling seagulls. Her herbal scent mingled with the tang of salt spray and seaweed.

Stick to business. "Tell me about Santerre," he said. "How did you meet?"

She flicked a sharp glance at him. "You've spent three days studying the police files, and you have to ask me that?"

He sighed and ran a hand over his hair. "Come on, Claire, the files aren't exactly a complete biography."

Her Gallic shrug, a lift of one shoulder accompanied by pursed lips in a sultry pout, expressed reluctant acquiescence. "Jonathan and Paul were best friends and roommates at Yale. I met both when they came home for Christmas their senior year." She made no effort to continue.

A little irritation might loosen her tongue. "Jonathan was your cousin's stepson. Convenient, living under the same roof. Seeing you traipse around in a negligee would jump-start any romance."

The image of her tousled and warm from sleep hardened him instantly. Damn.

"*Espèce de*—damn you, Quinn." She turned on him, fiery flecks burning in the depths of her eyes. "Don't make it into something sleazy."

He'd pushed her buttons for sure. Most of the time she spoke flawless English, albeit with a sexy Acadian lilt and some trouble with *th*, but emotion popped French phrases from her mouth.

"Then you tell it. Don't leave me room to infer."

She looked over the water for a moment, then nodded. "Jonathan and Paul invited me to a few parties with them during the holidays. When Martine could give me the evening off."

"They? You dated them both at the same time?"

When she shook her head, tendrils escaped from the long braid. Curls twined around her ear and begged for his fingers. Or his tongue. He stared deliberately at the lobster boat.

"No, not dating." A sign of her annoyance was that she spoke slowly and distinctly, as if to a child. "It wasn't like that. We were all three friends at first. The three of us went to parties together."

"But that changed."

"Yes. When they came home for the summer, a rivalry sprang up. It was… oh, tense. I should have seen it coming. They were rivals in everything—sports, academics. Both had scholarships."

"Did they actually fight over you?"

"No, for some reason, Paul backed off. By the end of the summer, Jonathan and I were engaged. A year later we were married. I didn't know until after Jonathan's death how much that hurt Paul. He concealed it well at the time."

Two buddies in love with the same desirable woman. That might have led to bloodshed. Perhaps it did, but not in the typical way.

Jonathan Farnsworth, son and heir of the town tycoon, versus Paul Santerre, son of a lobsterman. No contest. Did Santerre realize that? Is it why he backed off? "Did you love Jonathan?" Love the boy? When they met, he was only about twenty.

Her delicate chin trembled a beat before she controlled it. "Whatever I say, you'll believe what you want. Ask me for whatever facts you need to solve this, Quinn, but some things are too personal." She started toward the SUV.

Michael stepped in front of her. She'd have to navigate the slush to pass him. "As far as the cops are concerned, personal reasons are the key."

"I see Pratt told you his theory that I planned all three deaths from the start. He has no evidence to back that up."

"No evidence against anyone else, either."

"That's because he hasn't investigated anyone else. Only me." Her cheeks colored and her eyes narrowed. "*Merde!* Are you so obtuse you don't understand why I've hired you? Maybe Fitz was wrong about your abilities."

Michael drew a deep breath, recalling the financial statements he'd snitched from the police files. The only evidence of motive they had. "I'd bet a poll of every couple under forty in Weymouth would find fewer than ten percent with wills. Most young couples are thinking about a happy future together, not about dying."

"What are you getting at, Quinn?"

"Isn't it strange that all three men made out wills leaving everything they owned to you?"

"Coincidence." Her eyes snapped with fury and something else he couldn't decipher. "You're blocking my way again."

Her gaze lowered to his chest, as if she could bore her way through him. Then she wheeled and plowed into the slush.

With her second step, a patch of hidden ice sent her into a skater's glide. Her arms flailed as she tried to maintain her equilibrium. Then, out of control, she reeled sideways.

He caught her around the waist and pulled her tightly to his chest. He felt the warm puff of her breath and smelled the coffee she'd drunk. If he bent his head, he could kiss her soft red lips, temptingly parted. And damn, he wanted to. Even through layers of wool and insulation, the softness of her breasts penetrated to his body. The reaction in his loins was instant and intense.

And damned troublesome. Attraction could derail his assignment, blow apart the case. Control had always been his middle name. With her he couldn't trust himself.

Sympathy for her was plowing inroads into his natural skepticism, but now uncertainty set up a roadblock. His years as a cop and in the DEA had trained him to read people. Usually that didn't help him a hell of a lot with Claire. Just now, however, he observed the gamut of emotions on her usually wary features. Anger. Pain and pride. Desire and uncertainty. And more. Secrets hid in Claire Saint-Ange's dark eyes.

"In a span of seven years, you've moved from poor relation to one of the wealthiest women in Weymouth, living in what this Boston Southie thinks is a damn mansion." His voice sounded thick with desire. Could she tell?

"If that was a crime, they'd have locked me up long ago. Quinn, why are you—"

At that moment, a dark blue vehicle making a U-turn swung past them, spraying slush. When Michael realized that the sports utility vehicle might sideswipe them, he lunged away, dragging Claire with him.

A rental car. He couldn't be certain, but the three men inside appeared dark, maybe Hispanic. El Águila's men?

Mopping at her coat hem, Claire appeared not to notice the car's occupants. Were they attempting to contact her? Or attack her?

\*\*\*\*

When Claire recovered her composure, she allowed Quinn to hold her arm for the walk to his car. The sensation of his big hand on her elbow gave her an incongruous sense of security beyond mere physical support.

The careless driver had barely dampened her coat and boots. Her protective shell suffered far more damage.

Quinn seemed to relish baiting and badgering her about Jonathan and Paul, as if investigating *her*, instead of investigating *for* her. Both hot and cold glittered in his gunmetal eyes. He desired her as well as distrusted her.

In spite of annoyance at his accusations, she clutched at his rock-hard arms and melted against him after her misstep. What was it about him that roused her emotions so?

"Well, well, well. Looks like the Widow Spider's wrapping up her next victim."

At the voice, Claire looked up at the man beside the vehicle. There stood the last person she wanted to meet, even if he might have helpful information.

Hard and lean, with shoulders burly from a lifetime of physical labor, he looked younger than his seventy-odd years except for his ruddy, weathered face and sparse hair. If the expression in his eyes could kill, she'd be stretched out on the ice.

"Hello, Russ." Turning to Quinn, she said, "Michael Quinn, meet Russell Santerre, my former father-in-law. Russ bought Paul's business from me."

The two men didn't shake hands.

"Don't be fooled by her," Russ said to Quinn. "The female of the species *is* more deadly."

"Quinn is an investigator I've hired to look into Paul's and the others' deaths." Claire would not rise to his taunts. She would not.

Russ gazed at Quinn with interest. "Investigator, huh? Plain to see what you were investigating a few minutes ago." His mouth twisted.

Apparently seeing no point in explaining their embrace, Quinn said mildly, "I'm sorry for your loss, Mr. Santerre. I hope to uncover how Paul died. Will you answer some questions?"

He maintained his grip on her elbow. Could he feel her trembling? She understood Russ's antagonism, but that didn't keep her stomach from knotting. The warmth and pressure helped. Quinn's cool manner reassured her of his professional skill. As a bonus, judging from his reaction, it disarmed her father-in-law.

"O' course I want the whole truth, but I'm

surprised she does." Russ tucked his thumbs in the pockets of his quilted vest. Sour-faced, he leaned back against the SUV's tailgate.

"This is no place for an interview," Quinn said. "Is your office nearby?"

Russ snorted. "Office? Ayuh, you can come over to my office." He waved a callused hand toward the other side of the landing where a metal chimney puffed smoke from a cedar-shingled shed. Beside it stood a large refrigerated, straight-body truck, Paul's truck. "It's warm inside, at least."

When they fell into step beside him as they walked to Santerre Seafood, as the truck's sign proclaimed, Russ wheeled stiffly, belying his robust appearance, and raised one palm. "Whoa! Just you, mister. Not her. Not the Widow Spider."

Quinn slanted an I-told-you-so glance at her. But he said to Russ, "My client insists, Mr. Santerre."

"Ain't my problem." His chin jutted.

"I'll just have to tell her everything later."

"Russ, I'll listen only," she said. "Pretend I'm not there."

"Suit y'self, but you might hear things you won't like." With that, he stomped ahead of them to the shed.

Chapter Five

ONCE INSIDE, MICHAEL observed Claire slip to a small window overlooking the docks. Maybe keeping her back to the two men would restrain her and allow him to do what she'd hired him for.

"Ain't fancy, but it beats standing outside," Santerre said. "Belongs to the harbormaster. He lets me use it while I'm waiting for my suppliers."

Mooring buoys, rope coils, and cartons of motor oil and paint filled the corners of the tiny shed. Wood smoke mingled with the odors of old fish and new paint. The only other contents were a scarred wooden desk and a few folding chairs. If the drug smugglers had a base in Weymouth, this sure as hell wasn't it.

"Is that what Paul did? Did he use this shack?" Michael asked, keeping it friendly.

"Sometimes. Mostly Paul met the fishermen at sea in that boat of his. A real go-getter, my son. That way he could brag to the buyers about freshness."

"So he must have bought the *Rêve* for business reasons." Or the drug cartel bought it for him.

"Ayuh, had her built special. He hustled more business after that. Struck it rich. Seems like he—" Santerre's glance slid away as he dropped whatever he'd been about to say. He wiped a meaty hand across grief-filled eyes. Was it grief or was the man holding back something?

"But you let the fishermen come to you?"

"Have to. Sold my own boat when my arthritis got too bad to keep haulin'." He rubbed his hands together, then held them over the wood stove. The knuckles, weather-reddened, were swollen, the fingers twisted.

"Do you have a real office someplace? Or a warehouse?"

The older man responded with a derisive hoot. "My phone's my office, and the truck's my warehouse. Santerre Seafood's a one-man operation, mister."

"But you do a good business?" Michael prompted.

"Still have most of Paul's customers—restaurants and markets in Boston. Folks is always eager to buy Maine seafood." His gaze flickered away, and he bent to add wood to the fire. "It's a comfortable enough living, even if I don't make near the money Paul did. I got no need to work my butt off to buy fancy furniture and clothes for a grasping bitch. Didn't even take her husbands' names. Not Farnsworth's neither."

At the window, Claire stood motionless. If not for the tight set of her shoulders, he'd think she wasn't listening. Seeing her so determined to stay strong filled him with unwanted admiration. Later he'd ask her about the name.

"You think Paul worked that hard just to please his wife?"

"Damn straight. To please her. To win her. To keep her." His face contorted with vehemence.

Stiff-spined, Claire remained at her inconspicuous post but bowed her head.

Santerre continued, "You seen that big house young Jonathan Farnsworth set her up in, the one Paul renovated?"

"First-rate." Michael would rather steer the conversation another direction. "Did you see your son the day he died?"

The older man lowered himself onto one of the folding chairs. "He come over to the house for coffee before he took out the *Rêve*."

"Do you remember anything unusual about your conversation? Or about your son?"

"Unusual? Nope. Cops asked me the same thing."

"What did you talk about?"

"Hard to remember now. It was five years ago, you know." He scratched his head and glanced away. "He had a lead for some new supplier out on one of the islands. I think that's where he was headed that day. The day she whacked him over the head and killed him."

Michael stood and zipped his parka. "How do you account for that, Mr. Santerre? Can you suggest how Claire could have gotten on and off the *Rêve*? There's no trace of anyone with her description renting or borrowing another boat. An old seaman like you must have some ideas."

Claire turned slowly, her gaze glued to Michael, her cheeks pale.

"I've thought on it some, I admit," Santerre said. "Must've been a boat. Cops found nothing back then. But trying to track somethin' like that five years after a murder's like tracin' the course of a ship after the wake's disappeared."

Michael thanked him for his time and suggested that they would talk again.

On their way out, Claire continued to avoid her former father-in-law's gaze.

Had she feared what the old man might say? Could she be innocent and genuinely want to solve the crimes? Or did she hear what Michael heard between the old man's words?

Russell Santerre was hiding something.

****

"Stop! Stop here!" Claire shouted.

As soon as Michael slammed on the brakes, she dashed from the vehicle and charged up the drive as if to a fire. He scanned the area for signs of trouble, but saw nothing, not even smoke rolling from the rooftop. He watched her scoop up something dark from the middle of the pavement. Once she'd moved out of the way, he pulled in.

"What the hell's going on?" Once again, he wanted to strangle her. "You could've been hurt, jumping out like that. What a fool th—"

"Shh, you'll frighten him." Ignoring his tirade, she faced him, chin in the air.

"Who?"

"He was there in the drive. You almost ran over him." In her arms she cuddled a small black kitten, its matted fur tipped with ice. "*P'tit bébé*, he must be frozen." Her liquid tones rippled up Michael's spine. "Come in, Quinn. You can light that fire you laid."

The dog Alley greeted them at the door with whimpers and wags. Claire patted her and showed her the kitten, no more than a smudge of wet fur in her hands. With her mistress's reassurance, Alley sniffed, and then licked the newcomer.

Claire's soothing tones sent shock waves of lust through Michael. Fighting off that and other feelings he refused to examine, he strode to the wood stove.

In a few moments, she'd dried the foundling into a ball of fluff and tucked it into a cardboard box lined with towels. "I'll let him warm up, then give him some food."

She set the box beside her wing chair and sipped her reheated coffee. With her legs curled beneath her and the black, flowing skirt tucked around her rounded bottom and sleek legs, she resembled a kitten herself. A kitten with sharp claws, he reminded himself.

"How will you find the owner?" he asked over his steaming mug. The unspoken codicil to that question was that the neighborhood doors were barred to her. He sure wouldn't volunteer to go house to house. Hell, his dangerous attraction to her was making him grouchy. Maybe door-to-door canvassing wasn't a bad idea. A way to question the neighbors about her.

"*Mon Dieu*, I would like to find them." A flush stained her cheeks. "The people in the house behind mine moved away two weeks ago and left behind four kittens about six weeks old. I suppose they kept the mother cat. I don't understand that kind of casual cruelty."

"Four kittens?"

"This is the last one. I've been feeding them, leaving a dish of food on the back porch. One by one, they came to me."

"Where are the others?"

"At the shelter where I found Alley. Kittens are easy to place, especially at Christmas." Her mouth softened, and her eyes grew maternal. "But this one I shall keep."

"Your dog. They must have had plenty of healthy dogs at the shelter. Why choose a crippled one?"

She lifted one shoulder. "Let's say Alley chose me. They would have euthanized her unless someone adopted her and paid for the surgery." She stretched out her left arm to the pup in question, who nuzzled her hand. "I could afford it, and her situation was not unlike mine."

"Wounded and fighting for her life?"

Her mouth narrowed in a stricken expression. As if in response, Alley whined. Composing herself, Claire rose. Her skirt swirled up to flash a glimpse of shapely thigh. "I'll bring more coffee when I bring his tuna."

Alley trotted behind her.

After she left the room, Michael relaxed into the depths of his chair.

She'd done more decorating. A fir garland dotted with gold stars draped the mantel. The Christmas tree sparkled with gold, silver and red. More formal than the ones his boisterous family threw together, on hers, every star and ball was evenly spaced, but nice.

With Christmas only a couple of weeks away, his mom was probably baking her special Italian pastries, almond biscotti, and spice cookies, enough for an army. With his brothers' kids, they had at least a regiment. This Christmas would be tough for everyone. Agony for him to miss seeing them, but, hell, facing them would be worse. Especially this first holiday without their family elf.

The first Christmas without Amy.

The mug shook in his hands. Afraid it would shatter in his tight fingers, he set it beside his chair. He'd get through it. When this case was over, he'd return to his wilderness isolation. As a tough street kid headed the wrong way, he had turned in a new direction thanks to the same sort of survival experience. Now he counted on that and time to help dull the pain and the guilt of failure.

But for now he had this first Christmas to endure without any family. Only the Widow Spider. At least she kept him busy. Busy, and more.

He didn't want to like Claire Saint-Ange, didn't want to care about her. But today's events had brought out such contrasting facets of her personality. The passion in her duels with him, in her determination to find the truth, in her eyes when he held her. The courage to listen without flinching to Russell Santerre's accusations. The gentleness and patience to coax four abandoned kittens to trust her. The generosity and loneliness to adopt strays.

Strays. More than one. She hadn't allowed the handyman to shovel the porch, but Michael saw in her backyard a brand-new snow blower still bearing tags. He'd bet Fogg wouldn't bend his frail old back over a shovelful of snow again. And her attachment to the three-legged dog was real.

The episode with the kitten sliced through Claire's antagonism where his clumsy challenges had failed. No matter her lush beauty, she hadn't lured three men into marriage with a prickly personality. He'd bet his sub-zero sleeping bag that she recently cultivated her hostility as protective coloration.

Hostility worked for him too, as a defense against her beauty and courage. Involvement with the target? Bad idea in more ways than he cared to list. Here it was barely noon on the second day he'd ever seen her, and his libido threatened to compromise his mission. Dangerous Curves Ahead signs should be posted all over that woman.

This assignment didn't require Gestapo tactics, but either he attacked her or he kissed her until they both couldn't breathe. And if he kissed her, he'd want to lay her down and bury himself in her until this clawing need burned itself out. Hell, already every bone in his body ached for her. And one part that wasn't a bone.

A muffled cry came from the direction of the kitchen.

"Claire?" he shouted, already halfway down the hall.

He found her opposite the kitchen entrance. Dark eyes wide with fear and cheeks pale, she stared at a partially opened pocket door. Her dog stood at her feet, hackles raised, a fierce rumble emitting from her throat.

"Did you go in this room?" Claire asked him.

"In there? No. What's the matter?" Taking her trembling shoulders in his hands, he turned her to face him.

She wavered, eyes luminous and vulnerable, as if she longed to seek safety in his arms. Then the defenses slid into place, and she withdrew. "Someone has been in the house."

"What is this room?" With one smooth maneuver, he positioned her behind him.

"My... my office." She clutched at his sleeve. "Are you going in? Do you have a gun?"

"Yes. And no." He didn't carry a damn gun. Hadn't for eight months. "Get back, Claire."

When she didn't move, he shoved her sideways at the same time he slid open the door. In an alert half crouch, he burst into the room.

In his search for movement, for telltale sounds, he

had a vague impression of dark wood, a breakfront like his mother's, a computer and printer positioned on a side table. No closet, nowhere an intruder could hide.

"They're gone," Claire said from the open doorway. She held Alley in her arms.

"Why'd you think someone had been here?" Michael resumed an erect stance but remained alert.

"Some things were moved in the kitchen, and I'd closed this door." After depositing the wriggling dog on the floor, she darted to the computer table, where she examined stacks of papers and books. "I left this printout evenly stacked. You see how the pages are twisted, um, askew? And the books?"

"You're sure?" He admitted to himself that she usually arranged everything precisely—their mugs on the tray, the candles on the mantel, even the tree decorations. A vision of her straightening the magazines on the side table winked into his mind.

"Quinn, I know how I do things in my own house." She glared, arms folded.

"You're the damn boss." He scowled back. "What is all this, anyway?" The printout was in English, something about a moose and a bear, but the reference books had French titles. This woman had more damn mysteries than David Baldacci. "Are you a writer or something?"

"Or something." She sighed. "I didn't mean for you to see this. It's private. But now that you have…"

Obviously temporizing, she reached back to tug the fastening from her braid. The movement stretched her sweater across her breasts and shot heat directly to Michael's loins. When she shook loose her rich fall of mahogany hair, he clenched his fists. Dammit. Was she trying to kill him?

"Are you going to explain or not?"

"I do translations. English to French. French to English. This one is a children's book written by a Quebec author."

Another side to her multifaceted personality. "Why?"

"I enjoy it. I'm good at it, usually. I like having a means to earn at least some of my own income. Is that enough reason for you?"

"Just asking." He raised his hands in truce. "Any reason someone would want to rifle through these papers?"

"Children's literature is a stiff market, but I doubt publishing houses send burglars to spy on rivals." She evened the edges of the papers and arranged the books in a stack. Still frightened but in control.

"Were there any other signs of intruders?"

She shook her head. With her hair wild around her shoulders, she looked sexier than ever.

He had to get out of here. "I'll check the rest of the house."

Chapter Six

CLAIRE FOLLOWED, UNWILLING to stay in the violated room without Quinn. Who could have entered her house? Why? And how did they get in? She'd locked the back door before the drive to the harbor. It was still locked.

To Alley she said, "Some watchdog. You used to growl at everyone. What happened?"

But the dog merely gazed up at her mistress and wagged her tail.

When Quinn was halfway up the stairs, Claire called, "Without me, you won't know if things are out of place."

"Stay there." It was a clear order, issued in a tone of crisp command. "You can check after I make sure it's safe."

Straining to hear, she waited at the foot of the stairs. But no sounds betrayed Quinn's path through the four bedrooms and two baths. On bare floor or carpet, he made no sound. For such a big man, he moved with a cat's stealth, no doubt due to his DEA experience.

Rather than stand here wringing her hands, she dashed to the kitchen, then to the living room with the kitten's food. The tiny creature lapped his meal greedily. Alley peered over the box rim and sniffed the fishy aroma, then lay with a sigh on the hearth rug.

"I'll feed you later, sweetie, after *he* is gone." Her

gaze strayed toward the stairway. Still no sounds upstairs.

Why had Quinn left the DEA? A man with his training and talents. *"I'd had enough."* His curt response to her question had left more unsaid than it revealed. Any personal inquiry was answered briefly, with no invitation to probe. In the DEA, he must have carried a gun. Why didn't he carry one now?

What had happened to the man?

Quinn was a skilled interrogator. He'd wheedled more out of Russ than anyone had. That Paul intended to go out to meet a new supplier the day he died was new information to her. And she had a feeling there was more Russ could have said. Did he hold back because of her?

"All clear. You can come up now."

At the sound of Quinn's voice, Claire rushed up the stairs. Seeing him grim-faced at the door to her bedroom didn't give her the sense of security she'd anticipated.

All hard-edged masculinity and rugged appeal, he was too attractive for comfort. Slipping past him as she entered the room, she felt his body heat, saw his mouth quirk. Would that hard mouth mold sensuously to a woman's and give pleasure, or would it simply take?

A flutter of awareness in her belly, she trailed around the bath and bedroom under his intense scrutiny. She knew he desired her, and being together in her bedroom, in sight of her king-size bed, was too intimate.

She tugged at a corner of the damask bedspread and smoothed the pillow. Remembering his powerful yet light embrace after her misstep, she imagined being entwined with him on her satin sheets, with no heavy parkas, no clothing to separate them. A vision of that hard, muscled body sent heat rushing to her cheeks, and she ducked her head.

"Everything is okay." She struggled to control the tremor in her voice. "But some jars and bottles have been moved around in the bathroom."

"Nothing missing?" When she shook her head, he said, "You have a maid or someone come in to clean?"

"No, Elisha Fogg's the only one crazy enough to work for the Widow Spider. Even he doesn't enter the house." Unable to meet his gaze, she slid past him and hurried to the other rooms. "Why?"

He waited as she scanned dresser tops. Unyielding, a granite pillar. "Since there's no sign of forced entry, I wondered who had a key. Maybe Fogg?"

She rearranged perfume bottles on the vanity. "I have the only keys. Elisha doesn't need one. I'm usually here."

"What about Paul's? And did Alan Worcester have a key?"

"Alan didn't have one, and Paul's are somewhere on the ocean bottom."

"Okay, let's leave that for now." He rubbed his nape. "Then who might want to snoop around?"

"Other than the police, you mean. They are not so careful. Pratt and his men left everything above below."

Quinn paused. "You mean upside down?" His unexpected smile softened his features and lit his gray eyes to silver.

Her heart did a little flip. "Yes, upside down. Bilingualism has its limits. I do occasionally mix up idioms." Now her equilibrium was *above below*. She plopped onto the vanity's padded stool. "Who would snoop in my house? Many people fear me, hate me for what they believe I did, but simply to prowl around? I don't know."

"Russell Santerre sure as hell didn't conceal his hatred for you. Did you do what he said? Pressure Paul to turn this place into a museum?"

At the accusations hurt coming from the man hired to help her, pain constricted her chest.

"Did you push him and the others to write wills in your favor? Did you—"

"*Mon Dieu, non!*" Hands raised in fists, she flew at him.

He easily caught her and held her hands against the rock wall of his chest.

She struggled, tears burning. "No, Quinn, I made no demands of either man. Or of Alan."

"Then why the wills? You put me off before. Tell me now." He was so close she could taste the vehemence of his words, see flecks of green in his gray irises, inhale his masculine scent. "Tell me."

"I told you before. I don't know. Jonathan came home one day saying he had written the will, that it seemed like a good idea. And Paul made one because Jonathan had. Alan knew about it, I suppose." Drawn by his heat and strength and tired of the struggle, she rested against him, didn't resist when his arms slipped around her.

"Paul's workaholic drive and creating this tasteful Taj Mahal—was all that to keep your love?" His gruff voice wrapped around her like a wool blanket.

Paul had never had her love, but she couldn't say that to anyone, least of all Quinn.

She shook her head and leaned her forehead against his strong neck. The pulse in it throbbed to the same rapid-fire beat as hers. She needed to trust this man, but she had to fight her attraction to him. "Paul set his goals for success before he married me. I told you he and Jonathan were competitive. Right out of college, he worked constantly to build his seafood business."

"Seems normal." The deep rumble slid down her spine.

"You don't see. They couldn't compete in business, since Jonathan joined his father's company. Jonathan and I bought this house, but Paul had to have it professionally decorated. He had to buy the cabin at Caribou Peak and—"

"Caribou Peak? Isn't that the ski resort where Alan Worcester was killed?"

"Yes, we were staying at Paul's cabin." Without that, Alan would still be alive instead of crushed beneath an avalanche. She drew a deep breath.

"And?" Quinn urged. "The boat? The *Rêve*?"

"Yes, he had to have that boat designed for himself. And he had to have…"

"What?"

"He had to have Jonathan's wife," she whispered. She'd never told anyone her conviction about that. The very idea made her feel dirty. Bought and sold.

"Is that why you didn't take his name?" He slid his hand up her arm and around to her chin. Like red-hot coals, his fingers burned into her flesh. "Why is it still Saint-Ange?"

"Family. My cousin Martine has a brother and cousins to carry on the Parent name, my mother's name, but I'm the last Saint-Ange. My mother and father are gone. With their debts, they left me little but my name. I needed to keep something… something of my family."

"Family means more to me than you can know. Believe me, I understand." His voice was a raw murmur as he tipped up her chin.

Her heart skipped a beat at the hope that someone understood. "You do?" The first step to believing in her. She searched his smoky eyes, but all she saw was heat and hunger. He was going to kiss her, and she was powerless to resist.

"I want to."

The warmth of his breath puffed against her lips. Her heart tripped on itself. His face hovered only inches above hers, tantalizing her.

His hand left her chin to tangle in her hair and cup the back of her head. Their lips met with urgency, with need that had simmered since their first meeting. His hard-looking mouth molded to hers with searing demand and sensuous skill. A leap of electricity scorched through her down to her toes.

His lips tasted of coffee and heat and need. Curls of pleasure sifted through her as she opened to his probing tongue. Reveling in the headiness of how perfectly their mouths and bodies fit, she let her tongue plunge and parry with his.

His scent, his hard body, his throaty growls of desire saturated her senses. Her heart clattered and her blood pounded. His caress glided down her back to her derriere, and she wanted more, more than this devastating kiss. The ridge thrust against her belly told her he wanted the same.

When he eased away, Claire blinked, dazed for a

moment before she recoiled at her own mindless behavior.

"Oh, hell! I didn't mean to do that!" He slammed a hand against the doorjamb.

"Quinn, I—" she began. "It was a big mistake, and it must not happen again." She was responsible for three men's deaths. She didn't want another. For both their sakes, she had to keep the relationship on a purely professional basis.

"It won't," he gritted between his teeth. Storming away from her, he pounded down the stairs two at a time. "I'll check the cellar. Just to be sure."

Claire took her time descending to the kitchen. Though the lock had remained in place on the cellar door, she was glad Quinn insisted on looking around. Just to be sure.

When he returned, all male irritation and aggression, awareness flared again, but the steel core that had armed her these past months held. She busied herself washing their coffee cups. Radiating competence and granite solidity, he leaned against the refrigerator.

She started as the quiet was pierced by a shrill jangle. He'd wonder if she didn't answer. Maybe it was time he knew. Drying her hands on a tea towel, she crossed to the telephone. "Hello."

What she heard stopped her heart, then caused it to race. She dropped the receiver and clamped both arms around her middle.

Quinn snatched up the instrument. He listened, then barked, "Who's there?" Shortly, he replaced the receiver in its cradle. "It's dead. Claire, what the hell was that?"

A spasm gripped her chest, and her heartbeat jittered. "I've been receiving anonymous calls."

"A man?"

"I don't know if it's a man or woman." Her nerves screamed, until Quinn's proximity calmed her pulse, lent her strength. To prevent curling into his arms again, she scooped up her dropped tea towel.

"How long? When did this start?"

"The first time, after the avalanche buried Alan, the calls were threatening, accusing. I changed to an unlisted number, but still they found me. I changed the number again, and finally those calls stopped. Until two weeks before I hired you, but these calls are different."

"How?"

"Nothing, only breathing." But she felt a threat in the silence, a palpable menace. Someone was there, plotting. When Quinn eyed her hands, she realized she was wringing the life out of the towel. She shook it and folded her arms.

He tilted his big head, suspicion in his eyes. "There's more. What?"

"In the background, sometimes I hear a sort of thumping."

"And this time, the same—only breathing, the thumping?"

She twisted her mouth, pressed the towel to it. Should she tell him? "I won't blame you if you want to quit now. This may be more than just an investigation."

He stood before her, hands fisted at his sides, as if he resisted reaching for her. "I won't quit. Did the caller speak?"

She nodded. "He said…" Paralysis gripped her throat, but she choked out the words. " 'He's next.' "

Quinn's jaw worked, and his eyes darkened to slate. He stalked around the kitchen, shaking his head like the bull she'd compared him to that first day.

"Now I've put you in danger." Jonathan, Paul, Alan—each had died while they were apart from her, off on their own and alone. Quinn was in the same danger now.

He stopped his pacing and faced her, his scowl a thunderhead.

Her next words shocked her as much as the caller's had. "Get your things from the motel and move in here."

## Chapter Seven

MICHAEL HAD DRUNK in worse bars. He must have. But no dive on the Boston waterfront could be any sleazier or dingier than Butch's Bar, located in the downstairs rooms of a squat wood-frame house with peeling paint near the Weymouth town landing.

At four in the afternoon, the day drinkers slumped at the bar. The happy-hour arrivals, tired and thirsty after a raw day scalloping or pounding nails, cared only about getting a buzz on.

The muscular bartender slapped down beers and shots on the rough-planked bar for three unshaven men in yellow rubber boots. Odors of fish and gasoline overlay the less pleasant ones indigenous to Butch's.

No one paid him any mind. Exactly his intention.

After another gulp of his long-neck, he thanked the common sense that prompted him to avoid the draft. The bottled brew tasted enough like piss. Besides, after a sleepless night, even a small amount of alcohol could blur his senses. Not something he could afford in this joint.

Sleepless, all right. And he suspected Claire hadn't rested any too well either. The lady had backbone, but that call had frightened her badly.

Circumstances were requiring that he add protection to his investigation. Bodyguard, the job he should avoid. Even though she thought he moved in for his own safety, he suspected she was in more danger than she knew. Foolish female, if she trusted him to protect her.

*God, I can't protect her. Don't make me have to protect her. Not another one.*

Maybe to shield herself from him after that incendiary kiss, she tried to stash him at the end of the hall—far away from her room. But he insisted on bedding down next door.

Where he heard her run the shower, imagining warm water sliding over her curves. Where he heard every slide of sheets as she turned over on that huge bed. Where remembering the sensations of their kiss and her sighed responses swelled him harder than the amber bottle he was gripping.

Shunting aside the daydream, he swallowed another gulp of beer. With a glance through the smoke and gloom, he leaned against the cracked plastic of his back booth.

He saw few females present other than a wide-bodied waitress who could double as bouncer. In front of the jukebox, a brassy blonde in a fringed leather miniskirt and a scrawny male in stained jeans and a black vest, no shirt, ground their pelvises together to a Merle Haggard lament. Another woman, shoe-horned into jeans and a leopard-print top sidled up to one of the fishermen. Both women looked like they spent most of their time at Butch's. Or on their backs in the rooms advertised on a wall sign: Rooms—Hourly Rates. A couple of other females, more serious drinkers, sat at rickety tables with equally serious male guzzlers.

A moment later, every female head, waitress-bouncer's included, turned toward the door. Michael looked in the same direction.

Ricardo Cruz had arrived.

Michael chuckled to himself. He should have known. Happened every time that Cuban stud entered a room. His dark good looks, dimple, and pirate grin lured females from five to ninety-five like nectar drew bees.

Michael's partner was the son of a Cuban refugee and a Miami lounge singer. Florida-born, Cruz had inherited looks, intelligence, and a sharp sense of irony from his parents—added to his dedication to justice.

Male heads turned to check out the new arrival. One glance at Cruz's biker boots and the leather jacket snug across his shoulders convinced even the most antagonistic drunk to let him join Michael unchallenged.

Every female gaze followed his ambling walk.

"Yo, Cruz, nice entrance. You practice that woman-slaying look in front of a mirror?" Michael signaled to the waitress.

"You bet, *mano*, just like you do that fearsome scowl. Must've scared the crap out of these drunks." Cruz slid into the opposite seat.

Michael grunted noncommittally and slugged down the last of his beer. Though he didn't rehearse his expression, his powerful build and grim countenance likely prevented a confrontation in a bar that welcomed only regulars. "You find this sty okay?"

"No sweat. Why here?"

"Two reasons. Figured a workman's local dive was the last place the Mexicans would hang out."

Cruz lowered his voice. "From the name, I thought Butch's was some kind of female biker bar."

"So that explains the get-up."

"Wait until the boss gets the bill for this prime leather." A grin slashed across Cruz's face. "And the second reason?"

"Got the list of Paul Santerre's suppliers from his old man. He owns the business now. I'm looking for a guy who hangs out here sometimes. A lobsterman named Larson. Didn't get along with Santerre."

The waitress brought their beers and mopped several days' sticky residue from the cracked plastic tabletop—a courtesy she hadn't bothered to perform for Michael.

"Thanks, sweetheart, you're a peach." Cruz gave her a bedroom-eyed wink. When she left, he turned to Michael. "What did this guy have against Paul Santerre?"

"Don't know, but word is he hated Santerre's guts. He might tell us something the others won't." Michael angled his head toward the bar's rowdy gathering. "But he's not here."

"You got a picture?" Cruz's gaze followed his partner's.

"No picture. Big blond guy." Michael chewed on his lower lip. "Larson had an accident on his boat. Got his arm caught in the winch line. Halfway severed at the wrist. Couldn't get loose and couldn't get help. He sawed off the rest himself with his boat knife."

"Tough son of a bitch. So you're looking for a guy with one hand."

"Artificial hand." Michael slid his half-finished beer to one side. "Did you find anything about El Águila's boys being in town?"

"Checked the license number you gave me with the

rental agency. Dark guy, middle-aged, name of Tony Colombo."

"Wonder what wise-ass thought that one up." Michael's lip curled.

"Description sounds like Raoul Olívas, one of El Águila's lieutenants. Cruel bastard, likes to do his boss's dirty work. The other two are probably just muscle."

"They still around?"

Cruz shook his head. "No reason to stay in Weymouth. Could be in Portland, even Portsmouth, for that matter. You think they contacted the widow?"

"Someone did." Michael explained about the anonymous phone caller and the intruder. But not the kiss. No need to reveal something that shouldn't have happened and wouldn't be repeated.

Even now the memory of how soft and warm Claire felt in his arms, how her lips fit so perfectly, so hotly to his, and how much he wanted her affected his body. With effort, he kept his expression bland when he said he was staying at the house.

"All right!" Cruz slapped him on the shoulder. "Quinn, I do like your moves. That close to the Widow Spider, you ought to be able to wrap this up quick."

Michael doubted it. "Russ Santerre's still tiptoeing around something he knows. I'll go see him again. If I can get away from my *partner*."

"How'd you manage today?"

"Told her I had an appointment with the state detective. She avoids the cops when she can. That prick Pratt's given her a hard time."

"She's getting to you, Quinn." Cruz grinned and hoisted his bottle in a toast. "The original hard case is softening. Don't forget what you're there for."

"You're damn right to doubt my reliability."

"Man, you got to let go of what happened with that kid."

"*That kid*'s name was Kathy." Michael ground his beer bottle into the table surface.

"Anyone can miss a shot. Even an old medal winner like you."

"Not like that. Not in a hostage situation. I was too strung out to be the sharpshooter that day. I should have known better." His voice barely carried above the nearby din. "Because of my arrogance, a child died."

Cruz heaved a sigh. "Not arrogance, grief. Boss should have known better. And it wasn't your fault, anyway."

Michael didn't want to drag his friend through yet another post mortem of his problems. "About the widow and drugs," he said, "I'm beginning to wonder."

"Next you're going to tell me you don't think she's murdered anyone."

Although doubts about Claire as a killer niggled at him, Michael would say nothing for the time being. The sensationalism surrounding the case had died down months ago. Why did someone telephone her now? And at least one threat against him.

Maybe the real murderer?

"Russ Santerre and the widow aren't the only ones with secrets," he said. "The damn DEA's holding out on us—on me, anyway. Why didn't I know from the get-go that Santerre Seafood was a one-man operation? That Claire Saint-Ange sold it to her in-law? And that Paul Santerre's boat has been in dry dock for months?"

"You're right, partner. All that info is easy enough

to dig up without an undercover agent," Cruz agreed. "What do you think the SAC is up to?"

"I don't know, but I don't like it. Any of it. If I find out our office is behind those anonymous phone calls and they've pitched me naked into a damn hornet's nest…" Michael slammed one fist against the already dented wall.

No one at the bar looked over. One man hunched deeper over his beer.

"About those phone calls…" Cruz began.

"What about them?" Preparing to leave, Michael levered out of the cramped booth.

"The caller said, 'He's next.'"

"Yeah. So?"

Cruz stood too. He slid on supple leather gloves, one finger at a time.

Female gazes homed in on his every movement.

"But only the widow heard those words. You didn't hear the voice yourself." One ebony eyebrow arched, he waited for Michael's acquiescence before continuing. "Then how can you be certain what was said? If there have really been other calls."

"If there are more, I'll need you to check on the cell numbers anyway."

A few minutes later when he started the engine, Michael admitted Cruz was right. Any calls that could've been saved on the answering system were gone now. Each time a different number, she'd said, and she recognized some as coming from cell phones. This one also, he could tell. Burner phones, for sure. Untraceable, prepaid, each probably destroyed immediately after the calls. Dammit.

She was getting to him. Anonymous calls, yes, but

threats? He'd never even thought of the possibility that she had fabricated the warning message.

Had the widow spun a trap for him?

\*\*\*\*

Pete Larson was a bear of a man. A polar bear, Claire amended, as she noticed his rolled-up shirtsleeves. He beckoned to Quinn and her with his prosthetic hand, then ducked back inside his garage workshop. A pickup sat in the driveway surrounded by bikes and saucer sleds, the debris of children in a hurry for lunch.

She exited Quinn's SUV and tugged her coat collar tighter around her neck. The promise of more snow hung pregnant in clouds' swollen bellies.

Larson agreed to talk to them as long as he could continue repairing his lobster traps. That meant shivering in an unheated garage. Again.

"What is it with these fishermen?" she muttered to Quinn as they picked their way up the toy-littered driveway. At the side of the garage stood two snow forts, and inside one a stock of snowballs. "Is it some Down-East code or a macho thing that requires them all to work without heat?"

His mouth flirted with a grin. "These temperatures shouldn't bother you. Where you grew up, nearly in Canada, doesn't it stay at zero until spring?"

"True, but we knew enough to heat our houses and worksheds. And here on the coast it's a damper cold that eats into your bones." Claire thrust her gloved hands into her pockets. She'd never seen Quinn with gloves or a hat. Yesterday when they'd met with another fisherman, she'd stamped her booted feet to assure herself they were still attached, and Quinn hadn't even zipped up his parka. "Cold doesn't seem to bother you, I've noticed."

He stopped at the walk-in door to the garage and gaped at her as if she were the odd one. "I don't mind it. If you spend enough time in the out-of-doors, your body adapts, and you don't feel the cold."

"I'll take your word for it. Was it outdoor stakeouts that gave you that winter tan?"

"No. Camping." The crinkles beside his eyes and the tan they revealed drew her gaze. He turned the doorknob.

"Camping?" Her eyebrows rose. "You mean like in a tent? In the tropics somewhere?" She and Jonathan had spent their honeymoon in a platform tent in the Virgin Islands. That kind of camping she understood.

"A tent, yes." He held the door for her to enter the garage. "But not in the tropics. In the White Mountains of New Hampshire. I trekked in and camped for two months before coming to Weymouth."

"*Mon Dieu*, whatever for?" Had Quinn gone after a fugitive or a survivalist? One of those people who wanted to be able to survive in the wilderness when the nuclear holocaust came? Or was he one of them? "For a client?"

He scraped his teeth on his lower lip as he seemed to contemplate his response. Sadness hovered in the depths of his gray eyes. "Something happened, a... loss in my life. It was an escape, a chance to experience the peace of nature, to live on the edge and challenge myself. A vacation, if you like."

"You folks comin' in or you goin' to stand out there gabbin'?"

At the sharp tone of Larson's question, Claire

scooted inside with Quinn close behind her.

What had happened to him? Her grief and trouble were paraded for all the world to see, but Quinn kept his bottled up. He'd opened up a part of himself that she thought he usually kept hidden behind the tough ironic facade he presented to the world. In spite of her resolve to avoid interest in his affairs, to avoid knowing anything personal about him, she wanted to understand.

Rather than muse further, she focused her attention on their host.

## Chapter Eight

AFTER CLOSING THE door behind them, Michael took a second to collect himself. Only yesterday he'd resolved to distance himself from the tempting widow, and today he'd blabbed more to her about his wilderness retreat than he ever had to Cruz, his friend and partner. What the hell was wrong with him?

Striding toward the lobsterman, he held out his hand. "Thanks for taking time to see us, Mr. Larson. Do you know Ms. Saint-Ange?"

The big blond man smiled and held out his good right hand. "We never met before, but I've seen you."

Michael watched Claire's tentative greeting. Both had expected the same fear superimposed with hostility projected by her father-in-law and the other fishermen.

She hurried to the lobster-crate seat Larson offered beside an ineffectual kerosene heater. Michael watched as she settled down and wrapped her long coat around her legs. He should've noticed before how the cold affected her. During the last few days, she'd trooped from fishing boat to dock to unheated shed with him. Uncomplaining. Until today.

Camping in the tropics. If he took her camping on some sandy island, he'd peel away the bulky coat and wool pants to bare her soft skin and sleek body to the sun. And to him.

Jeez, where did that idea come from? Maybe the cold was affecting him after all.

The Gallic head tilt and her quizzical expression snapped him to attention. He must look like a daydreaming fool.

"As I told you," Michael said to the lobsterman, "I'm talking to Paul Santerre's seafood suppliers. The police must have already questioned you, but I hoped you might tell us your ideas about his death."

"Funny you should say that." Larson scratched his head with the forefinger of his lifelike prosthesis. "The cops never asked me squat. Not that I could've told 'em anything. I hadn't seen Santerre in four months when I heard he died."

He reached inside the rectangular wire trap on his workbench. "Hope you don't mind if I go ahead with my repairs. Crabs and sea urchins tear up the pot heads somethin' fierce." He winked at Claire. "Uh, that's the nylon net contraption that keeps the bug from gettin' back out."

Michael knew he must have looked perplexed because Claire said from her crate perch, "Bug is the fishermen's term for lobster, Quinn. You go ahead with your work, Mr. Larson."

"Word is you didn't like Santerre much." The state detectives hadn't bothered to talk to Santerre's suppliers. Maybe it was as Claire had insisted. They had their suspect—his widow.

"Hell, that's puttin' it mildly. I hated the bastard's guts." Larson held up his left hand. "You see this bionic hand I got? With it, I can do my haulin' with near the same efficiency as before. But Paul, he weren't interested in givin' me a chance to prove it."

"I know my husband wasn't always easy to get along with. What did he do to you?" Claire removed her gloves and clasped her hands in her lap. Beside her on the crate lay five metal clamps she aligned into an even row.

"What did Paul do to me?" His face grew grim. "When I lost my hand, most everybody around town offered help. My oldest boy—he was nine—and my wife did my haulin'. Neighbors and other folks I didn't even know brought food and donated money for medical bills."

"That's the wonderful thing about a small town," Claire said. "Everybody pitches in."

That acceptance and community spirit didn't apply to her, the ostracized Widow Spider. And still she could express sincere sympathy for another's benefit.

"Except Paul," the man continued. "We went to high school together, but that didn't cut any ice with him. He dropped me from his list. Canceled all orders and replaced me. Guess I should've known what he was like."

"What do you mean?" Michael said. Understanding Paul's motivation seemed key.

Larson pointed to the lobster shell tacked to one wall. "My first bug," he said with a proud grin. "Did you know bugs are cannibals? If their claws ain't bound in the crate, they'll attack, climb on, fight, and even eat one another in competition for food. For being' top bug, so to speak. Paul was like that. Long as things went his way, his claws was closed and harmless. Cross him or defy him and he'd chop you to shreds."

"I'm so sorry. I didn't know about his ending your contract." Clutching her gloves, Claire came to stand beside Michael. "Paul didn't confide much about his business to me. If I'd known…"

His arm itched to slide around her shoulders. Claire was tall, nearly his height, but at this moment, trembling at his side, she looked small and vulnerable.

"Don't you fret none about it, Ms. Saint-Ange," Larson said. "Maybe I shouldn't say this, but I'm gonna speak my piece. I don't know if his death were an accident or if someone killed him. If it was you who deep-sixed him, I hope they never prove it. Good riddance to the son of a bitch."

**\*\*\*\***

Long past twelve that night, Claire stared at the computer screen. Her fingers hovered over the keyboard then dropped to her lap. Wakefulness had driven her to try working. Alley slept at her feet and the kitten in his box in the kitchen.

In frustration, she tunneled her fingers through her mass of hair and shook it back. Grégoire's moose story would simply not cooperate. She couldn't find the English words to match the rhythm and phrasing of the French-Canadian tale.

*Merde*, it wasn't the translation plaguing her. No, probing for evidence ripped open barely stitched wounds. The burden squeezed her chest like an ever-tightening vise. Sometimes she could hardly breathe.

Then there were the phone calls. She hadn't heard the voice again, but he'd called twice more since Quinn moved in. With no time pattern to them, she jumped every time the phone rang. When she did manage to fall asleep, she bolted awake, her anxiety fabricating its mocking jangle. At least now, she'd have proof. She'd turned off the answering system before, not wanting to hear the terrifying silence... and breathing. But Quinn had insisted she record the calls. He connected a small digital recorder as well, for a more permanent record. Evidence, she supposed.

For the rest of her sleep deprivation, she blamed Quinn. Her old uncles, who'd competed against the Irish immigrants for jobs at the mills, would call him *maudit Irlandais*. This cursed Irishman distracted her from her work and disturbed her sleep.

She should never have permitted him to hold her. To kiss her.

*The curse of your beauty is to be alone.*

She'd sworn to herself never to become involved with a man again, but one embrace, one kiss had her panting for him. For an embittered man who didn't want involvement any more than she did. For a man who yelled accusations at her one minute and held her comfortingly the next. For a man whose kisses aroused her more than Jonathan's ever had.

But why? What was there about him that enticed her? Sex had never preoccupied her like this.

Making love with Jonathan had been sweet and satisfying, though not the fireworks she'd hoped for. With Paul, sex was less than satisfying. He treated her like a porcelain doll, a vessel that was supposed to lie there passively. With Alan, no intimacy at all. But no caresses before ever caused these erotic dreams or tingling nipples or aching need. Or nagging guilt.

Dwelling on the kiss wouldn't erase the emotions and distraction it engendered. It didn't help to have Quinn sleeping under the same roof.

Except for showing an equal measure of distrust and desire for her, he masked his feelings well. Once or

twice, like today at Pete Larson's, she'd seen past the professional facade to something somber and sorrowful in his slate-gray eyes. She'd toyed with the idea of probing for more. Did his dammed-up emotions ever erupt in passion? Would he focus his fierce concentration on a woman when he made love to her?

*Mon Dieu,* if she knew what was good for her, she'd never find out.

Why couldn't her private investigator have been someone effete like Agatha Christie's fictional Belgian detective?

She giggled.

"So you do laugh."

"Quinn!" Pulse pounding, she spun around in her swivel chair. "What are you doing up?"

Alley lifted her head, then collapsed again in gentle snores.

Hair rumpled and shirtless, Quinn hovered in the doorway. He wore only a pair of faded, soft jeans that molded to his powerful thighs.

Once again he'd moved through the house with predatory quiet. That warrior aspect of the man fascinated her—his restraint, with tightly coiled emotion just beneath the surface. So different from other men she'd known.

She knew his large body was fit, but seeing the bands and layers of solid muscle sculpted by smooth skin made her forget to breathe. The angled light outlined every sinew and plane on his muscled chest and emphasized the hard angles of his jaw. Brown hairs curled in a wedge across thick pectorals and narrowed to a line that disappeared past the open top button of his jeans.

It was all she could do not to go run her hands over his chest to see how soft those springy-looking hairs felt in contrast to his hard body, to trace the tan line at the base of his neck.

"What am I doing up?" he muttered, in a low, rumbling tone that reverberated in her senses. "So I should ignore the hall light and your open door and snore away instead of doing my damn job?"

His jaw and brooding eyes should intimidate but instead captivated her. Wrapping her fleece robe closer around her legs, she said, "I'm not used to having someone concerned for my safety. I didn't want to wake you just because I couldn't sleep."

"You're not wearing black."

"Black? No, I..." The non sequitur confused her. Her gaze veered from the narrow strip of hair arrowing into his jeans to her pale blue robe.

"I didn't think today's women went in for mourning colors. But you wear nothing but black. Why?"

Swiveling away from him, she found the words with difficulty. "After so much tragedy, it was... respectful and necessary. To set myself apart."

"For how long?" He came one step closer.

"I haven't thought about it." That was a lie. She thought about it all the time. She punched a button to save her file, and then stood. "At least until... things are resolved." Maybe forever.

"Until you find another husband?" Another step closer. Too close. His body heat beckoned her.

"No, not that. I'll never marry again." She struggled to face him. "I can't go through that again, and I can't ask anyone else to take the chance."

"You sound like you believe the fable your aunts told you. A curse. A test from God."

She did. Nevertheless, the grief was beginning to wane, replaced by a kind of bleak acceptance. And finally she was taking action. But nothing dulled the fear.

She couldn't answer Quinn. He stood so close she could count the individual dark hairs shadowing his chin, could breathe in the mingled scents of shampoo and soap and man. So close her skin tingled when he swept a skein of hair from her shoulder.

"A beautiful, intelligent woman like you, alone? Jonathan bought you this house. Paul refurbished it. Still you needed more. Is that why you kept trying?"

The abrupt question broke the spell.

"Kept trying?" she snapped. "You don't understand, Quinn. It wasn't like that at all."

"Then explain it to me, Claire." When she tried to brush past him, he clasped her wrist in an unbreakable but painless grip. "We're obviously both awake. I need to understand your relationship with these three men if I'm to help you."

Electric excitement streaked through her at his searing touch. She swallowed. "Over the last few days, we've talked to several people. That's our investigation. Isn't that enough?"

With a glide of his wide palm up her arm, he released her. A shiver rippled through her. She was beyond questioning her reactions to Quinn.

"No, it's not enough." He folded his arms. Determination glittered in his eyes. "You've gone with me to talk to different men who used to sell Paul their catch. One-handed or not, Larson could have cheerfully drowned him, but he wasn't alone in his hatred. One way or another, Paul screwed over three men for his own gain. But none of them has any connection to Jonathan Farnsworth or Alan Worcester."

"Maybe… maybe one of those men killed Paul, but the other deaths were accidents."

"You don't really believe that, though, do you?" he said.

Thoughts of the ominous phone calls—one in particular, *He's next*—wouldn't be shoved away. "No, I don't. But the curse—"

"You're intelligent and educated, for God's sake. Why are you so hung up on this curse notion?"

"Not a notion. Please understand, Quinn. After my parents died, my aunts drilled it into me. *The curse of your beauty is to be alone.*"

"No curse, it's guilt. Your aunts heaped guilt on you for the loss. Guilt you can't shake even today. These aunts, um, in their day, were they knockouts like you and Martine? Were they attractive?"

She frowned, not understanding where he was going with this question. "*Tante* Odette and *Tante* Rolande? No. My uncles refer to them as *les boudins*. It means puddings or short, fat sausages. The uncles maintain that's the reason they're *vieilles filles*, old girls."

"You mean old maids." He swirled his tongue around his teeth. Concealing a smile at her confusion?

"Yes. But what does that have to do with anything?"

"Don't you think it's possible they're a bit jealous of your looks?"

"Jealous? No, impossible. They love me. They

Susan Vaughan

raised me. I was only a child when my parents died, but I think the curse idea was something they got from the priest."

"They might believe in the curse as a fact, and as a child, you were easy to convince. But you're no longer that child. Why would God single you out? There are millions of attractive people in the world who don't face punishments for features nature—God, if you prefer—gave them."

"I'd like to believe that. But then why these deaths surrounding me? Leaving me alone."

"It's possible the three deaths were accidental or unconnected, but I don't think so either. I don't believe in curses, and neither should you. But the connection has to be you. One way or another. What are you hiding, Claire?"

"Perhaps I killed them."

One brow sketched upward. "There is that." He turned away. "We need to talk more. I'll go start a fire."

He'd already started a fire, one she ought to extinguish.

Chapter Nine

MOMENTS LATER, WHEN Claire entered the living room, Michael looked up from the fire he was stoking. He instinctively fixed his gaze on the gently rounded tops of her full breasts, which were revealed in the gaping overlap of her blue bathrobe. Does she have anything at all on under it?

In her little office, the view had damn near sucked out his eyeballs and split his jeans. Seemingly unaware of his agony, she carried a decanter and two bulbous stemmed glasses on a silver tray.

Fortification or seduction?

"Don't say it, Quinn." Claire deposited the tray on a wheeled cart. "The Widow Spider isn't trying to snare you in her web. If I'm to bare my innermost feelings and secrets, I need some false courage. And I thought you wouldn't refuse sharing a glass." She flicked on the tree lights.

Humor mixed with the tension in her words, but he'd yet to see a smile on her kissable lips. He rose and wiped his hands on the old T-shirt he'd pulled on. And how the hell did she know what he was thinking?

Her dog trailed in, stretching and yawning. Alley's gaze moved from one to the other as if to ask what the devil they were doing up so late. With a noisy sigh, she collapsed on the hearth rug.

Claire handed him a glass. The lamplight through

the amber spirits cast a golden glow on her slender hand. A hand he imagined dancing over his skin... clutching at his back as he slipped— Hell!

Shunting aside that train wreck of thought, he asked, "Do you ever use the fancy room across the hall?" It was twice the size of this one, and he'd never seen her in it.

"The ballroom, you mean?" Her lips twisted. Swirling the brandy in her balloon glass, she stared at the vortex. "I dust and vacuum in there occasionally. That's all."

The thickness of her lowered lashes shuttered her eyes but didn't conceal the violet smudges beneath them. As he'd predicted, the investigation was wearing her down.

"More of Paul's extravagance?"

"So you're beginning to understand. He had a wall removed between two rooms to create that." She curled up among the throw pillows at one end of the camel-backed sofa. Apparently unaware of its effect on him, she pulled the robe together.

He'd thought her a calculating mantrap. She was nothing like that.

Relief and disappointment hitting him at the loss of his view, he eased down at the other end of the sofa. "I get the picture of a guy hell-bent on parading his raging success before all. Aggressive enough to demand everything his way."

"Everything." She continued to avoid his gaze.

Her reticence to discuss the son of a bitch might stem from the illegal activities—or something else more personal. Ice-edged unease speared his gut. "Claire, was he ever abusive to you?"

Her eyes widened. "Abusive? Physically? Never! Nearly the opposite." She hesitated, and her gaze slid away. "But controlling, demanding, as you said."

He tipped his head toward the Christmas tree. "I bet Paul's idea of decorations had a hell of a lot more glitz."

She rolled her eyes. "He hired decorators. A Portland magazine featured the house. We married in November, but he started the renovations six months before so the house would be ready. By October, he nearly drove the carpenters mad, he was such a foot-breaker."

"Foot-breaker?"

"*Zut*, another idiom." Her full lips pursed in thought. "*Casse-pieds*, a pain in the feet, I think."

He bit his cheek to suppress a laugh. "In English the pain's in other parts of the anatomy." He longed to skim a finger along her lower lip, to feel its softness.

She didn't smile, but at least she seemed more relaxed with him. More at ease, but no less sorrowful. Grief clung to her as an ever-present shadow. And guilt, but for what?

*Tell me the whole truth, Claire.*

When he'd decided, he didn't know, but he was going to help her to catch a murderer and a stalker. God help him, he didn't want to fail again. Anxiety crawled around in his gut like a scorpion preparing to sting. Seamlessly, he'd segued from total noninvolvement to full combat. He could authorize himself to broaden his mission without getting personally involved. He could do that. Solving the murders—for damn sure they were murders—seemed as important as tracing the drug smugglers.

For sure the answers were linked.

"I know how ambitious Paul was. Paul's various suppliers back up what you said." He had to frame his next words carefully or risk blowing the game. If only he could level with her. "Did you ever wonder how he was able to hit the big time so quickly? If he'd gone outside the law?"

She gaped at him as though he'd stuffed a pillow in his mouth and danced on the table. "You mean bribes or threats or something? Really? We were married only six months, and he didn't talk to me about his business."

She tugged at her mass of hair and flung it across one shoulder to drape across her breast like a fan. A fan he'd like to replace with his hand.

Frowning, she added, "Though it wouldn't surprise me if he cut a few corners. Some fishermen sell under the table to avoid reporting income. But Paul worked so hard. No, his earnings didn't surprise me." She tilted her head, slightly forward at an angle, in the French way that simmered his blood. "Nor did his lavish spending."

"All for ostentatious display. The *Rêve*, the cabin, renovating this mansion, and you—the trophy wife."

"As I said the other night, his reasons for marrying me were more complex than that, but, yes."

"Having Jonathan's wife. You and Jonathan loved each other. And it's clear why Paul married you." He lowered his voice and leaned toward her. "But why did you marry Paul?"

****

Claire's pulse stumbled with the question. Needing another bracing sip, she tipped up her brandy glass. She must have a trapped look, like a cornered mouse. How could she make him understand what she barely understood herself?

"Quinn, you have a family. You said the other night that family meant a great deal to you. Parents, brothers and sisters, perhaps? Where, Boston?" Her eyes snapped wide at a new thought. "Even a wife?" She adjusted the three small cushions so their edges overlapped.

"Changing the subject, Claire? Hiding something?"

"No. Bear with me. It all ties in."

"Yes, my folks are in Boston." He bit off each word. Clearly he didn't want to discuss them. "No wife."

"Kids? Have you ever been married?"

He shook his head in that characteristic bull-like way. "No and no. My job never left much time for anything serious enough to lead to marriage."

"Tell me about your family, then."

"Claire, do we have to—"

Her frown stopped him.

He sighed. "My dad's a Boston uniform cop, desk sergeant now, and my mom does temp work. Roark's the oldest, then me, then Sandro—Alessandro."

"No sisters?"

"None." He ground the word from between his teeth.

"Alessandro Quinn." Liking the sound of it, she tasted it with the tip of her tongue along the seam of her lips. "Interesting ethnic combination."

"My mother's Italian."

"Are you close? Christmas is only days away, Quinn. You must have presents to buy. Don't you want to spend time with them?" She scooted her chair closer. An Italian mother and an Irish father. What a wonderful, rowdy family it must be.

"They aren't expecting me this year."

From the steel in his eyes and the taut muscle in his jaw, she read pain behind his terse statement. But this wasn't the time. "I'll bet your mom's a good cook—special holiday meals, pasta, pastries. Family dinners with laughter and joking and music. Any grandchildren?"

"My brothers have produced a slew of rug rats." Features contorted with emotions she couldn't identify, he surged to his feet and yanked her up to face him. "Cut this crap! What the hell are you getting at, Claire?"

Her vision dimmed and shimmered with lost images. "The only family I'm close to, my aunts, drain what life I have with their talk of tests and curses from God and bearing up. Quinn, I have no one. No one."

He released her, and she stumbled away to hunch beside the twinkling Christmas tree.

"Even before suspicion alienated Martine, we weren't close. I was distant family she tolerated for her children's sake. A constant reminder of the backwoods she'd escaped." She failed to suppress a shaky sigh. "First my parents. Then Jonathan. You said family meant a lot to you, so can't you understand? I was so very alone. I needed someone."

"And Paul was there." Coming to stand behind her, he placed a hand on her shoulder. "You married him, but you didn't love him."

She turned around. The tendon in his jaw easing, he looked oddly relieved.

When both his hands cupped her shoulders, she didn't object. His warmth, his clean scent, the tiny white lights glowing softly soothed the gripping ache within her, and his nearness made her pulse race.

"I've never admitted that before. *Mon Dieu*, I couldn't."

"Too incriminating. The grieving widow." He said it without sarcasm.

Something like a fist squeezed her throat. "I did grieve for him. I do. He could be difficult, I know, but I wasn't unhappy. In spite of most of what you've heard about Paul, he could be very charming and persuasive. A born salesman. That's another reason he did so well with his seafood business."

"And Alan? You waited five years before chancing marriage again. Was it love? Did you fall hard?"

"Alan was my friend more than anything. And my attorney. After Paul's death, he helped me settle the seafood business."

"Again, there when you needed someone."

She turned toward him, gazing into his calm gray eyes. Rather than harsh and unyielding, his features now looked to her dependable and solid. "I suppose that's it. He was more than ten years older than me, but he was kind and gentle and wise. I can't expect you to understand. You've had a loving family, but I've been on the fringes all my life. I wanted a family of my own."

"A need as old as time," he said. "Easy to understand."

He was right. Because of his prodding, she'd put it into words, for herself as much as for him. And what she wanted now was to yield to her desire for this hard-shelled man with the soft center. Her own strength was ebbing, and she needed his. That he wanted her showed in his sensual touch and in the darkening of his eyes.

But since she wasn't one for casual sex, and anything else could be fatal, she forced herself to resist. *"He's next."* She couldn't let herself care for this man only to have him killed too.

A wry grin lifted a corner of Quinn's mouth. "You should be Irish with all that guilt weighing you down. Let it go. There's no curse. And what happened wasn't because you didn't love them. You lost the young husband you loved, so you settled for less."

She frowned at him for seeing too much. "No wonder you—"

At the telephone's shrilling, her heart tripped into over-drive, and she flung herself against Quinn's chest. Alley leapt up, barking at phantoms.

"It's him!" she whispered, as if the caller could hear.

\*\*\*\*

A half hour later, Michael punched the Return button on his digital recorder. He sat in the swivel chair at Claire's desk, and she stood at rigid attention beside him.

"One more time, Claire," he said. "Listen for anything you recognize. Phrasing, pronunciation, accent, background. Anything." Having Caller ID didn't help because a cell number didn't necessarily reveal the caller. Calling back resulted in a "not in service" message. Another burner phone.

But now he knew the threats were real, not part of some elaborate Widow Spider's web. He cast her a sideways glance, asking for a response.

She nodded, mute, hands fisted at her sides.

The recording began. Claire's wobbly greeting. Silence. Then the soft cadence of breathing. At last a raspy whisper.

"He... can't... have... you."

Claire's gasp. More silence. Finally a click.

"Well?" Michael swiveled toward her.

Eyes closed, she stood as if in a trance. Her sash had come undone, and the gaping robe exposed white silk. The nightshirt's V dipped below the shadowed valley between her breasts. His eyes strayed, and his body suffered.

She shook her head. "Only the lack of the thumping noise I heard before. But, Quinn, he... he thinks that we... you and I..."

"Have a thing going," he finished for her. Something he wouldn't turn away under other circumstances.

"Why would he think that?" She opened her eyes and walked to the window beside the desk. Outside, fat, white snowflakes fell in starry clusters against the windowpane. She yanked the curtains together. "That means he's watching the house, doesn't it?" Her voice was ragged. She pulled her hair into a knot, then let it fall, as if she wanted to collapse the same way.

"Or he's seen us together around town. We haven't exactly traveled incognito." Mostly they'd remained at arm's length from each other. Except for the day they'd gone to the *Rêve*. When she'd slipped, he'd held her in his arms longer than necessary. Maybe Raoul and his men had witnessed that little interlude. The taped voice had no Latin accent, but had to be tied in with the widow. He just didn't understand yet how.

"Okay. Okay." He rose from the chair to pace around the small office. "It's late. We're tired. Let it go for tonight. I want you to tell me more about Jonathan before we see Martine tomorrow afternoon."

She didn't appear to be listening. Forehead pinched, she stared through him, then dropped her gaze to the recorder. "We started with people who might have a grudge against Paul."

Ah. He'd wondered how long it would take her to deduce that his investigation was aimed in the wrong direction for her purposes.

"Much as I didn't want to believe it, *I* am the connection. If the threats are real, he killed them because of me." Her breath gave a little hitch before she went on. "We should be looking for someone with a grudge against me."

She rushed to him and clutched his arms. "He'll kill you, too, Quinn. You have to understand the danger."

He slid his fingers beneath her collar, with the innocent intent of closing that tempting gap. But she gazed at him with such torment in her chocolate eyes that instead, with a light tug, he drew her closer. She felt right in his arms.

"I can take care of myself," he said, a bit too gruffly. "Maybe it's not a grudge. Maybe he wants you for himself. No one else can have you. An obsession." She could easily become an obsession. His. But he couldn't let himself care.

The hard points of her nipples met little barrier in her silky nightshirt and his thin T-shirt. Their light brush against his chest shot his entire blood supply to his groin. Light-headed, he ached to touch her. She was the most desirable woman he'd ever known. Beautiful, sensual, intelligent, brave, and strong.

Was she murderer or victim? Was the caller a stalker or one of El Águila's American connections?

Dishonorable and dangerous to touch her. Hell of a mess. And damn the DEA for putting him in it! Hell, who was he kidding? He wanted her with an intensity he'd never felt before. And didn't like. But it didn't have to mean the hearts-and-flowers kind of involvement. That wasn't for him.

His fingers trailed down her collar line to caress the inner swells of her breasts. When she didn't turn away but merely gazed at him with her tragedies reflected in her eyes, he wanted to make her forget it all. To hell with honor and dereliction of duty. One night of unbridled, uninhibited sex wouldn't compromise his mission.

He closed his hand over her left breast and touched his lips to hers. Pleasure flowed through him like molten gold.

With light kisses, he cruised his way around her lips, soft as butter. When she opened to him, the first lazy sweep of his tongue against hers made his senses reel wildly. Through the silk, he rolled her peaked nipple between his fingers. Her delicate scent and her honeyed taste caused renewed need to explode in his loins. He went from hard to stone with devastating force.

He felt her small hands on his biceps, grasping.

Not grasping. Pushing.

"No, Quinn. Stop." Her voice was feather-light, her breath coming in short gasps. "I don't want this."

He released her, shaking his head to clear the

narcotic fog of their embrace. "But...you..." Not only hadn't she resisted, she'd leaned into him.

She tugged the robe around her and retied the sash. Her dark hair curled in a wild mass around her pale features. "I wasn't myself. The phone call... his threat... *merde*." She ran her hands over her hair. Her eyes were dark and opaque and unreadable.

"Claire—"

"Don't touch me again, Quinn. You're my employee. That's all."

Chapter Ten

THE SNOW TURNED to freezing rain and back to snow again. In the morning, an overly cheerful radio forecaster announced that the entire state of Maine was closed. Wind tossed great white billows, making for impossible road conditions and trapping Claire in the house with Quinn.

Last night had almost ended in disaster. Beyond stupid to prance around in her nightclothes, teasing him as he'd accused her of doing with Jonathan. Finally, common sense had overruled desire.

Their dealings with each other returned to forced politeness and latent hostility. Unfortunate but necessary. Aside from her attraction to Quinn, Claire liked him. He growled and snapped like a beast, but underneath his hard exterior hid an honorable man, a caring man who tried not to care.

Instead of wondering why he feared involvement so, she would return to aloofness. It was the only safe way since she felt the same. Any closeness to him would endanger him further. She'd kept her strength and independence for this long, and she could continue. But the temptation to lean on Quinn and yield to her desire for him sapped her willpower like the sun melting an icicle.

They spent the morning brainstorming names of possible stalkers. She described everyone she knew, including Elisha Fogg, her hairdresser, and the bag boy at the supermarket. Then she let Quinn use her office computer and the telephone for cross-checking names and whatever else detectives looked for. Escaping to the kitchen, she comforted herself with unnecessary Christmas baking—a *tarte aux pommes* and the preliminary steps for a *bûche de Noël*, a cake and meringue Yule log, and a *tourtière*, a pork pie.

By one o'clock, the snow backed off to light flurries, so Claire and Quinn set out on foot for the Farnsworth house. For a time, neither spoke. Side by side, they crunched through the new snow, heading deeper into the winter-muffled neighborhood.

"It's only two blocks this way, on a cul-de-sac," Claire said. At the corner, she turned right and quickened her pace.

"You said last night that Martine barely tolerated you. How did she and Jonathan's old man feel about your marriage?" Quinn tucked her arm in his, keeping her at his side.

She allowed it. He wasn't overstepping the boundaries she'd set up, not really. And the sidewalk was icy.

"Newcomb, her husband, was thrilled, even threw us an engagement party. But Martine—it's odd. At the time, I let it go. She said she was happy for us, but I never quite believed her. She acted resentful, even angry."

"Resentful of what?"

"I don't know. Is it important?"

"Any little thing might be. The slightest reason for being an enemy makes someone a suspect at this point."

"But Martine?" She sighed. Most likely her green-eyed snit arose from some petty reason now long forgotten. "Before you meet Martine, I should tell you about the resemblance."

Her feet stopped of their own accord, and she stared at the two children playing in the next yard. While Robert tried to push the huge snowball, little Adele, packed on snow. Claire's heart throbbed painfully. How she'd missed them!

Quinn pressed her arm. "Claire? Are they Martine's kids?"

She nodded, unable to drag her eyes from the children and their half-finished snow figure. Longing gnawed at her. "I haven't seen them in months."

Robert looked up, and then nudged his sister. "Hey, Claire!"

"Claire, come see our snowman!" Adele hopped up and down on the sloping lawn.

Daggers pierced her chest, and a strangled sob tore from her throat. She took one faltering step toward the dancing children.

"Adele, Robert! Come in the house!" The peremptory voice came from the house. When they hesitated, their mother called, "Have you forgotten what I told you? Come in this instant!"

Claire didn't wait to watch them run away from her. She buried her face in Quinn's thick parka and sought to calm her screaming nerves. Somewhere in the back of her mind, she realized she was once again clinging to him, relying on him.

Hating the reason but accepting the excuse to hold her, Michael put his arms around Claire. "Your cousin won't let you see them?" The boy looked about twelve, the girl, ten. Old enough to understand.

A deep breath shook her shoulders before she straightened away. "Not since, since…"

"Since the accusations began," he finished for her.

A few moments later, Martine Farnsworth opened the front door of her colonial-style home. "I know I agreed to this interview, Mr. Quinn, but I didn't agree to have that woman in my house." Her lips formed a line as thin as a razor blade.

"I'm searching for proof of how and why your stepson and the others died, Ms. Farnsworth. I'm sure you're interested in furthering that investigation. I'd hate to tell Detective Lieutenant Pratt that you refused cooperation." Unlikely she'd know he had no police authority.

"I won't contaminate your house, dear cousin," Claire said in a tight voice.

"Oh, all right." Martine led them into the house and seated them in a formal living room done in pale colors—beige and white and yellow. Silver swags and doves draped an enormous balsam fir in one corner. The dual wallop of the color scheme and the chilly atmosphere gave Michael the sense the woman had invited the snow in with them.

Obviously uncomfortable, Claire perched, ready for escape, on the edge of the loveseat beside him. Seeing the children had sliced through the defenses she'd rebuilt since last night.

What it must cost her to declare that she'd never marry and have that family she craved, he now grasped. She believed sincerely in that curse, damn her superstitious aunts. Generous and giving, she should have the children she'd forgone. A sliver of that sacrifice pierced his chest.

The resemblance Claire had begun to explain was obvious. A general facial similarity, the same thick mahogany hair, the same slender curves. The eight years Martine had senior to Claire didn't show. Likely due to regular spa pampering.

Even so, he would never mistake Martine for Claire. A little shorter and her wide mouth hadn't the same full lips. Most of all, she lacked the spark of warmth and sensuality that glowed in Claire's eyes. Not to mention her lady-of-the-manor attitude. He half expected her to ring a bell for the butler to serve tea.

Snobbery wasn't a quality he associated with Claire. He didn't count last night, when she deliberately called him her "employee." That was a defensive move. He still wanted her, more than ever, but she was right to stop him. For now.

"I can't imagine why you think I can help you. Newcomb and I told everything we knew to the police long ago." Martine made a show of consulting her Rolex. "And I can't give you much time. We're leaving for our condo at Caribou Peak as soon as my husband gets home." Her frigid tone should've left icicles on her lips.

Naturally the Farnsworths would have a place at Caribou Peak too. Interesting. "I'd appreciate anything you can tell me about your stepson, Mrs. Farnsworth."

"Newcomb's the one you should talk to, but I'll do my best. Jonathan was a wonderful young man, very devoted to his father, very bright. Loads of ideas and plans for expanding Farnsworth Enterprises."

"The company sells local products, I understand."

"Gourmet products. Pasta in bear or pine-tree shapes, blueberry syrup, locally ground pancake mix, pottery mugs, and herb teas. That sort of thing, all packaged in baskets to be sold in the country's finest gift shops."

"Claire." Newcomb Farnsworth strode in. "Martine, what's she doing here? What's going on?"

As if a general had barked for attention, Michael rose.

Gray-haired and nearing sixty, Farnsworth would present a commanding presence in any gathering. His snotty patrician demeanor, assuming obedience and deference as his due, typified other damn corporate suits Michael had run up against. The old-school type who considered himself layers above any shanty Irishman who'd worked on the docks to earn his way through school.

Damn, where did that come from?

Martine beamed a welcoming smile. "Oh, darling, I'm so glad you're home. This is Mr. Quinn." In a few words, she explained their presence.

"I hope you'll consent to help me clear my name, Newcomb," Claire said, breaking her usual silence during interviews. Her calm voice and expression belied the anxiety clearly eating at her.

"You're on a fool's errand, but I suppose we can answer a few questions." Hands in the trouser pockets of his custom-tailored suit, Farnsworth took a power stance beside his wife and before the hearth, an elegant marble structure filled with white poinsettias, not a warming fire.

"I appreciate your cooperation," Michael said. "Mrs. Farnsworth was just telling us about the family business. How heavily was Jonathan involved in the company?"

"I had placed him in charge of development. He showed great promise."

"Oh, yes," Martine put in, "he just brimmed over with ideas for European markets and adding to the product line."

"You were close, then?"

"We were friends," she said. "We used to talk a lot when he was home from college. Before *she* came."

"I can see why, since you were closer in age to him than to your husband. Isn't that true, Mrs. Farnsworth?"

"I suppose, but why not?" Her eyes narrowed, daring him.

Michael was trolling, but Jonathan's stepmother had risen to the bait. Instead of challenging her defense, he offered her his best disarming grin.

"He was a friendly boy, very outgoing," Newcomb added. "With his own mother long dead, I was pleased that he saw fit to confide in his stepmother."

"Tell me about his death." Claire and Pratt had filled Michael in, but he wanted the Farnsworths' version.

Claire remained poised for flight. Face composed, she stared at the hearth, as if into flames rather than flowers. Her fingers buttoned and unbuttoned a pocket on her long black skirt, over and over. If he could, he'd give her silverware or jars to line up.

"Jonathan had bought a fancy sports car at an antique car auction," Martine began. "Will you tell this, please, Newcomb?" She placed a hand on his arm.

After a long look at her, he acquiesced. The recital was obviously difficult for both. With lowered lashes, Martine listened.

"That night," Newcomb said, "Jonathan drove his

sports car out the Cliff Road—sharp curves, dangerously slick from a previous rain. Lord knows what he was doing out there." He shot an accusatory glare at his son's widow. "He... the car smashed through the guardrail on the sharpest curve and fell into the water. The police said he must have been going too fast."

"He'd been in this house before the accident. Had he been drinking?"

"We had a scotch together while we talked. That was all." The older man's lips compressed, and his eyes darkened.

More guilt. This family sure spread it around. Farnsworth blamed himself for his part in his son's death. But the amount of alcohol in Jonathan's system hadn't amounted to enough to affect his driving. "And you have no idea why he went out there?"

"I just told you that, I believe. We spent an hour or so talking business. He didn't say anything about Cliff Road."

"Or to you, Mrs. Farnsworth? You did speak to him before he left, didn't you?"

"Only... only to say good-night."

"That's all, Mrs. Farnsworth? You and your stepson were close friends, I thought. He didn't discuss his plans with you or mention going to meet someone?"

Her countenance tightened, grew brittle. "I told you, he said only good-night and left. If he didn't confide in me as he used to, it was her fault." Her eyes flicked a dagger at Claire. "I don't know how she did it, but she killed Jonathan. Sabotaged the car, the brakes, or the steering or something."

The cops had found no evidence of tampering. Of

course, a night of rinsing by ocean swells might erase evidence. They'd found no paint chips or tire tracks from another vehicle. Maybe it *was* an accident. "Did either of you leave the house after Jonathan?"

"Just what are you getting at, Mr. Quinn?" Newcomb's eyes glittered with indignation.

"Nothing." Michael shrugged elaborately. "I'm simply gathering facts. Did you leave the house that night?"

"Certainly not," Martine said. "We went to bed soon afterward. That's all we can tell you. Please excuse us now." She rose and led them toward the door.

"We have a trip to pack for," Newcomb added in final dismissal. He strode up the stairway without a backward glance.

A toss-up which of the cousins would win the ice-queen competition. Martine had haughty disdain down perfect, but Claire's untouchable, remote act was damn good—except for her trembling. He hooked her elbow with his hand so she wouldn't bolt out the door without him.

While they waited for their coats, a painting in the foyer caught Michael's eye. Father and son. Suit-coat formal.

Jonathan, tall and boyishly slim, posed beside his father's chair. While an air of command and power radiated from the elder Farnsworth, in Jonathan's eyes Michael saw humor and easy charm. The kind of charm, like Cruz's, that could melt even an ice queen.

Martine had married a man twenty years her senior. Stood to reason she'd be jealous when her younger cousin snagged the firstborn son and heir.

Didn't the biggest—and most dangerous—part of an iceberg hide beneath the water's surface?

Chapter Eleven

ALTHOUGH THE SNOW had stopped, Claire plunged mindlessly toward home, head down, feeling as if she were fighting her way through a driving blizzard.

Without warning, an arm plucked her off her feet and yanked her against a large immovable object. Her breath blew out in a whoosh, but she managed a breathy "Quinn! What the—"

He set her on her feet again but held onto one arm. "The car. It almost hit you."

She glanced up as a station wagon slithered away in the wet snow. Her heart tripped into an erratic tattoo. Fleeing the smothering hatred of the Farnsworth household, she'd paid no attention to where she was. Or to traffic.

"*Mon Dieu*, thank you, Quinn. I had to get away from there." She hugged herself. "I couldn't breathe."

She didn't resist when he guided her across the street toward her house. Having that familiar, warm pressure on her elbow grounded her, calmed her.

"You need to be home," he said.

"No, I like the air, the snow. Some activity is what I need." She hadn't realized it until she uttered the words. Instantly she knew where to go and what to show the big man beside her. "Quinn, you have cross-country skis in the back of your SUV. How would you like to use them this afternoon?"

His jaw worked, and his lips twitched toward a smile. "If you don't think it would compromise our employer-employee relationship, boss."

Touché. Heat rose to her cheeks. She said, more sharply than she intended, "You'll be on duty. I'll need protection, won't I?" She wrenched her arm from his light grasp to tromp up the snow-caked walk to her house.

Behind her, his rumbling chuckle triggered a sensual ripple through her, but his words stopped it.

"I thought I was the target, not you, babe."

\*\*\*\*

Half an hour later, following Claire's directions, Michael drove them north on Route One to a small state park a few miles outside Weymouth. Occasional glances in his rearview mirror assured him no one but Cruz had followed them out of town.

Frost-daubed pines and spruce arched tunnel-like over the closed park's narrow road. The scenery barely earned a glance. Michael forced his concentration on his driving, away from the woman beside him.

Constantly clad in mourning colors, Claire was stunning. But in her ski outfit of dark pink splashed with streaks of orange, she set him ablaze like the sunset she resembled. The soft fabric clung to her breasts and hugged the flare of her hips, and he wanted to rip away the damn outfit. Anger at his adolescent craving chased desire through his veins.

"You can pull in here." Claire pointed to a small parking lot where two other vehicles already sat. "Though the park is officially closed, rangers groom the trails with snowmobiles."

While she fastened her skis, he laced gaiters over his jeans. Out of habit, he'd left his skis and boots in the back of the Explorer, but hadn't considered packing the rest of his gear. A windproof anorak over a sweater and the leg coverings would suffice for their short trek.

Her sexy outerwear looked barely used, but her skis and boots had seen many miles of trail. "All this time I thought you didn't like being out in the cold," he said. "You're dressed like you do this every day."

"Idle standing in arctic sheds is what I hate." She pulled her hair back with a stretchy headband that covered her ears. "I grew up cross-country skiing. We had no money for fancy downhill ski resorts or equipment, but using my father's old skis set me free, allowed me to escape. Gliding across new snow like this through forest and field is wonderful, like discovering some new, wild place no one has ever been before." Her eyes grew dreamy.

Michael longed to touch his lips to her eyelids. He cleared his throat and inhaled deeply of the crisp, evergreen-scented air. "I know what you mean. Out in the Whites where I was camping, I felt I was on another planet, maybe the moon. Or I was the only person alive."

She angled her head in the way that always got to him. Then, without warning, her lips curved in a smile.

His breath stuck somewhere behind his breastbone, and his heart skipped a beat. Poleaxed. There was no other damn word for how she hit him. The smile painted color on her cheeks and danced lights in her eyes. Like the sun coming from behind a cloud—pure gold.

"*Allons-y.* Let's go." Before he could recover

enough to comprehend her words, she swished away into the woods, her arms working the poles in rhythm with the gliding skis.

He planted his poles and sprang forward in a racer's lunge. He was the stronger skier and could easily pass her, but then he'd deny himself the pleasure of keeping that firmly curved backside in his sights. So he hung behind her a few paces.

The groomed track zigzagged over the rolling terrain of the park's nature trails and then through the open camping area, past snowcapped charcoal grills and up-ended picnic tables. They passed two other skiers, a teenage couple in ragged jeans, but he saw no one he considered suspicious. After the last campsite, he followed Claire into the woods again. Moments later, she burst through an opening and disappeared.

Ice froze his gut, and he surged forward. When he emerged, he found the edge of the earth. A treeless snowfield sloped down, and then dropped off. To nothing. Nothing but cold white. Sky and snow merged to complete the illusion.

"Over here. Follow me."

The only color in a monochromatic world, Claire stood to his right at the edge of the trees. Only then did he exhale the breath he'd been unaware of holding. What the hell!

"Take off... your skis," she puffed out, her cheeks flushed from the exertion. "It's safer on foot from here to the edge." She bent and unhooked her boots from the bindings, then stepped away from the skis and headed downward along the tree line. "I want to show you something."

Hiking in slow motion through the deep snow

gradually brought more into view. Between snow and sky lay the pewter sea of Casco Bay, its roiling waters stretching to fir-spiked islands and beyond.

Claire stopped at a heavy wooden railing and gazed out. "Isn't this magnificent?" Apparently she'd seen the view many times before, but that didn't dim the awe in her voice.

"The end of the earth," he said. "You're a good skier."

"Thanks. I didn't know if I could do it again."

"Because of the way Alan died."

She nodded. "It was the last time I skied. I was out on one of the cross-country trails when the avalanche happened."

Michael wanted to know more details about Alan Worcester's death, but later. Right now, they had other things to discuss. His gaze dropped from the mesmerizing sea to the cliff falling away beneath him and down to a two-lane highway. "That's Cliff Road, isn't it?"

"That curve is where Jonathan's car went over the edge and into the ocean." She looked composed, but her fingers traced rows of even lines in the snow atop the railing.

Below them the highway turned sharply, and then wound its way out of sight. On the curve, a sturdy guardrail stood in place as if nothing had ever happened. Yet, seven years ago, on a clear October night, a sober Jonathan Farnsworth had crashed his sports car through the rail and hurtled to his death.

Major questions remained. Why had he been driving so fast? Why the hell this dangerous road at all? Had someone helped his death along? If so, who? And why?

"It made no sense to me then," Claire said, "and it still doesn't. What was he doing here?" Sorrow thickened her voice, and she fluttered a hand at the road below.

He longed to wrap her in his arms. "You don't think he could have just been putting his new car through its paces?"

"That wasn't like him. Unless... no."

"Unless what?"

"He might have done it if he and Paul were racing each other, but back then Paul had only an old pickup. And anyway, Paul was home in bed. He was the first person I telephoned when Jonathan didn't come home. I'd been up north and arrived home quite late, after midnight."

"There's no way to know any of that now, I suppose." From what he knew about the relationship between Jonathan and Paul, racing wasn't out of the equation. Even between a new high-powered sports car and an old pickup truck.

If the two friends had sped around those treacherous curves, Jonathan's death was an accident and not murder by some obsessive madman.

Had Paul the grieving friend then suffered the guilt of having left the scene and assuaged that guilt by caring for the widow? Or had Paul the competitive son of a bitch conveniently helped himself to his friend's widow?

Michael bet on door number two.

The problem with that scenario was it didn't explain the other two deaths, Paul's included.

Taking another tack, he said, "Are you ready to

talk about what happened earlier at the Farnsworths'?"

"What do you mean? Nothing happened. We didn't learn anything we didn't already know." She spun away from the cliff. "It's time to go back now. I have to feed Spook."

"Who?" A thread of panic wound around his throat at the doublespeak for spy. It was too close for comfort.

"The kitten, of course. He appeared like a ghost." She smiled. "Maybe Spook-*y* is better. Cuter, at least."

Exhaling, he halted her escape by clasping her hand. "Maybe you didn't learn anything new because you're denying what was right in front of you. Martine is hiding something. Jonathan could have told her something that night, something she's kept from her husband. They were close, maybe closer than they should have been. If something… happened between her and Jonathan ”

"You are implying that Jonathan and his stepmother…" He watched her struggle, unable to utter the damning words.

"Had an affair? Possibly. Whatever it was, she's terrified that Newcomb will find out." When Claire jerked loose and pushed uphill through the snow, Quinn let her go but followed close behind. "You said yourself she seemed angry at your marriage."

"I don't believe it!" Shaking, she stumbled halfway up the hill and fell in the snow. She curled into a ball on her side.

He dropped to his knees beside the weeping woman. He reached out a hand, then drew it back. What the hell had he done? His thoughtlessness had snapped the tenuous equilibrium she struggled to maintain on her emotional high wire.

"God, Claire," he began. Jesus, what could he say? "I know you loved Jonathan. Maybe it's something else with Martine. I spoke without thinking." He dug in his back pocket for the paper towel he used as a handkerchief. "Here."

She accepted it with wordless snuffles.

Without his permission, his hands reached out to pull Claire into his arms. To his surprise, she allowed him to comfort them both by holding her. While she cried, they remained on the snowy slope, on their knees facing each other. Michael struggled to ignore her herbal scent and his body's predictable reaction to her nearness. Hell, lately he spent most of his time half-aroused. Just chemistry, right?

When the tears subsided, she mopped at her eyes. "Isn't it strange? Those who hated Paul came right out with it, but the one who loved him, his father, is hiding something. And another who loved Jonathan, his stepmother, also has a secret."

"Do you have any ideas about that?" he asked the top of her head.

She eased back. Her eyes were dark and desperate. "I denied it just now as I've tried to deny it for years, but you're probably right that they had an affair before I met Jonathan. Poor Newcomb."

"How do you know?"

"There were… indications. Jonathan refused her calls, made me talk to her when she telephoned. At his father's house, he wouldn't stay in a room alone with her. It was nothing he'd ever discuss."

"He must have been just a boy when it happened. The sexy stepmother and an adolescent on hormone overload. A collision waiting to happen. Don't let it taint your memories of him."

She smiled, a sad, crooked one, but it still shot heat through his system. "Thanks, Quinn." She pressed a soft kiss to his mouth.

Even that light caress rattled his cage, but he managed to contain his desire. "You're welcome, boss."

She laughed, and they rose to finish climbing the hill. She'd regained her brave face, though it must hurt like hell to think the husband she'd loved had kept such a secret.

After clamping on his skis once more, Michael stared at the sea. "Could Martine have killed Jonathan to guard her secret?"

"She might do anything to safeguard her children," Claire mused, "but what about Paul? And the caller?"

No solution fit all the deaths, dammit. Regarding Jonathan, another possibility remained, one he didn't like mentioning.

"No one ever suggested Jonathan might have killed himself," he said, "but betraying his father had to weigh heavily on him."

"I don't know." Claire's voice wavered like the trembling pine needles behind them. She pointed a ski pole at the cliff. "But that turn... is called Suicide Curve."

## Chapter Twelve

AFTER ANOTHER SPATE of flurries overnight, Claire was glad that the weather front moved Down East to dump on the Canadian Maritimes. The next morning brought freshly washed blue skies and a dazzling if cold sun. Elisha Fogg's old truck chugged to her house for him to clear the snow.

As usual, she rose early. She waxed the kitchen floor and then dusted the living room. When Quinn suggested a meeting with the Weymouth police chief to cover his list of potential stalkers, she bowed out. He never questioned her reluctance to talk to cops, so after polishing the brass candlesticks, she was able to slip out alone on an errand she'd prefer to share with no one.

Not even with a man she was coming to care for. To care for more than she should. Damn! Couldn't she have a simple business association with the man? Her looks got in the way, and her own needs. Her curse. He wanted her, even believed in her now. If only desire and proximity were the reasons, she could fight the attraction. It should be easy.

But it wasn't.

She returned home at noon, relieved to see that Quinn hadn't returned and that Elisha's truck remained at the curb. He'd been happy to stay and walk Alley after finishing the snow removal. At least this once she hadn't had to worry about someone prowling in her house while she was gone.

The anonymous phone calls had become rarer lately. Perhaps the stalker was more circumspect because of Quinn's presence. Or perhaps he'd exhausted his supply of burnt phones. No, not *burnt,* what did Quinn call the disposable phones? *Burner phones*, that was it. Whatever the reason, she'd take the peace.

At the police station, Quinn should be safe enough. If her anonymous caller posed a threat to him, his safety was her responsibility.

It would probably do no good to advise the stalker that Quinn meant nothing to her, that he was merely the P.I. she'd hired. He was in danger any time he spent away from her. In spite of yesterday's revelations, she didn't believe that Jonathan had taken his own life. Nor that his death had been an accident.

Jonathan and the others had died while she was unavailable—at home, or at the library, or off on another skiing trail. Like today, when she went off on her own. Her heart thumped. Quinn was surely okay.

She carried her packages up the cleared walkway to be greeted by Elisha shambling around the corner with Alley.

Depositing her burdens on the porch, she clapped and called, "Alley, come, little one!"

Elisha freed the dog's leash, and she raced on three strong legs to her mistress. The old man shuffled closer and stood waiting while the dog twirled in frantic circles and yipped a happy greeting.

Claire lifted the dog into her arms. "Well, Elisha, how did you like the new snow blower?"

His thin shoulders lifted a fraction, and the

weathered lips pursed. "I managed. Not as reliable as a shovel, mind you. These newfangled gadgets got too many movin' parts to run for long without needin' work, but it did the job today."

"I appreciate you trying it out for me." She knew not to push his pride. "Mr. Quinn's not back, I see."

He doffed his patched cap. "Well, yes and no, Claire."

"What do you mean?" An uneasy chill invaded her spine.

"He come back a while ago, seems like. Left again in a wicked hurry."

"Did he ask where I was? Was he looking for me?" She didn't want him following her, prying, but out alone, danger stalked him.

The old man coughed and worried his cap as if trying to scrub off its innumerable stains. She focused half on how to locate Quinn and half on Elisha's meandering monologue.

She tuned in as he said, "That Quinn's a good'un." He measured out his words one at a time in his Down-East drawl. "The past year, folks has said terrible things about you, missy. I don't understand it all, but I know you. You ain't done nothin' wrong, and you deserve better."

"What are you trying to tell me?" Was it something about Quinn? Whatever he had to say, she'd have to be patient. Elisha Fogg chewed over every word before spitting it out. Letting Alley wriggle from her arms, she held the leash.

"He stood and talked to old Elisha like you do, Quinn did. Not like that Santerre you was married to a while back. Woulda stepped over my bleeding body in the middle of his own yard, he would. Not Quinn. Asked about the blower. Listened."

Claire mentally reviewed places Quinn could have gone. Maybe he was questioning someone on his potential stalker list. Without her? No, he'd promised. Judging from his restraint, despite his desire for her, he was honorable. She imagined the control behind his smoldering gray eyes, the power in his broad shoulders, the tenderness in his hands. *Mon Dieu*, where was he? He could have gone back to see one of the lobstermen. Or...

Now the old man's kneading threatened the battered cap's survival. "A young woman like you needs a good man like that to take care of things. A young man. Not a dried-up old crab like Elisha. Yes'm, Quinn's a good'un. Asked for my help."

That snapped her to attention. "Asked for your help?" She clutched the old man's sleeve. "What do you mean?"

"Asked if Elisha seen any suspicious characters snoopin' around the neighborhood." His thin shoulders straightened, and he plopped the cap back on his grizzled head.

"And have you?" She mentally kicked herself. She'd never thought to recruit Elisha, who like a seagull, watched all comings and goings.

He bent forward. "Told him I seen a big dark blue SUV, cruising back and forth. Stopped once or twice in front o' the house too. Don't belong to nobody on this street."

Claire's heart clattered, and her throat tightened. A Jeep SUV? Where had she seen such a vehicle?

"Weren't the only time I seen that SUV, neither,"

he continued. "That's when Quinn took off like a dog on a scent." He pointed a bony finger at Alley, who was sniffing at something under the porch.

"Please, Elisha, where else did you see the SUV?" She could barely restrain herself from shaking the information from him.

"Why, down to the harbor earlier this mornin'." He scratched his chin beneath his scraggly beard. "Saw it parked outside Greavey's Boatyard. You know, where—"

The clawing anxiety turned to daggers of fear. "Stay a while longer if you can. I have to find Quinn." Her breathing shallow with dread, Claire thrust the leash at the old man.

She backed her car onto the street and skidded away before Elisha could reply.

****

Michael could find no sign of Raoul Olívas's vehicle at Greavey's. If El Águila's men had been there, they were long gone now. He couldn't find out about anyone snooping around the *Rêve*. Greavey himself had driven home to lunch, and the secretary had spent her morning in front of a computer screen. Other than himself, no one had asked her any questions.

Inside the boat shed, the *Rêve* rested on its struts the same as it always had. Nothing seemed out of place. Except the ladder. It was nowhere near.

After checking out every other boat in the shed, he finally located the damn thing at the shed's upper end. Someone had propped that ladder and two others against a broad-beamed wooden sloop, where a radio blared an old Stones romp, and the odor of fresh varnish stung his nose. The varnishers had presumably gotten the hell out of there for lunch too. When he mumbled something about the world running on its stomach, his belly growled in reply.

He struggled back to the *Rêve* with the unwieldy ladder and with the pieces of a puzzle that wouldn't fit no matter what the hell he did, or which way he turned things. The Weymouth police chief had been less than helpful, adopting the state Major Crimes line against the Widow Spider. He did finally agree to run Michael's list through the computer.

Cruz could have checked the names on the DEA's computers, but Michael didn't want to explain it to him. Or to see his friend smirk. Clearing the widow of murder wasn't supposed to be part of his gig.

She'd kept some secrets from him, like where the hell she'd gone this morning when she'd told him she had translating to do. But he couldn't believe the Claire Saint-Ange he'd come to know had murdered three men.

Still, he couldn't help thinking it was all connected. How wide was the widow's web? The drugs. El Águila's men. The telephone stalker. The murders.

They were all murders, his gut instinct insisted. He agreed with Claire that Jonathan's death hadn't been suicide. She'd seen no indications of depression or extreme worry, none of the usual markers.

Michael leaned the ladder against the side of the *Rêve* and climbed aboard. A quick glance around the cockpit spotted nothing out of place. Pros wouldn't leave much of a trace, but a sharp eye could spot even a tiny discrepancy. A dial turned, a coiled line askew, something.

As he lowered himself to the captain's chair, a

flash of movement out the upper window caught his attention.

Damn! Claire.

The old man must have told her. The freshening wind blew her long dark hair back like a capelet above her coat. Sunlight glinted fiery highlights off her hair. Woman on a mission. Judging from her tight mouth and the way she was storming through the parking lot toward the boat shed, there'd be hell to pay for investigating on his own.

Hot damn! An argument with his delectable boss was almost as good as sex. Almost.

He grinned, a real grin for the first time in months.

\*\*\*\*

Icy fear encasing her belly, Claire ran through the snow-filled parking lot. A fish truck blocked the entry, so she'd parked farther up the hill, alongside Quinn's SUV. At least she knew he was here.

Spitting French curses, she slipped and slid her way. The mid-thirties temperatures were melting the snow into a slushy mess. It slowed her pace, making her plod along in slow motion as if a force, unreal, dreamlike, kept her running in place. Tears threatened to choke her, to blind her. She had to reach him in time! In time for what, she didn't know. Maybe nothing. Didn't he know he was in mortal danger? She had to save him.

Was he in there? *Please let him be all right.*

An icy patch sent her into a skid, and she fell to her knees with more Gallic imprecations on her lips.

In the next moment, strong arms lifted her to her feet and held her. Steel-gray eyes searched hers.

She clutched at his parka-covered chest, cupped his

116

strong jaw with her hand, brushed at the strand of chestnut hair on his forehead. The rock solidity and heat of his body reassured her he was whole and well.

"Quinn! You're all right. Thank God!"

"Yeah, boss. Why shouldn't I be?" he drawled.

After she allowed herself to breathe, his teasing comment registered, along with the wicked glint in his eyes and the mocking twist to his mouth. The man didn't even realize the threat painting a bull's-eye on his back. And when he called her "boss," how did he manage to make it sound like "babe"?

His arrogance lit a match to her cheeks and her temper. She didn't know whether to kiss him or pummel him.

"Idiot! *Bête comme une patate!*" she yelled. "Why did you come down here by yourself? Don't you know—"

The boat storage building behind Quinn erupted like a volcano.

The explosion flung them to the slushy pavement with the force of a giant fist. The roaring and rumble swept over them like a portent of the world's end. Shards of metal and fiberglass and wood rained around them, on them.

When the shock ended, Claire found herself beneath the protection of Quinn's large body.

"What in bloody hell!" He rolled off her, and then pulled them both from the wet and debris to their feet.

Claire stared at where the lower end of the boat shed—and the *Rêve de coeur*—used to be. Angry flames leaped from the building wreckage. The fire's heat and the cognizance of what had just happened reached her at the same time. She couldn't speak, could only gape.

"We have to move back," Quinn said. "There might be more gasoline and other flammables in there." Grim-faced, he led her to a retreat position near the harbormaster's shed, where they had met with Russ Santerre.

The whine of sirens announced the imminent arrival of the Weymouth Fire Department. Fire engulfed the lower end of the boat shed and threatened to spread to the rest. Claire spotted Greavey's secretary standing outside the so-far intact office. She must have called in the fire.

Claire tore her gaze from the blazing debris of Paul's dream of a boat. Quinn's face was unmarked, but his jacket was wet and nearly shredded. "You could have died," she whispered.

He grimaced. The hand he brushed over the back of his head came away bloody. "Some damn thing cut me."

"Here, let me see. You're injured from protecting me." Her voice cracked with emotion. "Oh, Michael, this is all my fault."

He grabbed her hands and held them between their bodies as if manacled. "Is it, Claire? Is it your fault?" His eyes darkened to a winter-sea gray, stormy with turbulence. The set of his mouth transformed him into the hard man she'd first met.

The fire trucks arrived and with them a flurry of focused activity. Soon water cascaded over the hungry flames.

At his accusatory tone, her heart fell in a slow, sickening spiral. "Wha— You said yourself you were the target. Because of me." She tried futilely to free her hands. "You're hurting me."

"I could have been a hell of a lot more than hurt, lady," he spat at her. "The cops will be here soon, and you'll have to tell them everything. But tell me now. You know I come down here sometimes. What happened? Did you set the bomb and then have second thoughts? Did you decide a bomb was too obvious? Or too soon? So you changed your mind and raced to my rescue?"

His words stung like a slap. An unholy buzzing rang in her ears, and panic made it hard to breathe. "You... you think I could have done this?"

"You know enough about explosives. I saw the reference books for one of your translation jobs. Motive? Was I getting too close to the truth? Or like the typical serial killer, you just couldn't wait any longer. Had to do your next victim."

He yanked her closer, so she tasted the harsh bursts of his breath and the venom of his words.

Despair and pain ripped through her, paralyzed her. How could he say these things? "No, no," she whispered.

"Opportunity? I was gone all morning. Where were you?"

She only shook her head in mute denial. If he believed she could do this terrible thing, divulging her secret errand would make no difference.

"What a damn fool I was!" He shoved her away so abruptly she nearly fell. "To think I believed you. Believed the Widow Spider. I even..." With a growl of rage, he turned aside to stare at the smoldering ruins.

A hard lump clogged Claire's throat and spread downward to crush her chest.

No. She was the damn fool to have fallen in love with him. The future held nothing for them no matter what, but loving a man who hated her stretched the future into an agonizing wasteland.

Chapter Thirteen

WHEN THE WEYMOUTH police chief
ascertained that the explosion and resulting fire began
on a boat belonging to Paul Santerre's widow, the case
rapidly leapfrogged to the state detectives. After Pratt
questioned him, Michael had little to do but wait for the
investigation to proceed.

"Yow! Watch it. That's my skull, not a damn
wood-shop project. Feels like sandpaper you're
scraping me with," he bellowed at the ambulance
attendant who was cleaning the glass shards from his
scalp.

The EMT made some soothing comment and
continued probing the back of his victim's head.

Michael heard further mumbling about stitches and
going to the hospital, but he ignored them. He gritted
his teeth and concentrated on the black smoke rising
into the overcast sky.

Once the police arrived, they had separated Claire
and him for questioning. He hadn't seen her since.
Where the hell did they take her?

God Almighty, he'd acted like a flaming jerk. He'd
said terrible things out of fear and shock. Fear at how
narrowly they'd both escaped death. Fear of all the
unknowns in this damn case. Fear for Claire. And shock
at all the emotions whirling around inside him.

Worst of all, he'd destroyed the trust she'd given

him.

He did still believe in her, didn't he? True, she had a book on explosives. And she wouldn't tell him where she'd gone that morning. But if she was guilty, wouldn't she have a ready alibi? She'd had no pat alibis for the alleged murders, either. Shit.

Cruz would say he wasn't thinking with his brain but with a lower part of his anatomy. Hell, he didn't know anymore. He wanted to trust her. He did trust her. She didn't plant the bomb that could have blown them both up. No more than she'd murdered three men or smuggled drugs.

In the past few weeks, he'd pierced her prickly shield and seen past the beauty to the gentleness and generosity inside. From the beginning, he'd wanted her, and now he cared about her too. More than he wanted to.

Somehow he had to repair the damage he'd inflicted on their fragile relationship.

When the EMT jabbed at his head wound for the seventeenth time, Michael nearly turned to jab *him*. Damn, was this guy into S&M? He gritted his teeth through the last of the torture. Bandaging mercifully completed, he went to sit on the tailgate of Cruz's SUV. His head reeled, and someone pounded steel drums inside his head, but he would wait as long as it took to know about the bomb.

By late afternoon, he wasn't surprised to see local DEA and U.S. Customs agents join the MCU at the town landing. Next they'd call in the Alcohol, Tobacco, and Firearms guys because of the explosives.

Half the agents already swarming around the boatyard had worked with him at one time or another.

So why not add to the ATF and bring in the freaking FBI? They'd have a damn party to announce this whole undercover operation. When a Customs agent he recognized strolled by, he hid his face in his hands.

A frustrating hour later, Rick Cruz and Detective Sergeant Pratt walked toward him through the slush and debris. High clouds obscured the sun and threatened a new front.

"Yo, Pratt, where's Ms. Saint-Ange?" Michael barked.

Pratt's mouth twisted into a sneer. "One of my detectives took her to the police station for questioning. You worried about the poor little Widow Spider?"

Michael wished for the strength to slug Pratt in his smart mouth. "Damn right," he said quietly. Shouting would hurt too much. "That firecracker in there nearly nailed us both. She didn't set it, and I want to know who the hell did."

"Just what's going on with the DEA?" Pratt asked. "If you guys would lay it all out for me, we could get this over with sooner. I'd like to get home sometime. Tomorrow's Christmas."

Today was Christmas Eve. At that realization, the pain in Michael's head couldn't match the ache in his chest. On Christmas Eve, the whole Quinn clan stuffed themselves with his mom's lasagna and biscotti and then gathered around the enormous tree, where each opened one present. His dad told bad jokes. Roark played carols on the piano. Sandro sang off-key and rolled around on the floor with his kids. And Amy—

His eyes misted with the thought of all that without his sister Amy in her handmade elf hat to hand out the gifts.

"Yo, Quinn, you okay, *mano*?" Cruz said. "You look white as that seagull poop over there."

Michael passed a hand over his eyes and pulled himself back to the present problem. He zipped up the remnants of his parka to the neck. Cold. He was never cold. "Yeah, man, I'm fine. Just fine." If he ignored the claws ripping at the back of his head. "Can we get out of here? I don't want some ATF puke blowing my cover."

The state detective puffed out his chest and jerked a thumb toward the ruined boat shed. "Don't need no damn ATF help. Our own bomb squad can handle this one."

"We're finished here for the time being," Cruz said. "SAC said to report everything to Pratt here. This operation has changed course."

Three men in protective jumpsuits clambered from the rubble with evidence bags to be analyzed in the police lab.

Claire.

That could have been her—or him—in a body bag. Nausea roiled in his stomach and twined up his throat. Hell of a Christmas Eve. He gaped listlessly as the bomb squad loaded their booty into the state fire marshal's van, then drove past them. The smoke from the fire must be hanging in the air because everything looked oddly foggy. He wanted to clear his head, but the pain...

"Suppose you two DEA wonder boys come to the MCU field office and wait for the preliminary lab results," Pratt said. "I'll lean on the bomb squad to hurry it along. In the meantime, you can tell me all about your undercover op." His authoritative tone implied more than an invitation.

"Will do. Always glad to cooperate with the state boys," Cruz said with what Michael, even in his shaky condition, recognized as exaggerated amiability.

Michael scowled when his friend hunkered down to scrutinize him. He shivered again.

Cruz's mouth thinned. "But it will have to wait until we get back from the hospital. My partner's in shock. His head's bleeding pretty bad."

\*\*\*\*

When Claire finally entered her house at ten-thirty that night, she found Alley wriggling happily in greeting. The dog sat on command, and the black kitten mewed and pounced on Alley's swishing tail. Claire knelt to hug Alley and pat Spooky's head.

*Dieu merci.* Thank God they were all right.

A note was taped to her coat tree. The sight of the torn envelope and black ink stopped her heart for a beat until she recognized Elisha Fogg's cramped scrawl.

*Fed critters. Left 5:00 p.m. E.F.*

Tears stung her eyes. The old handyman had spent the entire day there. She hadn't telephoned because she didn't think he'd dare enter the house. Just this morning, didn't he express his faith in her innocence?

Now he was the only person who believed in her.

Folding the note, she wandered into the living room and flicked on a lamp. She was right to rush to Quinn's rescue. Without her, he'd have remained on board the boat and died.

Ironically, because of her actions, he once again thought her a murderer.

Where was he? Chief Snow had hustled her away so quickly, she didn't see if anyone tended his wound.

Was he all right? Would he return tonight? He'd have to retrieve his belongings, anyway. The safest thing for him would be to drop her case and leave town.

Which would also be safer for her heart.

Still, she needed to know he was all right. After the hours of questioning and explanations, she had more questions than answers. She'd told Snow everything—the phone calls, the interviews, the blue SUV. She finally remembered where she'd seen a dark blue Cherokee. At the town landing. Maybe Quinn found out more. Snow didn't tell her anything.

Exhausted, she wavered beside the unlit Christmas tree. She should eat, but she didn't feel hungry enough to fix anything. At the police station, they'd offered her a deli sandwich, but she'd only picked at it.

Christmas Eve. The traditional *tourtière* she'd planned to share with Quinn would make Alley several festive meals. Now the most she could manage was to build a fire and pour a glass of wine. She still wore her boots and coat, which had dried. If she could just get moving.

"Up you come, Spooky." Scooping up the kitten, she trudged to the kitchen, Alley at her heels. She deposited the bundle of black fur in his box. "Soon you'll grow big enough to climb over the top. But for now, I don't trust you not to scoot out the door and disappear."

Head cocked, Alley stared at the back door. A whine, then a growl emitted from her thirty-pound form.

"What is it? Is one of those sassy squirrels at the bird-feeder again?" Claire flipped on the porch light. "I'm sure you need to go out."

As soon as the door opened, the little dog raced away into the darkness beyond the arc of yellow light. She woofed warnings at the invisible intruder.

Claire smiled. At least twice a day, Alley had to reassert her dominance over the backyard wildlife, usually during daylight hours. This visitor had better be a raccoon and not a skunk. The barking stopped, but Alley wouldn't return until after her routine circuit.

Claire stopped at the porch steps. Three new boards framed the latticework. Elisha. Not content to merely pet sit, he'd found repairs to do. Again tears threatened, but she berated herself for uncustomary weepiness and made her way to the rows of wood.

She began lifting logs into her arms, but stopped when she heard a whimper from somewhere beyond the light's reach. Adjusting her burden, she turned and peered into the darkness.

"Alley, where are you? Alley, come."

All lay silent on this moonless Christmas Eve. With the privacy hedges at either side and the empty house at the rear, no light illuminated the dense black depths of the large yard.

A movement to her left caught her eye, but it vanished. Nothing. A bird. A bat.

"Alley, come! *Viens!*"

The porch light winked out. Darkness cloaked her and the woodpiles.

Ice congealing in her stomach, she edged toward the house. A flashlight. She had to get to the kitchen to bring the flashlight. She had to find Alley. She dropped the logs. What if the light hadn't merely burned out? What if someone turned it off? Someone who could still be in the house!

Her heart pounded. Was it the anonymous caller? Or the bomber? Were they the same?

Her lungs clogged and her throat closed. She couldn't call out. Not for Alley. Not for help.

A creaking noise came from the high double row of wood behind her. Quinn was right. That one would tumble over soon.

Another creak. A scrape.

Before Claire could react, the entire stack crashed down on her. A scream tore from her throat. Agony exploded on her back, through her whole body, with bursts of white light before her eyes. She crumpled to the snow-covered ground, buried beneath an avalanche of sixteen-inch-long split maple and birch.

"Alley." She managed the muffled cry before black oblivion engulfed her.

Chapter Fourteen

THE TINGLING ON his nape alerted Michael an hour later as he entered Claire's house. Something wasn't right. Tense and alert, he slipped the key in his pocket and locked the door behind him.

In addition to the hall light, another shone from the living room, but the tree remained dark. The rooms felt colder even than Claire's usual money-saving temperature. French economy, she'd told him. Her coat didn't hang on the rack. The house lay silent, waiting.

His head still pounded, and tension tightened a knot behind his eyes.

"Claire?" he called, though he wouldn't blame her for not answering him.

A clattering of claws came as the immediate response. Claire's three-legged dog arrived in a flurry of yelps.

"Yo, Alley. Where's your mistress?" He knelt to pat the animal.

The tan mongrel sat for his caress, then whined and dashed to the kitchen. Another light on in there.

A quick glance didn't locate Claire.

He wandered into the living room. No glass on a table. No magazine left open. The woman was too damn neat. She hadn't gone to bed, not with lights on. Where was she?

Alley returned to bark insistently at him. She

danced around him, and then raced into the kitchen.

"You want a biscuit, do you? Just a minute, girl."

Expecting to find Claire at work, he trailed to her dining room office. Empty and dark.

Once again the dog emitted her vociferous plea. She nudged his ankle with her long nose and gazed up at him, ears pricked to full attention.

Tendrils of alarm crawled over Michael's skin and curled in his gut. "What is it? What are you trying to tell me?"

Unless he was mistaken, worry filled the pup's liquid brown eyes. If the odd situation hadn't already alerted him, he would probably have continued to ignore the dog's behavior. Only movie critters or K-9 dogs led people to the rescue, didn't they?

"Okay, girl," he said. "Where do you want me to go?"

Continuing to bark, Alley scampered across the hall to the kitchen. She disappeared through the half-open back door as he entered the room. No wonder the house was cold. Was Claire outside fetching wood? He couldn't imagine that she'd leave the door open.

Strange. All was dark outside.

He reached inside the anorak he'd borrowed from Cruz. No gun. For eight months he hadn't carried a gun. He couldn't stop to examine why he'd suddenly gone for it. He flipped on the back porch light and stepped outside. Alley continued to bark and whine. Breathing easier but maintaining alertness, Michael crept down into the yard.

The only things he saw were the damn wood stacks. What was different? Hah, that precarious one had finally tumbled over. Now, where had the dog run off to?

Alley darted toward him from the other side of the fallen wood. One bark, then she raced off again.

Michael trekked through the snowy yard and around the strewn wood to the sound of the little dog's distress. At first he saw only the pup on her belly nosing at something under the wood. When she spied him, she stopped barking.

"What is it, Alley?"

He spotted a hand, almost as pale as the snow. Then dark, flowing hair like black blood against the white ground.

*Claire!*

His heart raced and the knot behind his eyes throbbed. "Oh, my God!" He knelt beside her and clutched her hand. Ice cold. He flung log after log away. "Claire! Answer me, Claire!"

She stirred, lifted her head from where it rested on her other hand, and squinted at the source of the voice. "No... the quilt... don't take it. So warm..."

*Just let her be all right.*

Hallucination, a sure sign of the onset of hypothermia. He tamped down the panic and inhaled deeply to quell the riot in his head and in his chest.

In the name of God, how long had she been lying here? His survival training kicked in. He had to get her out, get her warmed up. The logs fairly flew away with his effort to remove the weight trapping her to the icy ground.

The occasional snowflake had turned into a steady snow.

In what seemed like hours, Michael cleared enough space so he could check her limbs. Please, please. He ran his fingers over her legs, her back, her arms. No broken bones. Thank God for the coat and boots. It came to him that finally he had his hands all over Claire, but not in the way he wanted.

She mumbled something unintelligible and tried to swat his hands away. Then she lay still. Her lips were blue. Ice clotted her long, luxuriant hair. Drying it was a priority.

Grimly clamping his lips together, he lifted her into his arms. "You're safe, babe. I've got you."

The front of her coat, which had been pressed into the snow, glistened with moisture and caked ice. Michael hoped to God she wasn't soaked through.

"Come on, Alley, let's warm her up." He carried Claire inside and kicked the door shut behind them. Claire raised her head from his shoulder. "M-M-Michael, why are y-y-you here?"

Relief swept through him that she was conscious and recognized him. "I'll take care of you."

The little dog followed, ears pricked and never taking her eyes from her mistress, all the way to Claire's bedroom. Ever watchful, she curled up on the chaise.

After depositing his limp burden on the king-size bed, Michael ripped the sodden black coat away. If it wasn't ruined from the explosion, he hoped this had finished the job. If she were his, he'd never let her wear black again. He kicked the coat and his jacket out of his way.

All that wet hair clung to her scalp, leaching heat from her. He strode to the connecting bathroom to grab towels, one of which he wrapped turban-style around her head.

She lay on the bed, pale as paper. Her dark eyes widened in desperate concern. "You h-have to p-pack up and go. He'll try to k-k-kill you again." With clumsy fingers, she pushed at his arm.

Hell and damn. He'd accused her of trying to blow him up, and here she lay cold and injured and fearing for *his* life. On top of what Cruz had told him, it was enough to make him feel as low as a cockroach. Lower.

"Shh, let me take care of you. I should have been here." Failure tasted bitter as bile. Once again, he'd failed to protect a female in his care. This time, at least, she hadn't died. Her shivering meant she was warming up.

Her hands felt icy but thankfully exhibited no white spots of frostbite. He wrapped his hands around hers and held on, willing his heat into her. The black sweater and pants had absorbed the cold but not the moisture. A good sign. Wet cold penetrated faster. But they still had to come off.

"Where's your nightgown?" he said, tugging off her boots.

"In th-there."

He dug around in the drawer until he found a long flannel thing, definitely not something slinky like the other night. His constitution couldn't take that. "Okay, sit up."

When he started to remove her sweater, she twisted out of his grasp. "I can d-d-do it."

He doubted it, but trying might help warm her up faster. "Be my guest."

Claire's fingers dabbed stiffly and ineffectually at the sweater hem. "*M-m-merde.* Quinn, what's wrong?" Her chocolate eyes pleaded with him.

He sat beside her on the bed. "Sweetheart, your hands are numb from the cold. Let me help you. You have to get under the covers. You're on the verge of hypothermia. It's dangerous."

With an exhausted sigh, she nodded, still shivering.

"I promise not to peek. Much."

As matter-of-factly as he could manage, he peeled her black sweater from her perfect, rounded breasts and over her head. Skimmed her woolen slacks down her smoothly muscled legs. If his hands happened to brush her flesh in the process, so be it. He hadn't promised not to savor the soft feel of her skin, living silk his hands would remember.

Warming silk. Though her legs and arms still felt chilled, her belly was not. Another good sign. The cold hadn't penetrated to the vital organs. She'd be fine.

*Thank you.*

The heavy coat and boots had protected her from cuts and broken limbs, but angry red and purple marks already blossomed on her skin. Tomorrow she'd be stiff and sore, but whole.

Removing her lacy bra and panties would be too much temptation, so instead he tossed the nightgown over her head.

Clad in the enveloping flannel, she allowed him to bundle her beneath the covers. He left her to make hot cocoa, but when he returned, he found Claire still quivering in the bed. "What is it?"

"C-covers are c-cold," she said.

"I've turned up the furnace. The house will warm up now." He helped her sit up. Keeping an arm around her shoulders as support, he brought the cup to her lips. For such a strong, brave woman, she felt small and vulnerable. Using him as a heating pad, she huddled against him, one soft breast pressed into his side.

His body acted predictably, dammit, hardening him painfully. He'd just have to take it. Aches and pains all over. What was one more? "Drink this, and I'll call the cops... and an ambulance."

"N-no, no c-cops, n-no one. I've had enough c-cops f-for one day. P-please, Quinn."

He knew her aversion to the police, understood how much they must have grilled her tonight. Snow was already covering any footprints, anyway. "Okay, but first thing in the morning."

After finishing the cocoa, she said, "Quinn, s-stay with me." She plucked the towel away and gazed at him expectantly, lips no longer blue but still pale. And tempting.

He wanted to hold her, to dive into the dark pools of her eyes, to warm her with his own body.

Dangerous. Wrong.

"Maybe Alley will let me share her chaise. She's the heroine of the night. You saved her life, and now she's saved yours." He explained how the dog had nagged at him to follow her.

"I... remember she kept my hands warm for a while." Claire's brow furrowed with thought. "I thought someone had hurt her. She whimpered from the darkness but wouldn't come. And then... and then—"

"The wood fell on you?"

"Yes. But it didn't just fall. I saw someone. Someone who pushed it over on me." Her head fell against his shoulder. "I'm too tired and sore now. I'll explain in the morning."

When Michael started to rise, she clutched at him.

"No, not over there on the chaise. Here. Stay here and keep me warm." She snuggled closer. "I need you, Michael."

God. She needed him. He didn't want to be needed. He'd failed her like he'd failed the others. Claire needed only his heat. And wasn't holding her all night what he wanted?

He'd never allowed himself to lose control with a woman. Over the years, he'd had several relationships, none serious or long lasting. He'd always, always held himself in check so his strength aided pleasure but provided no pain. This woman he desired more than any other had the power to snap his restraint like a matchstick.

He struggled for the strict professionalism and disengagement that had the other DEA agents labeling him a hard case. His head wound throbbed. Exertion and stress made his struggle impossible. He needed rest as much as she did. She was hurt, and he had to take care of her. Helping her warm up wouldn't compromise his detachment. What was left of it.

After dousing the light, he removed his boots and sweatshirt, and then stretched out under the covers in his T-shirt and jeans, his arms around her. Just hold her felt healing, having her softness beside him.

Never mind that he was as hard as one of those logs and aching with need. Never mind that some forgotten organ in his chest raced with joy merely at the closeness. Never mind that she'd called him Michael.

Chapter Fifteen

WARM. SHE'D FEARED she would never be warm again. In a drowsy half-asleep state, Claire smiled, luxuriating in the quilt's heat.

Even her pillow radiated heat. It was summer and hot coffee and a wood fire all in one. She wriggled in the delicious warmth, propped her head higher on the firm pillow, and curled her leg over—

Quinn!

Sound asleep on his back, his head turned toward her, he slept on. It was his hard arm not her pillow cradling her head, and his jeans-clad leg beneath her bare one.

Then she remembered. The woodpile. Alley.

Twice in one day she'd nearly died. Trapped beneath the heavy wood, she'd called and called for help, but the same trees that sheltered the yard muffled her cries. Finally Alley appeared from the darkness to whine at her and lie on her hands. The intense cold and ceaseless shivering metamorphosed into a dreamlike limbo, where she stayed until Quinn had rescued her.

Carefully, stiffly, she slipped off the bed. On the way to the bathroom, she noticed the empty chaise. During the night, Alley had gone to her own bed in the kitchen.

With every movement, muscles and flesh protested. A paint palette from head to toe, she bet, but didn't want to look. After brushing the worst tangles from her hair, she returned.

Gray light through the window told her dawn approached. She ought to dress and go brew coffee. But instead, she crept back into bed to watch Quinn sleep. Breakfast could wait.

As soon as she lay down, he rolled toward her, throwing his left arm across her waist. She stifled a groan at the impact on her bruised body, and then gradually relaxed again into the luxury of his loose embrace. She couldn't move now, could she? Not without waking him.

In sleep, his chiseled features looked not softer, but less hard-edged. A wave of hair fell across one eyebrow, and his firm yet sensuous mouth was only inches from hers. If she pressed her lips to his, would he awaken?

Would he recoil or would he kiss her back? What would it be like to make love with this man? He distrusted her, didn't even like her, but he did desire her. So in control most of the time, would he lose that restraint in passion? Heat pervaded her at the images that thought conjured. Sweat-slick skin... his hard body covering her... his hands, his lips on her sensitive flesh....

With Quinn, she imagined sex would be neither sweet nor subdued, as it had been with Jonathan and Paul. Emotion and need steeped inside him in a volatile brew, ready to boil over in erotic greed.

Impossible. She shouldn't think like that.

She didn't want to love him. She didn't want to plunge from soul-deep, piercing intensity to tender warmth and back again or to feel such need to be with him and protect him, such giddy pleasure at just gazing at his stubborn jaw, such sizzle that blistered her from the inside out. No, she didn't want to feel like that.

Edges of white gauze peeked around the side of his head. Someone had bandaged his injury.

Tears burned at the reminder of danger. Despite that, he'd stayed to protect and care for her. For his own safety, he should leave. She loved him. Did that alone doom him?

What was she going to do?

"No…no… can't be true," Quinn mumbled. In the throes of a nightmare, his shoulders flexed and his legs twitched. "Not Amy… Amy. No! No!"

Claire reached out to place a steadying hand on his shoulder. He thrashed, and then stilled.

His eyes flew open in a wild and disoriented gaze. He lifted his arm and threaded fingers through his tousled hair.

"It's okay, Quinn. You were dreaming." A pang of jealousy pierced her. Who was Amy? What had she meant to him? What had happened to her?

Pain contorted his features. Then the shadow of his nightmare vanished, and awareness sharpened his eyes. And when his gaze scanned her, heated male hunger. "I think I must be still dreaming, if you're in bed with me." He settled his arm across her and gathered her closer. "Are you all right?"

Not too sore for what she needed. What they needed. "I'm okay. A little stiff."

She wanted him more than she would have thought possible. It was dangerous. It was wrong. But he understood her. She needed him. She needed his strength, his honor, and his humor. Just this once, for today, she wouldn't think of all the reasons not to love him. Except— "Yesterday you hated me. You accused me of planting the bomb."

He wrapped his big fingers in her tangled hair. The corners of his gray eyes crinkled. "We barely escaped being blown to atoms. I was afraid and confused. I *know* it wasn't you." A callused finger trailed across her cheek, leaving searing tingles in its wake.

"You? Afraid and confused? Impossible." When his rough thumb glided over her lower lip, she kissed it, and her insides liquefied.

"How about in a daze from a slight concussion? I have fifteen stitches to prove it." He angled his head to display the expanse of bandage. "Doc said my hair protected me, or it could've been worse. Guess I'll leave it long."

Breasts straining with need against his chest, she laced her fingers behind his muscular neck. "If I haven't already said so, thank you for saving me yesterday—twice."

"Can we talk about this later?" His eyes darkened, and his voice grew raspy.

Molding perfectly to her mouth, his lips found hers. His tongue tested the texture inside her lips, swept across her teeth, caressed her tongue. With a sigh, she gave in to the primal thrill of his heat.

He wanted her as desperately as she did him. He treated her like a desirable woman, not a doll or a goddess, and she was on fire for him, body and soul. Now was the time for boldness, not modesty or restraint.

"*Oui*," she agreed breathlessly against his mouth. Disengaging herself, she slipped her nightgown off over her head. Then she undid the clasp of her bra and removed it. "My fingers work fine now. No more clumsiness from cold. In fact, I feel positively overheated."

Desire shimmered between them, a palpable entity.

"Stop talking, babe." His moist lips brushed her nipples, teasing each in turn to a hard pebble.

"I have just one more thing to say, Michael." She could barely find breath to speak.

A sigh. "Mmm?"

"*Joyeux Noël.*"

"Merry Christmas to you too," Michael murmured.

The reality of what was happening dashed the remnants of sleep from his swimming brain. He lifted his head from nuzzling her lush breasts. "Are you sure you want this? Gratitude would be misplaced. Hell, if I'd stayed here with you, you wouldn't be hurt now."

Her lips were rosy and swollen from his kisses and her eyes filled with longing "Maybe, but who knows what else might have happened? I've fought this attraction since we met. I don't want to fight it today. Let's say it's a Christmas gift to myself."

"And to me."

Her soft hands glided over his torso while he struggled with his T-shirt and jeans. Damn, as never before, he ached to possess this woman, to touch and taste her every way a man could love a woman.

He tossed back the bedcovers from her creamy-skinned curves. "No secrets, Claire. I want to see you."

As he'd visualized, her body was beautiful. A sigh escaped him as he cupped her plump, round breasts, not large but perfectly proportioned to her figure. Slender but womanly, not model-thin. He took possession of her mouth again in a kiss that hardened him to desperation. He trailed his hands over her curves, down the firm satin of her belly, along the silken slopes of her hips, to the heated secrets of her body.

"You're so soft, Claire. Wanting to touch you like this was making me crazy."

Her answering murmurs of passion, her herbal scent, and the hot-honey taste of her mouth rocketed urgency through his body. When he probed her moist folds and tight depths, she whispered his name, her breath sweet fire against his mouth.

"Open for me, Claire. I want to be inside you."

"Yes, now, Michael."

When she flinched at the press of his arms around her, the memory of her injuries slammed him back from the edge. It angered him that he'd been so out of control, so blind with passion that he would have hurt her. "I don't know if we should do this." He combed his fingers through her long curls and massaged her scalp.

"There's protection in the bottom drawer." She apparently misunderstood his restraint.

"Not that." He stroked the lower curves of her breasts. "I don't want to hurt your back, your bruises."

She smiled, her dark eyes luminous with arousal. "And your head." She bent and swirled her scalding tongue around one of his nipples, sending flames over his skin. "I'm sure with a little creativity, we can manage." As if to emphasize the point, her warm hand closed around his rigid shaft. Shock waves coursed through him in bombshells of pleasure-pain that mocked his control.

"The... bottom drawer, you said." He reached for the bedside stand. With passion-clumsy fingers, he grabbed a foil packet from a small box.

"Let me." Chocolate eyes dark, she kept her gaze on his as she ripped the foil and slowly slid the condom on him.

The blood thundered in his head. "Claire!" She was lightning striking him, searing his body and scorching him to his soul. He burned for her. Only for her. Caging her with his arms, he twisted across the satin-sheeted bed so he lay on his back, his injured head projected over the edge.

She let out a little gasp of surprise, seemingly bewildered at the position. Then she straddled his hips and with agonizing leisure took him deep into her body.

He stroked the straining muscles of her thighs, then held her hips in place. She moaned and gripped his arms. Shuddering with the sheer joy of being inside her, part of her, he vowed to make it last. In tandem, they moved, rocked as if they had always been together, forged as one. The power and perfection of their union awed him.

He brought her down for a thorough kiss that staggered them both. She sighed, then arched back and, curls flying around her in a wild mahogany cloud, rode him with a frenzy that matched his own.

The ultimate spark sizzled within him, effervescent in his veins, building, building.... He heaved and bucked, his pleasure building to the inevitable, then stiffened, poised on the edge. He slid his hand between them to caress her intimately. At last, he felt the tightening of her contractions begin. "Oh, yes, Claire, yes!"

Low, gasping moans and French words he couldn't distinguish shuddered from her lips as the climax took her. When her inner muscles spasmed around him, his whole body stiffened as he convulsed, joining her with the white-hot fireworks of his own completion.

Collapsing on his chest, she kissed his throat. "I never knew it could be like that. I never knew."

It had never been like that for him, either—this frenzy to oblivion, the tingling aftershocks, the heavy pounding of his heart. The need to possess.

He didn't want to examine or question his feelings now. All he wanted to do was hold her. They rested that way for endless moments. Separating their bodies, he held her gently and rolled to his side.

Claire's brain slowly swam up from a swirl of sensation and emotion. Beyond merely pleasant, this was elemental linking. With the primal connection of their bodies, she'd reveled in his power and potency, in the currents swamping her with each thrust, driving them both to an overpowering climax. How wonderful to yield to her own sensual nature—and his. To fully enjoy each other's passion.

What she felt for Michael came so unexpectedly, not a soft warmth but a frantic emotional flight, full of need. Warmth and companionship too. A happiness she had never experienced radiated through her as they lay curled together, their legs and arms entwined, with the scents of sex and each other mingled on their skin.

At last, up close, she could look and touch her fill. He was Rodin's *Thinker*, broad and heavily muscled like a boxer. Beneath whorls of coarse hair rock-hard pectorals banded his chest. In repose, his shoulders bulged with solid sinew. Not a body-builder's exaggerated musculature, but solid as if from hard work. So strong he'd lifted her easily atop his body, and

Always a Suspect

she was no doll.

Too curious for further restraint, Claire said, "Do you lift weights? How did you become so…?"

"Muscle-bound?" His self-deprecating grin softened his hard-edged features and warmed her heart.

Muscle-bound? No. He was as much a deep thinker as Rodin's subject. "You said it. Not me."

He dropped a kiss on her forehead. "You could say the body type runs in the family. Even in his sixties, my old man is still a tough Mick."

"Genetics can't account for it all."

"You're not going to drop this? To help pay for college, I worked on the docks in Boston."

"A stevedore? Is that what they call them?"

He nodded. "Summers and weekends during the school year, I tossed around boxes and crates. Now I lift weights in a gym to keep fit."

"So you can protect clients like me."

A shadow of emotion darkened his expression. Jaw muscles taut, he said, "Not protect. I'm an investigator, not a bodyguard. I didn't do you much good yesterday."

Something had happened that continued to torment him, to weigh him down with guilt. Whatever it was, Claire would bet it involved the mysterious Amy of his dreams. Now was not the time for serious discussions.

"You've been alone a long time." He nodded toward the bedside stand. "Yet you have those—"

Mortification heating her face, Claire pushed away from him to no avail. She might as well try to launch Gibraltar into space. "Paul's! Those were Paul's."

Amusement quirked one corner of his mouth. "They've been there five years?"

"And why not?" Acting offended was impossible

when entwined with a large naked man. Her reason for not throwing them out was silly. "I... thought the trash men might make jokes at my expense."

His roar of laughter skipped tingles through her veins. When they'd first met, she was certain he never even smiled. He cupped her chin and kissed her softly.

"I believe you, though you're full of contradictions. As brave as you are, living here and throwing the murder accusations back in everyone's faces, you still care what people think of your morals."

"I'm not promiscuous."

"I never thought you were. In spite of two marriages, you're... inexperienced."

His skimming finger left a track of sparks around each breast and down her belly. "But hot. Definitely hot." He lowered his mouth to hers for a slow, steamy kiss.

When they came up for air, she murmured, "A hot babe? You called me that once." The way he said it now, the term didn't seem demeaning. She preferred it by far to being an object of remote worship.

As she slid her leg up and down his thigh, she felt his arousal hot and hard against her. Liquid heat pulsed within her. She heard the rip of another foil packet.

"I was right, babe—" he drew her leg higher across his hip and slipped inside her "—as long as it's me you're hot for."

"Ah... burning."

Chapter Sixteen

LATER THAT EVENING, Michael was slicing tomatoes for their salad. Fresh vegetables didn't last long on his winter camping trips, so while in civilization, he found them essential. They were finally going to eat the Yule log cake and that mouthwatering pork pie she'd made for Christmas Eve.

He'd never felt this way, had never wanted just to hold and be held like that. She'd revealed the reasons for her inexperience. Farnsworth and Santerre hadn't looked past the beautiful façade to the beautiful inside. They were fools. She was a passionate and enthusiastic lover.

If it hadn't been for the animals, they would have made love until neither one could move. But Alley's pitiful whine reminded them the dog needed to go out and both animals needed food.

Even though it was Christmas, that morning Michael had driven to Major Crime to fill out a report on the attack and to check on the bomb analysis. Results could have taken days, even weeks, but they'd gotten lucky. Most of it he could share with Claire, but for now he wanted only the pleasure of her company.

For him, for this day, she abandoned her widow's weeds in favor of a clingy pink sweater. The way her black leggings displayed her legs, he didn't even mind their color. In the afterglow of sex, she appeared even more beautiful, her complexion luminous, her vibrant spirit free of defenses.

Claire reached around him to snatch a carrot strip. He grabbed her hand and kissed it before pulling her into his arms for a more thorough embrace. Heat licked through him from every pulse point, from every touch of skin. His need for her was insatiable, like an all-consuming wildfire.

"All this for stealing a carrot? In that case I may turn to a life of crime."

Too close to the truth for him to laugh, but her sly smile tempted him to drag her upstairs again.

"I know it's not funny." She trailed her index finger across his furrowed brow. "But these days, gallows humor is all I have."

He did laugh then before releasing her.

She was arranging their dinner on a tray. "Before we eat, tell me what you learned this morning. I don't want my Christmas dinner spoiled with detecting." She folded each napkin precisely around the silverware.

"All right." He leaned against the counter. "The explosive was RDX, a volatile and tricky plastique only a professional could use."

"And that takes the hook off me?"

"To Pratt's regret, yes, it lets you off the hook." He grinned. "A sensor under a mat was hooked to a timer, set for probably two or three minutes. It started the countdown as soon as someone stepped aboard."

"You triggered it."

"And your arrival saved me." He reached for her.

"Oh, no," she retorted, backing away. "You will distract me. Tell me everything first. Who planted the bomb?"

"Major Crime may be on the trail. Early yesterday morning, a man gained access to the *Rêve* by showing the boatyard owner a fake MCU badge. From the description, it sounds like a known hit man."

"Someone hired a killer? Who? My anonymous caller?" Her dark eyes troubled, she wrung her hands, then refolded the napkins. "Then he tried to harm me? Bizarre."

He might as well tell her the rest. The local cops had already let it slip to the press. "It may have been someone different. After the first guy left, Greavey says three dark men who sounded Hispanic asked about him. Greavey didn't admit them to the boat shed."

"It makes no sense. Hispanics?" When she shook her head as she glanced out the window at the darkened backyard, he knew what she must be thinking.

"I know," he said. "It's exasperating to have that couple inches of snow obliterate any tracks."

"That's not it. Three men. It could have been two or three last night." Corkscrew in her hand, she slid a bottle of Côtes du Rhône from beneath the cupboard.

"What do you mean?" He took the bottle from her and opened it.

"If one person held Alley to keep her quiet, a second had to turn off the porch light."

Claire carried the pie, cloth place mats, napkins with holly designs, wine goblets, and white china on a large tray. He followed with the salad and wine.

"Maybe a third to push over the woodpile on you." That had been the collective conclusion of the MCU and DEA agents that morning.

Cruz had confided that the DEA didn't place credence in Pratt's theories about the Widow Spider.

149

An attack on her by her dead husband's crooked pals added to the confusion, but tended to exonerate her for drug dealing as well as murder. For some unknown reason, the DEA wanted him to continue his undercover investigation. Quinn told Cruz to pass along the message to the Group Supervisor that if he didn't get some straight answers soon, he'd walk away.

"But why? Who are they?" Her hands trembling visibly, Claire arranged the place settings on the low coffee table. She'd lined up the flatware at precise distances from the dishes.

Fear was stark in her eyes. Michael set down his lesser burdens and drew her into his arms.

"So much of it seems to have something to do with Paul. What could it be?" she asked.

Damn, he wished he could level with her, wipe away all the subterfuge and stop lying to her about who he was and why he was there. When DEA red tape coughed up his resignation, he would. How she would react, he didn't want to contemplate.

Some Christmas. The only gifts beneath the tree were for the animals. Distracting them both from their problems, their short idyll in bed that morning had been the only gift for the two humans in the house.

"I wish I had some answers for you. You have every right to be frightened. This attack on you has raised the stakes. They could return any time for another shot. We have to catch these guys and find the truth. And soon." He kissed the top of her head. "Let's enjoy our Christmas dinner now. My damn stomach is going to hold my mouth for ransom if it doesn't get some of that pie soon."

Claire seated herself on the floor and dished out the

meal. "In *Mémé*'s—my grandmother's—family, this dish was usually made with oysters, a great delicacy, instead of pork or beef." A wrinkle of her nose indicated her opinion of oysters. "When I was little, all the family went to midnight mass and then came home for a late supper called a *réveillon*. We children waited for *Père Noël*—Santa Claus to you—to come fill our stockings. In France, originally it was wooden shoes called *sabots*. In our Acadian culture, it's just shoes."

"A mingling of customs and cultures." Michael scooped up a mouthful of the pie. "Mmm, this is as good as—" with an inner twinge, he stopped himself from comparing it to his mom's cooking "—anything I've ever tasted."

The scents of balsam, fine red wine, and meat pie swirled around them, blending with Christmas carols from the stereo. She told him more family customs. He told her about the blending of Irish and Italian traditions at his home on holidays.

She told her great-uncles' tall tales about logging and farming in the St. John Valley. He told tales of growing up with his rowdy brothers on South Boston's mean streets. She talked about attending college and beginning to do translations. He described his days on the Boston police force and his move to the Drug Enforcement Agency. But not his reason for leaving.

\*\*\*\*

Later, replete with wine and dessert, they stretched out beside the festive tree. Claire leaned against the sofa with Michael's head in her lap, angled to protect his bandaged wound. He'd persuaded her to delay cleaning up after their meal. For once, she had a good reason to put it off.

Alley snored before the wood stove, and the kitten romped with a feather toy on Michael's chest.

Though their time together was only temporary, Claire would always remember this day and keep it in her heart. Would always keep *him* in her heart.

The only safe way to keep him.

Watching him play with Spooky tugged at her emotions. This big, square, rock-hard warrior with such strong hands tickled and teased the tiny kitten with a gentleness that brought a smile to her lips.

"Are you sure you don't want to telephone your family?" she said. "It's not too late."

"No."

"Christmas isn't the time to hold on to anger. Maybe—"

"No, dammit!"

Setting the kitten aside, Michael levered around and up to a sitting position, facing her. Then, more calmly, "No. We're not estranged. I can't face them yet. I…"

The play of emotions on his face made his torment clear. From anguish, doubt, torment, grief, to exhaustion. She saw the moment he decided to tell her what had happened.

"I didn't exactly level with you about my family." His jaw worked. "When I joined the police force and again when I moved to the DEA, I wanted to clean up the streets, to eradicate the drugs that ruined so many lives. And I thought I was making a difference until…"

"Until what, Michael?"

"I had a sister. Amy. She was seventeen."

*Had* a sister. Oh, no, so young. Did she really want to know? "What happened?" She took his big hand in both of hers and waited, heart battering her ribs.

"She was a surprise baby for my parents, and a joy to us all." He ran his free hand over his shaggy hair. "How can I describe her? A sprite, an elf, full of mischief and laughter. And daring. She bounced all over Boston alone, no matter how many times Dad warned her.

"About eight months ago, she was attacked on the street near my apartment. Killed by muggers, kids her age who wanted money for damn drugs. It tore my family apart."

"Tragic. I'm so sorry, Michael." She wanted to hold him, but could see from the tension in his shoulders, his fisted hands, that he needed to be left alone. "You seem to blame yourself. Why?"

He pulled away and rose to his feet, paced the room. "It was my fault. Amy had mentioned earlier that she might drop by that evening. But hell, I forgot and went to target practice. I was one of the agency's best shots. If I'd stayed— Instead, those damn sewer rats battered her, broke her, and left her bleeding to death. If I'd gotten my hands on them, I..." He passed a trembling hand across his eyes.

She reached out to him then, but he rose and crossed to the stove. Giving him time to master his emotions, she waited. His sister had ignored warnings about being on the streets alone. She'd said only she might drop by. He was torturing himself needlessly. "Michael, you—"

"There's more, Claire." He dropped into his usual chair as if his feet would no longer carry him. His expression was bleak, his complexion gray. "The next day I screwed up again. The DEA had been hiding a witness in a big case. A woman and her five-year-old daughter. Kathy. When the watch changed, one of the gang, a brute named Tunk, snatched the girl and drove away before anyone could do a thing."

"They would kill her if her mother testified?"

"Yes. We followed Tunk, cornered his car in a park. Kathy was in the front seat beside him, his nine-millimeter pointed at her head."

Claire went to him, kneeling between his legs. She wrapped her arms around his big torso and pressed her cheek to his chest. His whole body was rigid, solid granite.

"I can still see the ugly bastard," he continued in a strained voice. "While the hostage negotiator kept Tunk busy, my boss had me get a bead on him with my laser scope so I could take him out if he gave me an opening."

"The day after your sister's murder? What shape were you in to even be there?"

"Doesn't matter. It was my duty as an agent."

"Go on. Let it all out, Michael. Tell me."

"That bastard Tunk screamed obscenities at us and lowered his gun a fraction. My shot just missed him."

*"Non!"* She drew back, her gaze riveted on his ashen face. "Your shot, did it...?"

"Hit her? No. But as soon as Tunk knew what had happened, he killed her. Shot that beautiful little girl in the head at point blank range. You don't want to know what a hollow-point bullet does to a small skull. I nailed him, but too late for Kathy."

She shuddered at the image. "That's why you don't carry a gun."

He nodded, his gray eyes savage. "It's why I can't

protect anyone. Protect you. You can't depend on me in the clinch."

"But Michael, neither one of those deaths was your fault. Anyone can miss a shot, even you. And you were probably in no shape to attempt it. Your office should have given you time off. You can't hold yourself responsible for what other people do."

"You don't know what you're talking about, Claire. You weren't there. I only told you so you'll understand why I'll try to solve this puzzle, but you can't count on me to safeguard you."

"We've both been threatened. Or have you forgotten?"

"How could I? Just don't try to rearrange my damn psyche like you do the napkins or the candlesticks. Find some other poor bastard to rescue." He shot from the chair, strode to the hall and snatched up his coat. "I need air."

That said, he slammed out the door.

"*Merde*! Alley, I've made a mess of things." Tears slid from her eyes and splashed on the whimpering dog. He'd opened his heart a crack, and she'd trampled on his feelings. Now he'd slammed the door shut again—literally.

She was a fool to want what she couldn't have. Better if she didn't grow too accustomed to intimate sharing with him. Better if her heart broke now and not smash his later.

He kept insisting there was no curse, but how could she leave that behind as long as people around her kept dying? The curse of her beauty was to lose those she loved, one way or another.

Chapter Seventeen

"SMALL WONDER RUSS Santerre uses the harbormaster's shack as his office. No supplier could ever find his way through this rabbit warren of streets." Grimacing, Michael steered down the pothole-pocked lane. "What exactly did Santerre say when he phoned last night?"

"I already told you, Quinn. Only that he had something else to tell me—us, and that he'd see us today." Claire stared straight ahead, her protective thorns reinstalled.

After his emotional outburst last night, they were back to employer and employee. He was Quinn and not Michael to her. He didn't blame her. She'd tried to comfort him, and he'd rebuffed her. After their spectacular intimacy earlier yesterday, that had to hurt.

It sure was hurting him.

Last night he'd walked around town for a half hour before realization slapped him that his absence put her in jeopardy. But the house had been locked, and her bedroom door closed tight.

He'd wanted to go to her, to explain and apologize. Hell, that and to climb in bed with her, to taste her luscious breasts, and sheath himself in her until she called his name. He was so engorged at the need for her, he thought he'd split open. Instead he'd thrashed through the night in his lonely bed.

Given the circumstances, reconstructing barriers seemed wise. His failures twisted too painfully fresh in his gut.

Even if what she'd said made sense.

She pointed. "That's the house, the small gray-shingled one."

He slowed in front of the one-story bungalow. It might have once been charming, but now had mildewed and missing cedar shingles, a sagging roof line and plywood patches on the front door. Michael pulled into the rutted dirt drive and parked behind the fish truck.

"Doesn't look like Paul helped his old man out much." Michael opened Claire's door. The fish business should be lucrative enough for some home repairs.

"Russ wouldn't accept help from Paul and certainly not from me. I think he likes the sympathy it invites." Maneuvering as if to avoid touching him, she slid from the vehicle. "Stubborn old man."

Wily old man. Maybe nearly as wily as his son. Michael trailed after her to the side door, where Russ Santerre awaited them with his big revelation.

"Come in before the heat all escapes," he said. "I don't got all day, you know." In threadbare corduroy slippers, he shuffled ahead of them into the kitchen, where a teakettle whistled on a wood cook stove.

Without offering them refreshment, the old man set the boiling kettle aside, then motioned them to seats around a worn pine table.

Claire unbuttoned her coat and left it loose around her. She held herself erect and apart from the men. "What do you have to tell us, Russ?"

Her former father-in-law's gaze shifted from the

scarred tabletop to Michael's face. Though he'd talked to her on the telephone last night, today he rejected her as usual.

"Did you think of something new?" Michael asked.

"Ayuh. Somethin' new." He pulled his pipe from his shirt pocket and proceeded to fill it and light it before continuing. "'Bout the explosion over to Greavey's. I seen in the paper about the suspects bein' some South American types. That true?"

Michael nodded. "One of them talked to Greavey."

"Cops sayin' anything about them and other illegal goings on? Did they seem like rich guys?" His glance lit on Michael only to skip away.

"I wouldn't know."

"There's somethin' about Paul I didn't tell you." Russ averted his gaze to stare at the cooling kettle. "Paul and the seafood business. My boy wasn't always on the up an' up as I'd have liked him to be. Always had an eye out for the main chance, he did."

At Claire's intake of breath, Michael squeezed her hand as if in warning. "What was he into, Mr. Santerre?"

The old man chewed on his pipe stem. "I ain't exactly certain, you understand. I didn't want to tell them cops because they might think I was involved. But I don't think Paul bought that big boat with fish profits."

"Russ, what did Paul do?" Claire leaned forward, her mouth tense, one hand flattening on her stomach.

"You drove him to it. He wouldn't o' done it except for you and that fancy house," the older man spat at her. "He never come out an' told me, but I knew. Drugs. He was smugglin' drugs."

Claire's mind reeled from Russ's startling assertion. "I don't believe it. Paul involved in drug smuggling? *Jamais!* Never!" Even as the denial left her mouth, she accepted the veracity of his father's statement.

Michael had placed the suspicion in her mind with his questions, and upon reconsidering, she'd recalled too many inconsistencies, too many evasions when she'd discussed business with Paul. She felt tainted living off his money. She had to find some way…

"You said he didn't tell you." Michael said. "What makes you think so? Did Paul use the boat to bring in drugs?"

The old man hung his head, and Claire's heart ached for him. Losing his son hurt terribly, but to discover that Paul's overwhelming success had been due to deception and theft had extinguished his pride in his son's accomplishments.

"I just put two and two together, and it come out five. 'Bout the time he bought the *Rêve*, he weren't making enough dough for a down payment let alone monthly payments. All them islands out there. More miles of coastline than mackerel in the bay. Easy to sneak anything in. During Prohibition, boats used to smuggle rum."

"And the South Americans? Where do they fit into this scenario?" Michael asked.

Russ shuffled his feet. "I dunno. That's for you to puzzle out. Them foreigners might be part of the gang. Beats me why they'd come here five years after Paul's death."

"This is just speculation, you understand. Suppose someone else picked up the ball and is running drugs again into this area of the coast."

"Makes sense. Hope they catch 'em."

Claire expected Michael to respond, to explain further his amazing assertion, but he simply wagged his head in commiseration.

Russ set his pipe in a saucer and slanted her a glance piercing enough to slice her in two. "I think Paul were afraid he'd lose her if he didn't make it big fast. That even before the wedding."

"Think whatever you want, Russ." She was unable to restrain her tongue any longer. "I knew nothing about the drugs. Quinn, I'll wait for you in the car." She rose slowly, her soul heavy with her new burden.

"I'll come with you."

"Maybe you didn't know, missy, but you should've. He done it for you. Instead of my boy, it should've been you died on that boat." Santerre's words punched her in the heart.

## Chapter Eighteen

THREE DAYS LATER, the combined law enforcement forces had come no closer to finding the bomber or Raoul Olívas and his thugs. Although Michael and Claire continued interviewing people who knew both Jonathan and Alan, Michael's gut instinct told him they were just treading water. Somehow their murders were tied to Paul Santerre. So far he couldn't figure out how.

In the evening, he sat in Claire's living room, once again poring over his copies of the police files. Major Crime hadn't tumbled onto Paul's drug trafficking, especially since their investigation began so long after the fact. Russ sure as hell hadn't told them about the drugs, only his suspicions about his daughter-in-law.

A file drawer banged in Claire's office. Likely frustration at her search of old files and account books. She was searching for proof one way or the other about Paul and drugs.

Seeing how Russ's revelation had slammed into her ripped pain through Michael's chest. The burden she carried, already weightier than Atlas's, expanded with each new fact they uncovered. She blamed herself even though she did know Paul's avarice and ambition had nothing to do with her. She'd told him as much. The need to lift her millstone dragged at him, but he wasn't even close to the truth.

Something about the way Paul's body had ended up bothered him. The medical examiner reported body trauma and seawater in the lungs—death by drowning. Nothing suspicious there. But the tingling on his nape told Michael to dig deeper. Rarely did someone who drowned have the luxury of remaining with his skiff. A week after his disappearance from the boat, what the fish and the rocks left of Paul Santerre had been found wedged beneath his overturned skiff.

As if someone wanted the body found.

A bang and a crash from the next room shot him from his seat, but before he reached the doorway, Claire stepped into the living room.

She held out a flat maroon ledger. "I found this taped behind a drawer. It might be records of Paul's smuggling. I hoped not to find anything. Or to find a record of the boat sale or some proof he earned the money legitimately. But hidden like that…" The corners of her mouth turned downward and her shoulders slumped.

They sat side by side on the sofa. Michael longed to slide his arm around her shoulders in solace, but her stiffness mandated distance between them.

He watched as Claire flipped the ledger's pages to a date more than five years past. Down the pages, a blue-inked scrawl detailed amounts of cocaine and marijuana, dates of receipt and delivery, names and places.

Everything was there.

Five years ago, if the DEA had had this damning evidence, they might have arrested Paul Santerre before fate had meted out a permanent sentence. Instead of a widow suspected of murder, Claire would be a prisoner's wife.

And Michael Quinn would never have known her.

That notion tightened a steel clamp in his chest. He wasn't proud of being glad for someone's death, but there it was.

"I suppose I should have guessed," she began, "should have realized—"

"No!" He tossed the ledger to the floor and grasped her shoulders, turning her to face him. "Dammit, Claire, don't you dare blame yourself. Not for this. Paul's pact with the damn devil was his alone. He kept no computer files, only this hand-written ledger, and made it all look on the up and up."

Dark eyes wide at his outburst, she allowed him to draw her closer until she leaned on him, soft and yielding. At her lack of resistance, a tendril of warmth eased the tightening in his chest. His heart stumbled, then resumed its regular beat, as if her nearness were essential to its rhythm.

"What should we do with this?" she asked.

"*Do* with it? This ledger could lead to the capture of the stalker or the drug gang. We turn it over to the cops." Then maybe the DEA would allow him to disclose everything to Claire.

"Will they release the information to the press? It will destroy Russ."

He eased back to scrutinize her expression. Intent, utterly somber and earnest. To assuage the father's grief, she would suppress evidence against the son, evidence that might clear her in the public eye. "You seriously care about that old man after the way he's treated you?"

"He loved his son, the only family he had."

"Is that why you didn't deny his charge that it was your appetite for luxury that drove Paul?"

"I suppose. Persuading him that Paul's ambition was strictly his would only chip away more of his already shattered good-son image. I couldn't do it." On a deep sigh, she shrugged, that Gallic shrug he found so sexy. "Russ wouldn't believe me, anyway."

"In answer to your question about the press, I doubt the police will release the information right away. Once the bad guys have been taken out of circulation, the whole story will come out. This disclosure will bring the DEA into the case, as well." If only he could tell her they already were.

Before her sensual mouth could lure him to taste her again, he dropped his hands from her shoulders. He lifted the ledger from the carpet and leaned against the sofa.

Her arms cold at the loss of his touch, Claire remained perched on the edge of the seat. She cast a shuttered glance at Michael reclining beside her.

His denim-clad, muscular legs crossed at the ankles, he lounged with animal grace against the cushions. The black mock-turtleneck pullover encasing his torso emphasized his powerful build and warrior aura. To maintain her restraint, she rearranged the white candles on the low table before her.

When he'd embraced her, she greedily inhaled his scent—soap and after-shave and something distinctly Michael. Blindfolded in a crowded room, she could locate him by scent. She longed to cuddle against him, but distance was imperative, necessary and safer, if painful. The problem of understanding the deaths was becoming more and more complex and compelling. As devastated as she was at the truth about Paul, she knew the dirty business of the drugs conformed to the rest of his character. His connection with the drug gang might have led to his death. And the ledger could be the key.

"Do you think this ledger is what the drug gang wants from me? The reason they keep coming to Weymouth?"

"That would be a neat solution." His sexy half grin almost had her reaching for him. "But I doubt it. Someone's been in your house twice, but whoever it was didn't seem to be searching for anything. Drug gang flunkies wouldn't toss a house without ransacking drawers or cupboards and overturning furniture. I'm certain they don't know about the ledger."

For the first time, she wondered if the three deaths might be totally unconnected. It didn't absolve her if they were, but with the ledger, they had the chance to solve one of the puzzles.

She chewed her bottom lip while she worked out her idea. "Suppose they would go for the ledger if they knew about it. What if we used it… to set a trap?"

Chapter Nineteen

CLAIRE'S PROPOSAL LAST night was worse than nuts. Michael wrenched the steering wheel harder than necessary onto the Weymouth exit off the interstate. Although piles of plow-driven snow framed the roadway, the pavement was dry. A deep breath settled him for the suburb's quiet streets.

After trying to dissuade Claire from her trap scheme last night, he'd spent the morning doing the same thing with Pratt and Cruz. Independently, both agencies came up with the same idea as Claire's. The MCU and the DEA thought setting a trap for Raoul and his men was a hell of a good idea—with Claire as bait.

The reasons for his superior's decisions were a mystery. Involving Claire in trapping the drug gang would be too damned dangerous. And still the GS wouldn't allow him to tell her everything. Keeping her in the dark was like stranding her in a skiff on the open bay. He winced at the inadvertent parallel to Paul Santerre's death.

Damn, it was frustrating! Even Cruz didn't know why Michael had to remain in his undercover P.I. identity.

He didn't trust the cops—or himself—to protect her. He hated leaving her this morning. Who knew where Raoul and his henchmen might show up next? The anonymous—and silent, thank God—calls had dwindled to only about twice a week, but that wacko could switch to an overt attack any time. Claire had promised to stay home, if even that was safe, working on her overdue translation.

He adjusted his position in the seat to accommodate a familiar hard lump. Once again carrying a pistol in his small-of-the-back holster, he vowed to do everything in his power to keep Claire safe.

Sirens of emergency vehicles wailed behind him from the direction of the small community hospital and more ahead. Hairs rose on his nape. He gripped the wheel and accelerated as he approached the well-groomed avenue leading into Claire's neighborhood.

At the corner of her street, he had to pull over to allow the ambulance to pass. Seeing the flashing blue police lights and red ambulance ones clamped a vise on his chest.

*Claire!*

He tamped down his incipient panic. A moment later, he parked just beyond the police barrier and raced toward the house. A few neighbors stood by and two uniformed cops were talking to a woman across the street. He ducked under the tape and continued.

He slowed when the EMTs rolled a gurney from the ambulance. One white-coated attendant unfolded a black body bag.

Then he saw the body.

He stumbled to a halt, unable to fuse the connection between his brain and his legs.

She lay crumpled like a boneless doll in the dirty plowed snow at the curb. He recognized the black coat. Dark brown hair fanned around her head. A shaft of sunlight glinted on its red highlights and on the ragged halo of crimson-stained snow around it.

His heart slammed against his ribs, and his ears roared. He'd left her alone, unprotected, and now she was… he couldn't even think the word.

He'd failed her.

He'd lost her.

He stood frozen a dozen feet away in the drive, incapable of moving closer to the lifeless form in the street. "No! Claire, God, no!" He swiped one hand across his eyes. He would personally kill whoever did it.

"Michael?"

He reached for the gun at his back then stilled. No, shooting would be too quick. And not nearly painful enough. He'd beat the crap out of him. Then he'd kill the cowardly bastard with his bare hands.

"*Michael*, over here."

The lilting tones penetrated the crimson haze in his brain before the words did. On stiff legs, he turned toward the voice. Dressed in a long black sweater, she stepped from the porch.

"Claire?"

Shock and anguish ashen on her face, she hurried down the walk to him.

"You're… I thought…." He touched her arms, her cheek, her hair. Moisture dimmed his vision, and his heart drummed with the dawning realization that she lived.

"Yes, Michael, I'm all right." Tears spiked her lashes, and her eyes were haunted, but she managed a crooked smile. Without any resistance from her, he drew her into his arms. Her slender body trembled, her heart thumped against his chest.

"Thank God." He held her tight. Someone was dead, but he couldn't prevent his relief that it wasn't Claire. "I shouldn't have left you. If I failed again…"

She lifted her head. "I was perfectly safe. And if I'd ventured out unprotected, it wouldn't have been your fault any more that the deaths you blame yourself for."

"Who was it? Martine?"

On a nod, she eased back and turned toward where the technicians were sliding the gurney with its gruesome burden into the ambulance.

"A hit and run. She—" Tears overflowed Claire's red-rimmed eyes. "Oh, it was terrible! She'd just left when I heard the scream and the screech of brakes."

"Did you see the driver?" Ice colder than the late December air gripped his throat. It could have been Claire. They meant it to be Claire.

"No. The car was gone by the time I made it outside." She swayed like a birch in the wind, and he pulled her close again. "Michael, they were after me. I know they thought it was me. Oh, poor Martine!"

"She was wearing your coat. Why?"

Claire swallowed hard. As he had observed her do before, she forced herself to rally, to focus. "She came to the house. I've never seen her like that—nervous, so agitated she couldn't sit down. She ran out of her house with only a sweater, so I lent her a coat when she left. She wanted to get back before Newcomb knew she had left."

He kept his arm at her waist. "That's why I thought it was you. The hair and the coat. The killer must have thought so too. Why was she here?"

"We were right about Jonathan and her. A brief affair the summer after he graduated from high school. When he went to college, he broke it off. She was afraid we knew and begged me not to tell Newcomb."

"Does Newcomb know about his wife's death?"

Her mouth turned down. "He's inside now. With one of the policemen. I telephoned him after I called the ambulance."

"Have you told him the truth?"

"I can't do that. I said she came to patch things up, but I don't think he believed me." She glanced toward the street, where an SUV with a state license plate was pulling into the spot just vacated by the ambulance. "Oh, no, it's Pratt. Quinn, if I have to tell him about Martine and Jonathan, Newcomb will find out. And the children."

He heard her words, saw the Major Crimes detective approach, but his world narrowed to Claire. To her singular scent, her creamy skin, the vibrant life that was almost snuffed out. Nerve endings scraped raw, he fought to maintain a grip on calm. "Let's wait and see what develops."

"Afternoon, Ms. Saint-Ange," the detective said. "You keep popping up in the middle of things."

"Like a hair in the soup," she rejoined with acerbity.

Michael blinked at the oddity, and then assumed it was another French idiom. He stayed at her side, his arm around her shoulder. Pratt could think whatever the hell he wanted.

The portly detective gave a negative wag of his head. "More like the center of a bull's-eye. Between you and Quinn here, this little town's had more violence this week than in the past five years."

"Does that mean you think we're onto something with our investigation?" Michael asked.

"Mighty chilly weather for stirring up hornets." He tugged his coat collar around his neck. "This kind of stinger comes armed and dangerous. And he doesn't care who gets hurt in the crossfire."

"Claire was inside when it happened," Michael added. "Whoever killed Mrs. Farnsworth must have thought it was Claire. They resemble each other closely." That must be as clear to the cops as it was to him. Someone wanted her dead. But why? To silence her? About what?

"Witnesses have confirmed that fact, Quinn. A neighbor spotted a dark blue SUV fleeing the scene. Could be those Hispanic guys again. Your client isn't a primary suspect."

He heard Claire's dismayed inhalation. "What do you mean 'primary suspect,' Lieutenant Pratt?" she snapped. "Do you actually think I might be responsible *indirectly*?"

"You can bet she's responsible." Newcomb Farnsworth stood a few feet away. His patrician features contorted with pain, he approached ramrod stiff and seething with rage. "Probably hired some thugs to kill my wife. Like she killed my son. The Widow Spider is extremely clever and devious, aren't you, Claire? But sooner or later you'll make a mistake."

Claire shrank against Michael's side. She reached a hand out to the grieving man. "Newcomb, they were trying to kill me, not Martine. Blame me, hate me more than you already do for that if you want, but I didn't have anything to do with her death."

"No, not personally. Maybe you hired someone to do your dirty work. My son and Paul left you plenty of money." He clenched and unclenched his fists at his sides. "Blood money."

Michael edged in front of Claire in case Farnsworth became violent. Keeping one hand on his nine-millimeter, he slanted a meaningful look at Pratt.

The detective stepped closer to the bereaved husband. "Why would Ms. Saint-Ange want to murder your wife, Mr. Farnsworth? It's my understanding that until recently, the two cousins were close."

His mouth thinned, his lips white with anger. "As family must be, yes. Martine and Claire were not intimate friends." His glare was meant to cleave Claire in two. "It had something to do with Jonathan, I believe. My wife and my son were close friends. Claire was very possessive of her husband. After their marriage, she hardly allowed my wife to talk to him. Jealousy is a powerful emotion."

So he didn't know. The truth would eventually come out and would be just as damning as what the man believed now. Days ago, Michael told Cruz and Pratt what he and Claire suspected had happened between the stepmother and stepson. Would the detective play that trump card?

"Your son has been dead for seven years, Mr. Farnsworth," Pratt said in a low tone. "Do you have any evidence?"

Farnsworth shook his silver-gray head slowly. "How else do you explain all the deaths around the Widow Spider? She knows how to wait. Just keep her away from my children." Then he turned to leave.

"No, oh no, the children!" Claire whispered on a

ragged sob.

Michael could come up with no pacifying words. No way would she be allowed to comfort those motherless kids. All he could do was hold her and let her cry.

After a uniform drove Farnsworth home, Pratt moved everyone indoors to review the details of the hit and run.

Michael sat beside Claire on the sofa while she explained her cousin's visit, omitting the crucial information about the illicit affair. Twinges about the ethics of holding back about the affair plagued him, but he held his tongue.

"So, Ms. Saint-Ange, you say you didn't expect your cousin's visit?" Pratt said for the third time.

"No, Lieutenant, as I explained, Martine and I had not spoken in weeks." Her heavier Acadian accent was a measure of how tired and worn she was. Her voice was mechanically hollow and her face wan and drawn, but as she spoke, her spine straightened and her eyes flashed with resentment.

"When she came to the door then, you were surprised. Did you notice any vehicles in the vicinity then?"

"The street was quiet."

Pratt proceeded methodically with his questioning, repetitive and thorough, like a videotape on endless replay.

Michael gritted his teeth and let the state cop do his job. Dammit, he knew this was necessary, but all he wanted was to wrap Claire up and take her away somewhere safe. "Pratt," he finally bit out, "don't you think you have enough for now? My client has had a bad shock today and needs some rest."

The detective's astute glance darted from one to the other of them. "I suppose you're right, Quinn. I can return tomorrow if I need more information. Ms. Saint-Ange, my condolences on the loss of your cousin."

Once the detective had closed the door behind him, Claire leapt to her feet like a racer ready for the gun. Black skirt flapping around her tights-clad calves, she dashed around the room. It was late afternoon, dusk, and she plucked and slapped at light switches as if enough wattage could hold off the night.

There was no longer a holiday tree to illuminate, since she'd followed local custom and removed all decorations except the door wreath on the twenty-sixth. The drooping poinsettia on a corner stand added to the mood of gloom and emptiness.

"Are you all right?" He circled her with his arms. Damn, but he needed her, needed to hold her, to kiss her soft lips, to be inside her.

Bad timing.

"Yes, I was just afraid I'd slip and tell him something about Jonathan and Martine." On a wrenching sigh, she leaned into his embrace.

It seemed she'd forgotten about maintaining a professional distance. He sure as hell wouldn't remind her. "I'm not certain preventing a scandal is worth the damage caused by concealing information. There are worse things."

"Yes, there are worse things." Her dark eyes shone liquid with the knowledge. "Wait until I tell you what else Martine said."

Without further explanation, she whisked to the hallway, leaving him to trail in her reckless wake. More lights. Then the so-called ballroom, where a bank of switches set three brass chandeliers and several sconces ablaze.

"*Merde*, I can't stand it, Quinn!" she yelled, her voice breaking with emotion. "Every time I think we have a chance of reaching the truth, of solving this damn thing, it gets worse. And it injures more people." She twisted her mane of curls over her head in a gesture of exhaustion and exasperation. "I'm surrounded by death and darkness, and everything I do seems to make matters worse. I need light. Something to take me away from the damn curse."

"No curse, Claire. Greed, jealousy, blackmail. You can't hold yourself responsible for what other people do. Didn't you advise me exactly that about my loss? Whatever the motives—yes, plural—for all these crimes, the deaths are on the murderer or murderers, not you and not the result of a curse. Try to see that."

Her mouth thinned and she looked away. "Perhaps. If you can accept that your sister's murder and the missed shot the next day weren't your fault either."

He swallowed hard. Their situations weren't the same. Were they? Before he could come up with something to say, the telephone rang, followed by urgent barking from the kitchen, where both animals had been confined.

"Enough!" She stomped to the kitchen to answer the jangling summons, muffled by the closed door.

Spacious enough for a reunion of both sides of Michael's large family, the room was sparsely furnished with a few sheet-covered love seats and one or two other pieces. Claire told him Paul had intended to rise in Weymouth society by using this room for charity events. He shook his head at Santerre's ambitions.

Let her have her lights, but it wasn't smart to display their business to the world at large. He pulled the drapes closed, then hurried to join Claire in the kitchen. Could be another of those weirdo calls.

She quieted Alley before answering the phone. "Hello," he heard her say. Then, "Hello, dammit!" When this was apparently met with silence, she spewed out a string of what he assumed were French obscenities, and then slammed down the receiver.

After her wrath ran its course, he'd have to find out what Martine told her before she died. For now Claire needed an outlet.

Ready for more eruptions, he waited in the kitchen doorway. Damn, but she was beautiful with fury painting crimson on her cheeks and sparking lights in her eyes.

"About time you let this crazy bastard know what you think of his harassment. I'd rather see you angry than frightened. Feel better now?"

Claire stood taut and quivering, as if all her muscles and sinews were plucked violin strings. Her breasts heaved with barely controlled sobs, and her depthless eyes were wide with desperation. She shook her fists to the skies. "I feel... I feel like a tornado is spinning around inside me. I don't know what to do."

Alley sat quivering at her feet, and the kitten Spooky crouched in his box. His black fur bristling, he peered big-eyed over the cardboard edge.

With a grunt of frustration, Claire let the dog out into the backyard. Apparently anxious about her mistress, Alley returned in record time. The animal gave a sharp bark at Michael as if to pass off protection to him.

"It's okay, girl." He bent to pat the dog.

Seemingly satisfied, Alley trotted beneath the kitchen table to lie on her cushion.

"You need some action. To break something." He understood. He'd had the same churning need, twice.

"I could chop wood, I suppose." She looked dubious.

He shuddered inwardly at the image of her wielding an ax. "No, in your state of mind, no. That's not good enough for catharsis. To be really satisfying, you need something breakable, something you can smash."

She placed her hands on her hips. Lips pursed and brown eyes gleaming with an unholy light, she said, "I know just what to break."

Chapter Twenty

BREAKING THINGS MIGHT make her feel better, but only for a moment. Everything closed in on her, smothered her. How could she fight her way past the hard knot binding her chest? Maybe Michael was right.

"So much of what's going on comes back to Paul. Russ still accuses me of murdering him, and all the sordid facts about Paul infuriate me so I wish I could slap him. That's stupid, isn't it?"

"I understand how you feel. I've been there." His arched eyebrow reminded her he was no stranger to tragedy. "So what are you going to break?"

"You see those?" Claire indicated the French dessert molds adorning the kitchen wall.

"Those metal things?" Michael's jaw tensed as if he thought she was crazy.

She shook her head. "My mama inherited them from her grandmother, who inherited them from hers, who brought them from France. When I wanted to hang them, Paul wouldn't have what he called peasant trash on the wall. You should have seen the painting he hung there instead."

"Bad, huh?"

"Alley could do better with paint on her three paws. But he bought it at an estate auction, so he deemed it high class. What I have in mind to break are some other things he bought at that same auction." The symbols of Paul's ambitions.

After shutting the door once again on her pets, Claire led Michael to the ballroom. She hurried across the polished parquet floor to the walnut curio cabinet.

Arms folded, he stood expectantly nearby at the marble fireplace. "This cupboard reminds me of one my family keeps my great-aunt Fiona's Belleek china collection in. What's in this one?"

She huffed loudly and slammed open the glass doors. One of the panes shattered. Claire forced herself to ignore the glass fragments peppering the floor and snatched one of the delicate pieces inside. "No family mementos, I guarantee. Inside are a dozen porcelain figurines, ladies in ball gowns, ladies in white lawn and carrying delicate porcelain parasols."

"Very, uh… nice. They look valuable."

"Hundreds of dollars each, I think, but they were purchased along with the cabinet. Paul insisted I have the kind of collection befitting a lady." Hefting an aristocratic shepherdess wearing molded lace ruffles and pink bows, she glanced at the marble and brick fireplace.

Hard. Very hard.

"Perfect for satisfactory smashing. Go for it." His sardonic grin dared her. "I'll move out of the way of flying shards." He sidled away a safe distance.

Claire positioned herself before the hearth. She swung the shepherdess back and forth. The cold edges of the figure's frock cut into her palm. Heart pounding, she eyed the adamantine surface of the hearth.

"Well?"

"I'm thinking about it."

She heard him move closer behind her, felt his heat, like that from a furnace.

"A few minutes ago, you were mad enough to chew up one of those trinkets and spit it out," he hissed in her ear.

Her reflection in the mirror over the mantel looked Medusa-haired, red-eyed and frantic. A woman on the verge of madness. "For so long I've taken care of this house and everything in it. I can't—"

"You can!" His voice was a rumbling growl. "You've been holding in all your anger and fear. You try to be Miss Perfect, to atone for the crimes you're suspected of. Your house is perfect, immaculate, a museum. You sneak in good deeds as if they were sins. You hire a proud old man so he can feel useful. You take flowers and jigsaw puzzles to a nursing home."

Shocked, she pivoted to face him. "How did you know about that?"

"Never mind how I found out. I had to know where you were the morning of the bombing."

"You didn't believe me?" Anger heated her cheeks once more.

"Dammit, you needed an alibi!" He grasped her shoulders and spun her back to the hearth. "Now, heave that baby. Pretend it's me, if you like. Wind up like Pedro Martinez and let 'er rip!"

"Who?"

He emitted a grunt of disgust. "An old Red Sox pitcher."

She hesitated. Trepidation and guilt sapped her nerve.

Clasping his big hands on her shoulders, he growled in her ear, "Make it one for your friendly stalker!"

That did it. All her fury returned at the reminder of the phone calls. She swung her arm back, and then forward so fast, the figurine flew to the back of the marble opening.

*Crash!*

Claire gasped in horror. Edges of pink lace and shards of shepherd's crook scattered on the surface. The figurine's head, her dainty nose missing, rolled into a corner.

"See, the world didn't end." After a warm squeeze of encouragement, he released her and backed away.

"No, it felt kind of good." It did. She'd felt a small rush.

Immediately another figurine was pressed into her hand. "This one's for Paul and the drug gang."

"No. No, this one's for Martinc! Why did they have to kill her? Why?"

*Smash!*

A flirt in a ball gown flew into royal-blue slivers.

She bit her lower lip. Her heart pounded faster, drummed with a new beat of excitement and passion. And release of tension. Tears tracked unchecked down her cheeks.

She crossed to the cabinet and with trembling fingers plucked out another figurine, a dark-haired beauty with Grecian curls and draped in a tunic decorated with seashells. The goddess Aphrodite. "I've always hated her. Paul said she looked like me. She doesn't."

She wound up as much like a baseball pitcher as she could. "This one's for Paul and his drug pals and his damned ambition and greed!"

*Smash!*

Arms outstretched, she stood panting. The stony ache inside eased, replaced with a swirl of new emotion that seared her nerves.

"Is that better? How do you feel now?"

She'd forgotten he was so close behind her. She faced him. How did she feel? Hot. Her skin burned, every inch hypersensitive and tingly. Jittery. Her heart throbbed in every pulse point, and in reaction to his assessing gaze, veered deep into her belly. Tension translated to a need she feared couldn't be met.

What she really needed was Michael's arms around her, his lips, his hands, his body intoxicating her, driving her to sweet oblivion. The way she looked, how could he want her?

He stood in what she recognized as his protective stance, arms loose, powerful legs apart. A bull ready to charge. Unrelentingly, he stared at her, his gaze intensified to molten pewter, its heat enveloping her like liquid flame. His chest rising and falling with rapid breaths as if he'd thrown the porcelain, he waited for her reply. The bulge testing the limits of his fly told her what she needed to know.

"Michael, no, not better. I need… you."

"Claire."

In one swoop, he embraced her, his arms banding her to him. At his scalding kiss, her heart raced and plunged, and she clutched at him. Excitement radiated to her fingertips.

Fervently, she kissed him back, with hungry lips and tongue and teeth. Reveling in the firm resilience of his lips, the rasp of dark stubble around his mouth, his spicy scent, the taste of salty heat and hunger that was

Michael, she ran her hands over his face, around his neck and down his wide back.

His hands found her breasts, pushed aside her bra to tease the nipples. The kisses deepened, moved, pressed, shot darts of tantalizing pleasure to her loins, penetrated her very soul. She grew light-headed with need.

The chandeliers glittered overhead and on the mirror and on the shards beside them, creating an incandescent aura, a surreal hollow in space and time.

"Michael, now!" she murmured, barely able to speak.

"Yes, Claire, now." His arms beneath hers, he lifted her off the floor. "Put your legs around me," he said, his voice intoxicating and rich as brandy.

Slipping off her clogs, she complied, and was instantly backed up against the wall between the hearth and the curio cabinet. His powerful torso muscles flexed against her sensitive skin. She clenched her thighs to get closer to his heat. A shredding rip of her tights and panties, and his fingers found her, slid and fondled and plunged. Shuddering with pleasure, she could barely hold on.

"Oh, Claire, you're like hot, wet silk, so ready for me." His lips traced a spangling path along her cheek, down her neck, over her breast. "I can't wait."

A frenzied groan escaped her lips. She reached for him.

"Hold on," he said, fumbling with his jeans.

As he drove deep into her, raw sensation shook her. Her inner muscles clamping down on him, she rode the rolling surge of pleasure. Her body welcomed him with the same exultation as her heart, and she wanted to hold him inside forever.

"Claire!"

Hot and huge and hard, he lifted her, filled her with thrust after thrust. Pounding into her, he swamped her senses with his heat and strength and groans of pleasure.

She twisted and plunged with him, forcing her body down against his, cradling him, enveloping him, and fusing their two souls into one. A fleeting awareness that he was as out of control as she drove her even higher. Urgent need brought spasms of pleasure and flooding undulations of sizzling, white light. Then he stiffened and contracted against her in one last powerful lunge of completion.

Michael wasn't sure who held who up. His forehead pressed against the wall, he leaned on it with Claire still wound around him. Her legs and arms clung to him. He buried his nose in her tangled mane and inhaled the fresh herbal scent of her shampoo—sweet and tangy at the same time, like Claire.

God, he'd been so out of control, he could have hurt her. When she looked at him all sad-eyed and said she needed him, she didn't mean he should pound her with all the finesse of a sledgehammer. Never in his life had he felt such violent urgency, such desperation to have a woman. Never before had he so totally lost control. Never had he felt such incredible, delirious joy in lovemaking.

Tenderly, he helped her slide her legs downward, separating their bodies, but continued to circle her with his arms. "Claire, are you all right? Did I hurt you?"

"I'm fine. I'm not like one of them." She angled her head toward the broken statuettes.

No, she was definitely real, definitely all woman. Damn the fools of husbands who hadn't treated her like one. Jealousy stabbed holes in him, but pride in being the man to give her pleasure plastered them over.

"But," she continued with a smile in her voice, "I don't think I can stand alone just yet."

"That's okay. I can hold you like this forev—for a long time."

He swallowed the word he'd bitten off, digested it, and absorbed the warmth from it. He'd never said that word to a woman before, but with Claire, forever didn't seem like such a bad idea. Maybe that would be the only way to keep her safe. Fear twisted in his gut every time he thought about those bastards, Raoul and his gorillas, trying to kill her.

He would do what was needed to protect her. He swore it. Whatever it took.

She shook back her hair and smiled. He drank in the rosiness of her lips, swollen from his kisses, the delicacy of her jaw line, the lush mink of her eyelashes, the sexiness of her gaze. Desire pulsed hot and wild through his veins. Impossibly, he wanted her again, so much he ached with the need. But this time…

He lightly rubbed his lips on hers. "Damn, babe, I don't know what happened. I lost it. I tore your clothes. I took you like some rutting—"

"Bull?" she said sweetly. "It's all right. Tights are replaceable. It was glorious. *Magnifique.*"

When he stepped away from her, his boot crunched porcelain into the oak floor. "Hold it. You'll cut your feet." Sweeping her up in his arms, he carried her from the glaring brilliance of the ballroom and into the cozy warmth of her living room.

Depositing her on the sofa, he snagged the quilt from its armrest. "Now we'll do this the right way."

With a flick of his wrists, he snapped out the puffy quilt like a sheet and spread it on the carpet near the wood stove. Shuddering from the primitive need, he kicked off his boots and removed his shirt and still unfastened jeans.

"What do you have in mind? A picnic?" Her lips quirked with amusement. Roving down his body to his rampant sex, her eyes clouded with renewed desire.

"Sort of."

With the matches from the mantel, he lit the white candles she had scattered around. He flicked off all the electric lights before tugging Claire from her perch. Smiling her assent, she helped him dispense with her clothing.

He jiggled his eyebrows at her. "More like a feast, but you're the main course."

Chapter Twenty-One

CLAIRE PLACED TWO logs in the wood stove, then eased shut the glass-and-metal door. Still careful not to wake her sleeping companion, she slipped on his discarded T-shirt and went to the kitchen to let Alley out for the last time that night. When she returned, she sat cross-legged beside Michael on the quilt. Hugging the oversize garment around her, she inhaled his scent.

In the candles' gleam, he was beautiful. Supremely male, he sprawled naked on his back, the glow flickering amber on his bedrock features and bronze on his sinewy body.

She found both solace and satisfaction in his arms. He worshipped her body, not as if she were an untouchable goddess, but with passion and patience and tenderness. A feast, he called it.

He'd kissed and licked and tasted every millimeter of her skin, adored and probed and speared her most sensitive places with his tongue and lips, until she'd writhed and moaned. And then he'd made love to her with his body, slowly stroking with maddening discipline until the two of them exploded into flames hotter than a thousand candles.

Against her better judgment, she'd yielded to her needs, and his. She had no regrets, although hers was a doomed love. The losses of Michael's sister and the little girl he'd been protecting had wounded him so deeply he didn't dare put his heart on the line again. Just as well. It would only endanger his life if he fell in love with the Widow Spider. But oh, how she would miss him when the inevitable happened and he left. Pondering the long, lonely nights and days to come, she thought she might wither like the neglected poinsettia in the corner.

"Thinking about Martine again?" A callused finger brushed her cheek.

She started at his question and at the moisture his finger wiped away. Until that moment she hadn't realized she was crying. "Uh, yes, I…" Ashamed that she was wallowing in self-pity instead of mourning her cousin's death, she let the reply trail away in silence.

Michael lounged, seemingly unconcerned with his nudity, propped on one elbow facing her. Heavy-lidded, his eyes focused on hers. He brought her hand to his lips. "Babe, we might have a problem. I was so wild for you—"

An ancient, secret warmth began in her heart, spread through her, and lifted the corners of her lips. "I liked you that way, so desperate for me that you lost it."

"But neither of us thought about protection."

Her stomach did a back flip, and then settled again. It was unlikely that she'd become pregnant. Her mind and heart spun the notion around, worrying, then savoring the possibility.

Her practical side dismissed the idea. "It's all right. After a year of trying to have a baby with Jonathan, I was about to go to a clinic. But he died before the appointment."

"That's not proof. And Paul?"

"Paul didn't want children." Once more the

whirlwind of anger and tension was building inside her. She drew a deep, cleansing breath. "He didn't tell me until after the wedding, the *salaud*. He kept that and many other things to himself, it appears."

"Are you referring to what Martine told you?"

She nodded. It infuriated her so much that she wondered if she could get the words out. "There was more than one reason my cousin thought we might know about her affair with Jonathan."

"Oh?"

"Paul was blackmailing her."

"Paul?" He shot upright. "How did he know? Jonathan?"

"Probably. Martine didn't say. But the blackmailing began right after Jonathan's death and continued until Paul drowned. He had some kind of proof, maybe a letter or a note. She was frightened enough to cooperate with Paul for over two years."

"How much was she paying him?"

"Not money. He wanted favors."

"What kind of favors?"

"Social-climbing favors. Introductions to the right people to get him into the country club, invitations to parties, things like that." The way Paul had used his best friend and Martine sickened her, and she swallowed down the nausea that feathered her throat. "Now I understand why she continually sang his praises before I finally married him. He also forced her to promote him with me as if he were a product and she the TV commercial."

"He forced her to pimp for him, the sleazebag." His brow knitted and his jaw worked in thought. "Once you said Martine might do whatever it took to protect her children."

Her heart seemed to skip a beat. "You don't mean... kill Paul?"

"She had ample motive for removing both Jonathan and Paul. One word to her husband about an affair with his son, and who knows?"

Claire's mind reeled. Not Martine, no, she couldn't imagine it. "But how could she have managed? There's no evidence against anyone for either death. Where would she have gotten a— Oh, *mon Dieu, non*!"

"What is it, Claire?"

A molten knot ached in her belly. "Martine and Newcomb have a powerboat. She could have taken that out to meet Paul. And Jonathan, could she have sabotaged his car?" Tears burned her eyes. "I can't believe it. I won't."

\*\*\*\*

Hating his devil's advocate role, Michael brushed the disheveled curls from her shoulder. Then he clasped both her hands in his. All the grief and mystery swirling around her were wearing her down, eroding her strength, like water dripping on stone. He wanted to hold her, to make love to her again, but they needed to talk this out.

"There's one more possibility," he said. "Suppose Newcomb knew all about it—the affair, the blackmail. Suppose *he*'s the killer, and it's fear of discovery rather than hatred you see in him."

"Kill his own son? That's even more far-fetched than Martine being the murderer." Dark eyes liquid with sorrow, she shook her head.

"Stranger things have happened." He cupped her cheek. "Babe, a good detective examines all possibilities. We still have no explanation for why the other bad guys are after you. And there's one more front to cover."

"What now?" She sagged, appearing smaller and more delicate than he knew she was.

"Alan Worcester. How do Martine and Newcomb connect to Alan's death?"

"We haven't discussed Alan's skiing accident."

"No, we haven't." He leaned against the chair and drew her into his arms. "You look cute as hell in my shirt. It breaks my concentration. Now, tell me about Alan."

Once she'd settled between his legs, her back against his chest, she replied, "As I told you, he'd asked me to marry him and insisted I wear his ring for the weekend at Caribou Peak even though I'd given him no answer yet.

"At Caribou, the trails are named for North American wildlife. The main trail is Caribou, the beginner's is Otter, and so on. The steepest, most treacherous, a double-diamond trail, is called Cougar. That Saturday, in spite of the danger signs, he was determined to try the Cougar, just across from the cabin."

"Why did he insist on that slope?"

"Part of it was the fact that Maine ski country hadn't had any avalanches in years. Usually it was safe enough. It was Paul's favorite trail. For Alan, it was part of proving himself worthy or some testosterone-driven need."

"Me Tarzan?" He winced, hoping he wasn't doing the same thing by trying to protect her alone. *Please let me keep her safe.*

"But I refused to be Jane." She held up a hand in a gesture of futility. "Anyway, I went off on the cross-country trails alone. I hoped that if he didn't have me as an audience, he'd give it up and ski the usual trails."

"But he didn't." He'd read more in the files. "Witnesses reported hearing what might have been gunshots just before the avalanche that buried Alan. Maybe it was a hunter. I have no idea, but that's why the police were called in."

She nodded, her soft curls brushing his chest, winding waves of heat downward. A mistake to think the thin shirt would shield him from desiring her. Against her back, she had to feel his growing arousal.

"When they asked me about a gun, I told them about Paul's pistol. The kitchen drawer I always kept locked wasn't, and the gun was gone."

"His gun license was for a standard military issue, a heavy-duty automatic pistol, and the glamour weapon in shoot-'em-up movies. Not your average Joe Homeowner protection, but given Paul's extracurricular activities, he might have thought he needed something that held fifteen rounds. Did he know how to use it?"

She nodded again and adjusted her position against him.

He nearly groaned at the sensual abrasion.

"He practiced frequently at a gun range."

"The missing gun. That's what triggered—pardon the expression—the authorities' interest in you. But a handgun wouldn't create enough of a blast to start an avalanche." He kissed the top of her head. "Were the Farnsworths at Caribou Peak that weekend?"

"That weekend and nearly every other weekend. They're avid skiers."

"Good?"

"Expert. That's how they met. Martine was teaching skiing and doing ski patrol at Sugarloaf. That's a resort a little northwest of Caribou. As a kid, she'd been on the school ski team, a natural athlete."

"Ski patrol, huh." Something from his wilderness training jogged into his brain. "Then she'd know about avalanches—how to watch for danger, and how to start one."

"What do you mean?"

"It's the ski patrol's job to check the mountains every day for dangerous spots. If the snow's unstable, they shut off slopes or set off explosions to cause avalanches before the paying skiers come out."

"The Cougar trail, I saw warnings the day before that they might have to shut it down. The notice at the lodge said something about the early season snows being light and fluffy, but recent ones deposited heavy layers of wet snow on top, and that made for very unstable snow. Especially on the steeper slopes. Like this winter. One more result of climate change."

"So anyone who'd been at the lodge could have known that trail was dangerous."

"But would just any skier know how to get an avalanche started?" Claire sounded as if she knew the answer.

"No, but a former ski patrol would."

"That still doesn't explain why they would kill Alan. Martine and Newcomb knew him only casually through me. And how could either one of them have stolen Paul's gun without breaking the locks?"

"The gun's a hell of a mystery. I'd have to see the cabin. But for the rest, consider two scenarios. Martine hated you so much for taking Jonathan away from her that she didn't want you to have any man."

"Jonathan had broken off with her long before he met me."

"A killer's reasons aren't always logical to anyone else." If only this case wasn't so complicated. The usual DEA cases were straightforward. They already knew who the bad guys were. It was more a matter of catching them and having proof. This situation was like trying to find your way through a maze with false exits at every turn.

"And the second scenario?"

"This one works whether it's Newcomb or Martine. The other started to become suspicious, or the killer thought the cops were, so he or she needed some way to throw suspicion on someone else—you."

"I know you're the detective, Michael, but I still find it hard to believe that either my cousin or her husband has murdered three people in cold blood. There are just too many problems with the theory."

"I agree the theory has more holes than cheese," he said.

"And there's one more thing you're forgetting."

"What's that?"

"The stalker. He telephoned again after Martine's death."

"We're left with Newcomb, then, in any case."

"And the drug gang," she concluded.

*And the freakin' DEA.*

Claire gave a long, luxurious cat stretch. "I'm dizzy from all these crazy theories, and this floor's hard. About as hard as what's jabbing me in the back."

So she did notice his reaction to her wriggling

against him. Turning her in his arms, he savored the sweetness of her lips. He never tired of her taste and the enthusiasm with which she returned his ardor. "Maybe we could try one of those condoms upstairs. On a soft bed this time."

She stretched again and rose gracefully. He caught a glimpse of a triangle of dark curls and a sweetly curved butt. The stove's fire had died down again, but his built to hotter flames.

"Paul always made sure he had an ample supply. To avoid contamination." With efficient motions, she swept up the quilt and folded it.

Michael contemplated her words as he gathered his clothing and doused the candles. "Contamination? What do you mean? You or him?"

"He insisted it was to protect me." Her laugh was bitter. "But now I'm not so sure."

Michael hoped the son of a bitch was paying in hell for his crimes. In addition to all his overt chicanery, he'd robbed a warm, loving woman of the future family she desperately wanted and needed. "A complicated, troubled man. Don't feel guilty about how you feel."

She snuggled close in the curve of his arm as they headed for the stairs. "The more I learn about him, the more it consoles me not to have had his child."

Thank God she had no child to bind her to her dead husband. For a child's sake, she would have had to put on a brave front and pretend he was a good man, no matter how he'd used and deceived her.

Like Michael was deceiving her now, a little voice inside him said. No, not like Paul. It wasn't the same damn thing at all. He had no choice. She would accept his reasons, and after she was cleared and the bad guys caught, then they'd see where their feelings for each other led them.

If only he could tell her about the DEA now. Tomorrow he'd go to Portland and insist flat-out on that authorization. He'd demand to know what the hell was going on, why he was in the dark. Even his damn thickheaded supervisor had to see that Claire's life was in danger.

That was it. Once he got the go-ahead, he'd explain to Claire all about his undercover gig. It was part of his job.

She'd understand.

## Chapter Twenty-Two

CLAIRE ROSE EARLY the next morning to clean. Leaving Michael asleep, she donned black wool pants and a charcoal turtleneck. After brewing coffee and downing a few sips, she let Alley out and lifted Spooky from his box.

The kitten dashed off to explore in the living room. He would miss boxing at the Christmas tree decorations. She missed the tree too. For a holiday that had promised to be lonely and bleak, this one had brought her dramatic changes and danger... and love, if only one-sided.

Today was New Year's Eve. What would the new year bring? At least an end to the danger and mystery, please.

Her first chore was to clear away the broken porcelain from the ballroom hearth. Breaking the figurines in the first place—valuable and beautiful things—went against the grain, and leaving the mess only added to her guilt. Besides, Alley or Spooky could cut a paw on the sharp fragments.

Collecting the shards of royal blue reminded her of Martine. The figurine shattered for her. No matter how many ways they examined the events, twisting and turning them like a prism, she couldn't see either Newcomb or Martine as the murderer. A wave of pain and loss washed over her. Though they'd been estranged, Martine was family. As children, they'd played together, and later, her cousin trusted her to care for her children.

*It should have been me, not Martine.*

A sharp pain in her palm ended her preoccupation. Glancing down, she found blood welling up around a puncture from the blue fragment she clutched. Sadly, no blood sacrifice would compensate. She dug a tissue from her pocket and pressed it to her palm. Once the hearth was swept, she tackled the broken glass from the curio cabinet window. Maybe she'd sell the whole damn thing, just as Paul had purchased it. And once her nightmare ended, once the murderer—or murderers— was brought to justice, she'd sell the house, move away. To where, she didn't yet know.

By then no one could accuse her of running.

She gathered up her cleaning tools and gave the room a last appraising glance. All was in order. Ready for a Realtor.

*Oui*, she'd sell. Everything. The money would go into a charity fund with what Paul left her—his drug money. If the law didn't confiscate it, his tainted wealth might do some good.

Having made the decision, she headed for the kitchen.

The splash of water upstairs in the shower flooded her with warm memories of the night. Michael patiently helping her deal with her grief and frustration. Michael losing control in his desperate desire for her. Michael making slow, sweet love to her by candlelight. And Michael sleeping with his strong, protective arms around her.

Those memories would have to sustain her in her

exile.

Gripping her plastic bucket of porcelain shards, she stowed the broom and dustpan in the kitchen pantry closet.

The phone rang.

Claire dropped the bucket. It tipped over, spilling a handful of slivers. "No."

The stalker wouldn't call this early in the morning. Probably. Because of yesterday's tragedy, her nerves were drawn as thin as a cat's whisker.

On the fourth ring, she made herself lift the receiver. Relief at the identity of the caller washed over her. "Oh, Dwight, thank God! Usually you check in more often. If you hadn't called soon, I was going to fire you as my financial manager."

Her relationship with Dwight Cunningham being of long standing, she could joke with him. She pictured the dapper little man in his bow tie and double-breasted suit sitting at his giant glass-topped desk. She retrieved the broom from the pantry closet. Propping the handset with one shoulder, she swept the spilled porcelain bits into the bucket.

He cleared his throat. "I, ah, knew you were busy, my dear. My condolences on the death of your cousin. It was in this morning's paper."

"Thank you, Dwight. I haven't seen the paper yet. What did it say?" Had the reporters unearthed the mistaken-identity angle? Leaving the bucket and broom, she waited tensely.

"Let's see…" The unfolding of newspaper rattled over the phone. "That it was a hit and run. Maybe the same vehicle seen a few days earlier at the site of the bombing."

"Yes, everything that's happened seems to be connected."

"Thank heavens that federal agent is there to protect you. Frankly, Claire, I haven't called because I felt rather guilty for sending him, but now, well—"

Her heart and her knees wobbled. "What do you mean, sending a federal agent?" She yanked a wooden chair from the kitchen table and sat, hard.

At first, Dwight said nothing. "I, ah, thought they must have told you after the bombing. The DEA, the Drug Enforcement Agency, I mean. Michael Quinn is an agent, not a private investigator. Didn't you know? Oh, dear."

By now, the investment counselor was probably tugging anxiously at his bow tie.

Claire wanted to strangle him with it. "I think you'd better tell me all about it."

She listened with growing horror while the man described how the DEA came to him requesting help getting one of their agents close to Claire. They were seeking more information about Paul's drug smuggling cohorts. He insisted to her that he cooperated because he expected it to clear her.

After disconnecting, Claire lowered her head between her knees. Spots swam before her eyes, and she feared that the coffee she'd drunk might join the broken pieces in the bucket.

*How could Michael have fooled me so completely?*

Battling the nausea, she pulled herself upright and reached in her pocket for a tissue, but no tears welled up.

Dry-eyed, she struggled to understand. How could she have fallen in love with him? Why had she believed he might care about her? All along, she knew that loving him would gain her nothing. Her aunts' familiar words rang in her ears, this time with a more painfully discordant clamor than usual.

*The curse of your beauty is to be alone.*

****

When Michael came downstairs, he found Claire sitting quietly at the kitchen table. He kissed the top of her head in passing. He helped himself to coffee and three heaping spoons of sugar, then leaned back against the sink, sighing in satisfaction at the rich flavor and aroma.

When he registered her rigid posture and frozen expression, he straightened. "Was that the stalker on the phone just now?"

"It was Dwight Cunningham." Her voice sounded strained as if it pained her to speak. She drew a deep breath as he saw her barriers go up. "Were you ever going to tell me the truth, Agent Quinn? Or is that even your name?"

His heart kicked into high gear and his gut clenched. Cunningham had spilled his identity. Michael placed his coffee mug on the counter. He had to answer her carefully.

Folding his arms, he watched her. "Michael Quinn is my real name. I've wanted to tell you everything for a long time, ever since I realized you had nothing to do with Paul's activities. The DEA wouldn't authorize it."

"Wouldn't authorize it." Her voice was cold, flat. She rose to her feet and held his gaze. "But you knew all along, before you met me, about Paul and the drug gang?"

"That's why they sent me. Someone in this area

took up Paul's smuggling operation, and the DEA thought you might be involved."

"I remember you suggested a new smuggler to Russ. So you came here pretending to help me clear myself of murder, while you were really investigating me."

"Only to begin with. I—"

"*Mon Dieu*, the phone threats! I suppose the DEA's behind those too." Her voice held a note of hysteria.

"The DEA wouldn't do that." He hoped. One more thing to check on at headquarters. Someone would pay if they had. "Coincidence. The DEA approached Cunningham about the same time you asked him to find you a P.I." And the reason he'd had so little time to prepare for the assignment.

"And all that about your sister and the kidnapped child and leaving the DEA, was it all nonsense, designed to soften me up?"

Dammit, now she believed everything was a lie. He forced the knotted tendon in his throat to relax. He had to maintain a calm voice, an even tone. Then she'd listen. "No, those tragedies did cause me to leave the DEA. But until my resignation takes effect, I have this assignment. Claire, I swore an oath as an agent of the government. We have to stop these gangs that are ruining people's lives. It's my job."

He'd done what he had to do. That should explain his actions satisfactorily and close the matter. He grabbed his cup and swallowed another gulp of coffee.

"Your job." She clasped her hands together. "And was it also your job to make love to the Widow Spider? Or was that your own *coup de vache*, a dirty trick you and the other agents could laugh about?" The rose in her cheeks paled, as ashen as frost on the windowpanes.

The pain in her lusterless eyes shook him.

He started toward her, his arms open, but the icy warning in her expression halted him in mid-stride. "I never— No one in the agency knows. What I feel for you has nothing to do with my assignment. In fact, involvement with a subject is totally against the rules."

"A subject, that's what I am to you. You could break the damn rules to get into my bed, but not to tell me the truth." Tears choked her voice. Emotion thickened her accent and turned her voice shrill.

He'd hurt her, but the wound bled deep inside him too. He lifted his hands in surrender. "I wanted you. We wanted each other. And once I was certain you weren't involved and had murdered no one, I decided it was okay. I know it isn't logical, but lust isn't logical." He winced at his clumsy wording. That wasn't what he meant, but he didn't know what else to say.

"Perhaps then, neither is anger or betrayal. You may be on the opposite side from Paul, but you deceived me just the same." Seeming unable to bear his gaze, she turned away. As if she might shatter into as many fragments as the porcelain figurines, she clutched the edge of the table. "I want you out of here."

He couldn't prevent himself from touching her then, trying to comfort her, to reach her. He gripped her shoulders firmly.

"Claire, we have something good between us. Something special. If I had leveled with you, it might have jeopardized the operation. There's more going on, but they haven't told me everything. It was my job. Please understand."

Wrenching away, she spun on him. "Understand?

*Mon Dieu*, I understand, but I wonder if you do."

"Claire, *please*."

Her trembling shoulders betrayed her tension and distress, but her voice was steady and her eyes blazed with determination. "If the DEA wants anything from me, they can send some other agent. With an I.D. this time. Now pack up and get out of my house."

Clearly she was nearing the breaking point. No way would she listen to reason at the moment. After he knew the whole scope of the operation, he'd return. Then they'd talk again.

He turned and walked away.

****

Emotions crowding her chest, Claire remained by the table. While Michael mounted the stairs, while he moved around upstairs, she stood there, staring at nothing, unable to move. When the door clicked closed behind him, she flinched. He was gone.

Alley's bark roused her enough to let the dog in before she sank to the floor. The little one pushed her cold nose under one arm and wriggled her way into her mistress's lap. Claire hugged her while bitter tears flowed down her cheeks and soaked into the dog's fur.

His job, his job. It was a poor excuse. How he could keep his duty to the agency separate from his personal needs and emotions mystified her. If he truly cared for her, he would have told her the truth. It was as simple and as complicated as that. He didn't love her. She didn't want him to love her. No one should ever love her. Discovering Paul's duplicity had stung, but Michael's betrayal flayed her.

How long she sat there, she couldn't say. Minutes, hours, or days later, she dragged herself upstairs. If she cleared away every trace of him, maybe she could pretend to herself he was never here. She stripped the beds and changed all the towels, throwing everything in the washer. With robotic motions, she scrubbed every inch of the bathroom tile and polished and vacuumed every surface in the bedrooms.

And still his scent lingered. Impressed into her body, the fresh smell of his soap and his after-shave, the unique scent of his skin, tortured her senses and her heart.

Abrading her flesh with the loofah beneath the stinging needles of a long, hot shower restored feeling to her numbed body.

But the memory of him persisted.

Wrapped in a fresh bath towel, she sank to her knees beside the bed. Pain cinched her throat and constricted her chest. Her gaze swept the room where they had made love last night.

*I can't stay here.*

She couldn't run away and hide. The police would not allow it. And danger still stalked her. She couldn't remain under this roof with all the memories, either. She had to stay at least until after Martine's funeral. Then she'd get away. Gradually in her exhausted brain a plan took form.

Under the watchful and worried gazes of her animals, she dressed. Then she grabbed her cell phone.

Chapter Twenty-Three

MICHAEL SLAMMED HIS fist onto the heavy metal table with enough force to fell a tree. Then he gave it another whack for good measure and spewed out expletives scorching enough to char half the trees in the White Mountain National Forest, where he damned well wished he'd remained.

"That freaking bastard!" he roared. "Why did he keep that little secret from me this whole time? Didn't he see the difference knowing would have made?"

The new development complicated more than the DEA's operation. A lot more.

He prowled around the small conference room Ricardo Cruz used as an office in the Portland DEA suite. "Said due to my foul-up last year and my decision to resign, he didn't trust me with the whole story." Hands balled into fists, he punched at air.

"I didn't know either," Cruz said mildly. "The Group Supervisor is going through a messy divorce, and the Special Agent in Charge is on his case about that earlier screw-up. I heard he's on meds for depression. Must have skewed his judgment." Michael's partner lounged in a folding chair, his leather-booted ankles crossed on the metal table edge.

"Judgment, my ass. He likes to be in control, dance us around like damn puppets." Michael swung another folding chair out and straddled it. "All this time, he knew about another player in this farce and didn't tell us. The operation's been a trap for him all along."

"So you think this dude's the stalker," Cruz mused.

"And the one who snooped around in Claire's house. That's why I had to stay undercover even after the bombing. I bet you a week in your native land he's behind that."

"I hate to disillusion you, man, but this *is* my native land. I was born in Miami, remember?"

"Okay, a week in Cuba. Whatever." Michael waved away the distraction. He struggled to contain the flames jumping in his veins. "A hell of a waste of time. I even questioned Claire's damn hairdresser. I've been working a connect-the-numbers puzzle, only the GS had the most important number."

"Second prize, two weeks in Cuba." Cruz lowered his feet and leaned forward, grinning. His coal-dark eyes gleamed.

Michael couldn't stop himself. His mouth twitched into a smile. His partner's natural good humor never failed to ease his dark moods. "If that's the kind of lame joke you use on the female sex, it's a damn miracle you ever have a date."

"My jokes, lame or otherwise, are part of my charm. Women love a man who makes them laugh. I don't see you drowning in women."

"Buddy, I'm just drowning."

"Now who's making lame jokes?" At Michael's black glower, Cruz snapped his fingers as if in realization. "So what happened when that bow-tied banker blew your cover?"

What happened? Michael wasn't sure. "She threw me out. Thinks I'm lower than pond scum. Wouldn't listen to reason. Now she has no protection." He rose from the chair to stalk to the coffeemaker under the window. "You want some?"

Cruz gave him a thumbs-up. "So that's it. You and the sexy widow have made it together a few times?"

At that, Michael clenched his jaw, and heat rose to his face. *Made it.* The expression sounded crude for the most incredible sex of his life. For the connection and longing he felt with Claire. Struggling for nonchalance, he slugged down some of the steaming brew.

Cruz grinned. "Aha, I was right before. The lady's gotten under that tough hide. It's more than sex, isn't it? For both of you."

"Damn! This stuff's strong enough to fuel Air Force One around the world." Michael set the mug down so hard, the scalding coffee sloshed out onto the table. "What crystal ball told you that?"

"God knows why the lady cares, with your Alien Wild Man of the Mountains face. Must be your sparkling personality. Or another portion of your anatomy."

"Rick! Shut up."

"It's easy, partner—if you know something about women. Not that a guy can ever understand them completely."

Grinding his teeth, Michael glared at the other man.

Cruz lowered his feet from the table. "She wouldn't be angry if she didn't care for you. We're talking emotions here, not an exercise in logic, and you were acting like what you have with her is only a part of your job."

Michael blew out a breath. Dammit, his friend was

right. He jabbed his fingers through his hair and stared blankly out the dingy window. "I tried to tell her what was between us had nothing to do with the job, but she wouldn't listen to reason."

"Reason? Not what she wants, not what she needs, Quinn. She's listening with her heart, not her head. You have to show her how you feel." He stood and removed the leather jacket he'd taken to wearing regularly. After straightening the collar, he hung it on the back of his chair.

"How do you know so much about women?"

"I grew up with four sisters, remember? You learn what makes females tick or you don't survive." He feinted a few shadowboxing jabs and an uppercut at Michael. "And it's paid off big time in my social life. Love 'em and leave 'em, that's me, and they still love me. Take a lesson, *mano*."

"A lesson." Maybe. Michael had some thinking to do before he talked to Claire again. Cruz's advice could stew in his brain while she cooled down. *If* she cooled down. "In the meantime, we need a plan for this operation. I didn't want to do it, but it looks like we have no choice."

"You mean the ledger?" Cruz tested the coffee. "Not as good as Cuban coffee, but every bit as strong."

"Yeah, but I need to make sure Claire is safe." Fear for her chilled his blood, twisted his guts in a climber's square knot. "The GS's suppressing crucial information could have killed Claire. Probably did kill her cousin. We can't afford any more mistakes."

Cruz blew on his coffee, "So, like we discussed before, we have to set a trap. Only now we know who it's for. Boss wanted the widow in the dark. Does she know?"

Michael considered. "No, I'm certain she doesn't. She knows about El Águila's goons, though." She deserved to know about the stalker, but could he bring himself to tell her?

Working out the operation chewed up the rest of the day. Once word leaked that Santerre's widow had a ledger detailing his drug smuggling, they'd have a team of DEA and customs agents ready to arrest whoever came to Claire's house to retrieve it.

At nine o'clock Michael and Cruz left the DEA offices.

"Until the widow takes pity on you, you can probably get a room at my motel," Cruz said as they strode through the building's parking garage to their vehicles. "Coffee shop has dynamite blueberry muffins and a hot little waitress who slips me seconds when her boss isn't looking."

"Waitress, huh?" Michael said. "I thought you were seeing that blonde from MCU headquarters."

"Quinn, you've never been a party animal, and now that the widow's reeled you in and wrapped you up, you want everybody else to be tied down. When have you ever known me to ration myself?"

"Lost my head."

Only a few cars remained in the garage. Their pace slowed as they neared the SUV. Michael fished out his keys but looked at them as if he'd never seen them before. The urgency to go to Claire, for himself as much as for her, gnawed at him.

Instead of continuing to his rental car, three spaces away, Cruz halted. "Look, I've been trying to cheer you up, but I see how worried you are about your lady."

She wasn't his lady anymore. If she ever had been. "I don't like leaving her in that house all alone." Michael nervously twirled his keys. "She could be in danger even tonight. Can this office set up protection until her cousin's funeral?"

"Consider it done. I'll do it myself if these guys are all busy. Remember, buddy, it's New Year's Eve."

New Year's Eve. Michael had forgotten. A new year, a new beginning for them both, he'd hoped. But this development changed everything. He and Cruz would accompany her to the funeral, and afterward he would find the right words to explain. He had to. The hole he'd dug for himself seemed deeper than the Grand Canyon. Then what his partner had said hit him. "New Year's Eve. What am I thinking? Cruz, don't tell me you don't have a date."

The raven-haired agent ambled back toward the elevator. "I don't do dates on New Year's Eve. That midnight kiss seems to give them ideas about commitment. Something I'm allergic to." He grinned. "I'll see she's safe."

"Thanks. I'll feel better with someone outside the house."

Amiable and self-assured, his partner had another side in the face of danger. Cruz's marksmanship matched his own, and his lanky build and SEAL training allowed him to melt into shadows invisibly where Michael's bulk would stick out like ugly on a bad guy. He would trust no one more than Ricardo Cruz with his life. Or Claire's.

"Didn't you say using the ledger to trap the gang was her idea in the first place?" Cruz said.

"It was, and I tried like hell to talk her out of it

211

then. Too dangerous. I still think so, but the ball's in motion and time's running out."

In spite of accepting that he couldn't control what other people did, the idea of a third failure and that it could be Claire gave him the cold sweats.

****

Two days later, two vehicles pulled up in front of Claire's house. A leaden sky hung over Weymouth, and forecasters predicted flurries.

She peered through the sidelight. Not Michael, please no. Her heart tripped on itself. What was he doing here? The agent named Ricardo Cruz had said he would escort her to Martine's funeral. She couldn't bear it if Michael went too.

Her feet leaden as if facing the Inquisition, she dragged on her coat. Cool but polite, that was how she would face them. Him.

"Good morning, Ms. Saint-Ange." Cruz gave her a charming smile. "There's been a slight change in plans."

"What do you mean?" She fixed her attention on him, but her words formed automatically, her mind straying to the man beside him. Involuntarily, her gaze flicked to Michael.

She'd never seen him in a suit. He always wore either khakis or jeans and casual shirts, attractive enough on his muscled physique. In the navy suit, crisp blue shirt, and dark tie, he was devastating. The suit had to be custom tailored. No off-the-rack suit would fit those broad shoulders and massive arms, then taper so perfectly. Acute longing welled up within her. She forced herself to remember he wasn't honorable and decent, as she'd believed.

Before he could catch her staring, she forced herself to attend to what Agent Cruz was saying.

"—used to seeing Quinn with you. If anyone's watching, they'd suspect I was an agent."

Her cheeks heated as she strove to control her discomfiture. "You told me you would accompany me to the cemetery, Agent Cruz."

"Yes, ma'am," He ran his tongue around his cheek, and his eyes slid toward Michael, who stood by silently. "But this is Quinn's assignment. He knows some of the people who'll be at the funeral, and they know him. And Olívas—the drug cartel's man—has seen him with you." He shrugged as if that said it all.

"So, Agent Quinn, you plan to accompany me?" She eyed him as coolly as she could manage. She wouldn't let him know how deeply he hurt her.

"To guard you and to watch for suspicious strangers, anyone who shouldn't be at the cemetery." His familiar deep rumble flowed through her like a warm river.

She supposed she could survive if they weren't alone. "Will you accompany us, Agent Cruz?"

"Ma'am, I'll be there just outside the gates."

"I can go by myself, and both of you can wait outside the gates. I'll be perfectly safe at the cemetery," she said, with more confidence than she felt.

Cruz flashed her a dazzling smile. "Yes, ma'am, that might work if we frisked everyone before they went in."

"If we spot this Olívas or one of his men—or anyone else suspicious—I'll radio Cruz to follow them." Michael stepped to the side and angled one arm. "Are you ready?"

As ready as she could be under the circumstances. There was no way to avoid Michael's escort. But she didn't have to touch him or allow him to touch her. She swept down the porch steps and to the SUV. She was strong. Look how much she'd already survived. Grief for Martine and the critical scrutiny of everyone at the cemetery would demand so much of her, she'd have little time for concern about the nearness of the man who'd deceived her.

Chapter Twenty-Four

MICHAEL DROVE TO the Weymouth Cemetery north of town on a winding country road. In Maine during winter, bodies were usually stored until the ground thawed. Apparently Newcomb Farnsworth's influence extended to excavating frozen soil. This was merely the committal part of the funeral. By the time they arrived, he had to park at the end of the long line of mourners. He slipped on his parka and opened the passenger door.

Crossing the icy ground, Claire allowed him to take her elbow, but she studiously avoided his gaze. During the drive, she didn't say a word.

Doubt he could get her to listen to him tightened a knot in his gut. He had no right to expect anything from her, especially under the circumstances. Because of potential danger in this unknown crowd, he forced himself to set aside his feelings. For now.

They passed three cracked and mossy headstones that dated further back than the Revolutionary War. Toward the center of the burial ground, they stopped on a low knoll beneath a bare-branched maple tree. The Farnsworth family plot encompassed a house-size space in a corner.

"This is close enough," Claire murmured. "I don't want to attract attention, and Newcomb wouldn't welcome my presence."

To one side of the hundred or so mourners, they had a good view of the ceremony. In the plot's center rose a monolith, ornately decorated with wreaths and medallions, a one-story Washington Monument. The new grave, draped in fake green turf, yawned to the right of it. The family sat beneath a canopy in front of the coffin, where a priest read from a prayer book. A light snow fell, casting a veil over the proceedings.

Michael cast a sideways glance at Claire. Her eyes glistened with unshed tears. Clad in a new long black coat and matching wool hat, she stood dignified and solemn. A few people near them turned to stare with expressions of disapproval and contempt. She ignored them. Her gaze appeared focused on the two children in the front row of seated mourners. Martine's children.

"Perhaps you could speak to them after this is over."

She shook her head. "I don't want to cause trouble."

He asked her to identify the people around them. She named those she knew and pointed out others who looked familiar. Behind Farnsworth and his children sat an older woman she didn't know. Judging from her simple garb and deferential demeanor, a housekeeper or nanny, Claire told him. No one attending seemed out of place.

Even with Farnsworth's antagonism, it was odd that Claire hadn't attended the entire ceremony. "Why didn't you go to the church?"

Her lips thinned, and the hand clutching her small leather purse twitched. "I couldn't. As long as God has cursed me, I cannot set foot in His house."

Michael gawped at her amazing statement.

Dammit, she still believed. Hadn't they talked about it enough? He knew better than most that logic and emotions don't connect. And wasn't he a prime example? Shit.

Before he could press her—one more time—on the curse, his cell phone hummed in his pocket. *Cruz.* He'd have to ask her later. He stepped behind the tree to answer the call.

After he finished talking to his partner, he said, "Cruz saw a suspicious character nosing around the vehicles. When the guy took off in a tan pickup, Cruz followed him."

She drew a deep breath, but her mocha-colored eyes still looked haunted, with violet smudges beneath them. "That's it, then."

"Let's hope." He ached to hold her, to take her away where she'd be safe. Where he could persuade her of his honor, his sincerity. But that was impossible.

Cold prickles had him rubbing his nape. Experience warned him not to ignore this premonition of danger. Until he returned Claire safely to her house, he'd stay on the alert. He checked to make sure his service weapon rested safely at his back.

At the graveside, the ceremony ended, and people were drifting away toward the cars. The lowering sky continued to spit out great clumps of wet, starry flakes, some as large as saucers. The air smelled fresh and clean, with the salty tang of the nearby ocean.

When Michael saw Claire tense and her eyes widen, he knew why. Farnsworth and his children headed their way, the most direct path to the limousine. He slid his arm around Claire, but she shook him off and straightened her shoulders.

Aristocratic head held high and eyes on his destination, Farnsworth would have swept past them without a word. But when Robert and Adele spied Claire, they broke rank and sprinted to her. A sob breaking from her lips, she enfolded the children as if they were her own.

"Oh, how I've missed you both!" She kissed their cheeks in turn.

Adele hugged her cousin, crying her name and sobbing into her coat. Robert, at twelve less spontaneous, merely held Claire and allowed her to hold him. His brown eyes were huge and luminous, as if he were fighting back tears.

Their father snatched them from Claire's arms and hustled them away with the nanny. Robert turned back for a moment, puzzlement on his brow.

"How dare you show your face here!" Farnsworth spat.

"At least you haven't turned your children against me, Newcomb," she said quietly and evenly. "They know I would never harm their mother."

Without a word, Farnsworth stalked off to join the bewildered children in their limousine. Michael understood how the man must feel, but did he have to make an ass of himself? How anyone who knew Claire would believe her capable of murder was beyond him.

She turned to him and slipped her arm through his. "I'm ready to leave now."

Surprised that she requested his touch, he quickly understood. Against the dark background of her coat and hat, her face was ashen and drawn, as pale as the snow falling more heavily around them. When he noted her unsteady gait across the rough ground, he started to wrap his arm around her.

"No," she said shakily, "I'm all right." A woman on the verge of falling apart, but she was all right.

After an eternity of slogging through the deepening wet snow and past the curious and reproachful gazes of the other mourners, they reached his Explorer.

If Cruz caught up to the tan pickup, the danger might have passed, but the timing stank. Putting off too long squaring himself with her might mean losing his chance. If he drove around for a while, she'd have to listen to him.

****

Claire collapsed on the bucket seat. Pressure built in her chest. Letting the anguish wash through her, she lay back. She'd tolerated the sneers, snubs, and outright hostility, but the most wrenching part of the whole ordeal was seeing Adele and Robert, so alone, so sad. She ached for those poor, poor children, with only their coldly businesslike father and a strange nanny to shepherd them through the most traumatic time in their young lives.

She had vague impressions of Michael starting the SUV, turning it around, and pulling into traffic on the quiet road. Nearly everyone else had left.

How foolish she'd been to think having Michael with her would make this day harder. If anything, his support, his mere presence gave her the strength to endure it. She wanted to tell him, but she had to keep cool, not allow herself to be drawn into any emotional situation. There could be nothing between them. That was over.

"Quinn, I want to thank you for helping me endure that scene with Newcomb."

"You may not thank me when you hear what I've got to tell you." He stopped at an intersection, and then proceeded to the right on an even narrower country lane.

She sat bolt upright. "What do you mean?"

His gaze wary, he glanced toward her. "The day I… left, do you remember I went to DEA headquarters?"

She sighed. Did she really want to hear this? "Yes, you said there was more they weren't telling you. So?"

He nodded, his expression grim. "There are things you need to know about the operation. What it's really about."

"Does it really matter now?" She folded her arms and stared straight ahead. "It's a case of too little too late."

"Whatever you think of me, it's important that you understand the facts."

They wound their way leisurely through the hilly fields of the area. So far the roads weren't hazardous.

She distracted herself by gazing at the patterns of the snowflakes on the windshield. It didn't work. Her sensitivity to Michael's presence—his nearness beside her in this vehicle, his warmth, his scent, the rumble of his voice, his gray eyes—all kept her off balance. Maybe that was his aim.

"Why you?" she said, more irritated at herself than at him. "Why didn't Agent Cruz explain everything to me when he contacted me about protection?"

"Because you're not supposed to know this."

"Then don't bother." How dare the man try to placate her with official secrets.

He continued, ignoring her dismissal. "I learned

that day that I had been assigned to you as bait. I was the rabbit the greyhounds chase, the live lure for the big fish they wanted to catch. The agency sent me there to draw someone into the open. It was their web, not yours, that was spun."

She couldn't help but gape at him. She heard resentment in his voice and perceived rage in the set of his jaw. So he'd been a pawn as much as she. "Now you know how I felt. And just who was this master criminal?"

"The man who wouldn't want the murders of your husbands and fiancé investigated in too much depth, the man who wouldn't want you to remarry or even be involved with someone." His voice ground out harsh and bitter, as if the person were an old foe.

"The stalker. You know who he is? What's his name?"

"Paul Santerre."

Did she hear him correctly? "Paul?"

"We believe he faked his death."

"*Tu es tombé sur le crâne!* You're nuts!" Or *she* was going crazy. This was too much to be believed.

"It's true. With the DEA on his trail, he had to disappear. The DEA has suspected for a long time that the new player on the drug scene wasn't new after all. He had too many pieces in place, had deals set up too quickly after Paul died for it to be anyone else. Think about it."

"How could he fake his death? I buried him. They wouldn't let me see him, but his body was identified."

"You buried a body about his size and weight and wearing remnants of Santerre's clothing," he said. "Why didn't they do DNA tests?"

She huffed. "There was no reason to believe it wasn't Paul. If the DEA thinks he's alive, why didn't you exhume the body and order tests?"

"Didn't want to warn him off." He frowned. "How was the body ID'd then? He had no face, not enough fingers left to fingerprint. Scars?"

She shook her head to clear the swirling confusion. "Dental work. The dental records matched a bridge on his upper teeth." Impossible. She couldn't accept it.

"He and his drug pals probably found some poor homeless slob to take his place. I wouldn't put it past them to smash in the guy's face and put Santerre's bridge in his mouth. Maybe they counted on the fish and the rocks to take care of the fingerprints. Or maybe they—"

"No more. I refuse to listen to this." She lay against the contoured seat and willed herself to ignore his foolish talk. Why was he doing this? Beneath lowered lashes, she peeked at him to fathom his motivation.

He glanced in the rearview mirror, frowned, then squinted into the side mirror. As if in the Indy 500, he stomped on the accelerator, and the vehicle leapt forward.

"Claire, hold onto the safety handle. This could be rough."

Chapter Twenty-Five

THE VEHICLE SWERVED around a sharp curve, the torque throwing Claire against the door. A look in the outside mirror revealed the reason. A dark blue SUV followed close behind them. Too close. And gaining.

"What is it, Michael?"

"The Mexican drug gang. I should have known." Into his phone, he barked, "Cruz, where the hell are you?" Apparently receiving no response, he tossed the instrument down in disgust.

Claire kept a tight grip on the safety handle. They whipped along the narrow road and through curves. The giant snowflakes, like a child's folded paper cutouts, continued to fill the air and whiten the road. "Why? Do they think I have the ledger with me?"

"They were trying to kill you before they knew about the ledger. Maybe now they want to grab you instead."

She gasped. "Make me a hostage? To get the ledger?"

"Maybe it has something to do with Santerre." A jaw muscle jerked.

Her throat constricted. What did it mean if Paul still lived? Could he be behind all the terrible events? Even Martine's death? *Mon Dieu, non.*

"I don't intend to let them get close enough to find

out." He accelerated and wrenched the vehicle around another curve.

Claire's nerves clattered like a speeding train beneath her skin, and blood roared in her ears. In spite of their differences, she trusted Michael to get them out of this situation. Both their lives were on the line.

They weren't traveling the road back to Weymouth. Evergreens, spruce, and white pines, formed thick walls on either side of the road. Here and there dirt lanes led off to the right, marked by private-road signs.

And still the dark SUV pursued them. Though this interior had adequate heat, chills shivered through her. "We're heading north. Do you realize where you're going?"

"I have more horsepower than they do. We can keep ahead. As long as this damn snow doesn't get any worse." His grim voice matched his expression. At a sharp turn, he slowed, the powerful engine downshifting automatically, and then he sped up on the straightaway. "I don't know where the hell this road goes. I was just driving so we could talk."

A sudden bang and a hard jolt sent Claire's purse flying off her lap. She twisted to see the other vehicle drop back a few feet. "What was that?"

Once again Michael accelerated. "They rammed us."

They roared ahead, out of the tree cover. The tires spun on a broad turn, the vehicle swerving in a semicircle. Michael steered into the slide, and they sped forward. On their left rose a steep granite slab of cliff. On the right, a slender metal guardrail stood as the only barrier between them and the rolling pewter waters of

Casco Bay.

"The Cliff Road," Claire said, breathless. The accumulating snow obscured the road edges. Michael leaned forward over the steering wheel. "Up ahead is—"

"Suicide Curve." Where Jonathan's car had crashed over the cliff. They both knew the hazards of this road. She didn't need to voice them.

"Take my phone," Michael said. "See if you can raise Cruz. Just press Redial."

She did. "No response. It went to Voice Mail."

"Yeah, yeah." Muscles jumped in his tight jaw. "Talk, anyway. Tell him the situation. Tell him we need backup."

Claire described where they were and explained about their pursuers.

"Here they come again." He gripped the wheel as they headed into a blind curve.

Directly ahead loomed the water.

In horrified silence, Claire watched the dark blue hood approach in the side mirror. The magnification made it appear huge. A vicious heavy metal alien charging them. And they were its prey.

The other vehicle's bumper rammed their left rear fender. The shocking force sent Michael's SUV into a fishtail spin. Toward the steep cliff on the right.

Claire clasped both hands over her mouth. She bit back a scream. She could only watch as Michael struggled to turn out of the spin. He accelerated and wrenched the wheel to the left. Momentum propelled them sideways on the ice-spotted road.

With a parting growl of increasing speed, the other SUV passed them and disappeared ahead into the curtain of snow.

"Hold on," Michael bit out. "This might work."

He stomped on the brakes and yanked on the emergency brake at the same time. Almost imperceptibly, their slithering progress slowed. With a whine of metal, they stopped.

The jarring stop shook every bone in Claire's body and slammed her shoulder against the car door. Wincing at the pain, she glanced at Michael. He slumped over the wheel, but he was breathing.

"Are you all right?" To her ears, her voice sounded shaky and thin. "You did it. You stopped the car. We're safe."

"Not yet, babe," he said. "We have to get the hell out of here. This damn thing could take a dive."

Not until then did she notice the cant of her seat and the continuing whine of stressed metal. She stared out her window. Only the tarnished-silver sky and sea came into view, not the road. The Explorer tilted at a crazy angle, only partly on the roadbed. A rear tire hung over the cliff. Suspended, they teetered dangerously.

Only a severely strained guardrail held them back from an icy, wet death.

"I want you to remove your seat belt and slide toward me." Michael sat slowly upright and unsnapped his belt. Blood dripped onto his parka.

"You're hurt! What is it?" She reached toward him.

He caught her hand. "I'm okay. A cut on my forehead. It's nothing." Above his right eye bloomed an ugly gash and a purpling bruise, where his head must've struck the steering wheel.

For a second, she thought he was going to kiss her hand, but he released it with a gentle squeeze. Warm tingles spread up her arm from the contact. Dazed, she averted her gaze and flipped the belt's catch.

"Okay, now slide slow and smooth to me, and we'll go out my side. It'll be tricky since we're tilted at least twenty degrees." After zipping the cell phone into a pocket, he lifted the door handle and gave a gentle push.

Levering herself up and over with both arms, Claire slid onto the center console. Her legs made the move tight going.

On a shriek of protesting metal, Michael popped the driver's door. He shoved it upward and open. Violent paroxysms shook the vehicle. It lurched downward.

Through the windshield, Claire saw a guardrail support yanked from its cement bed. Like a rubber band stretched to its limit, the narrow metal rail twisted and thinned. Its harsh cry of protest whined on the wind. Rocks tumbled into the frost-tipped waters below.

Shock waves ripped through Claire. A scream crowded her throat.

Their precarious slide halted, but the metallic cry of the guardrail complained at the added weight. With the tilt increased, the SUV could tumble over the side at any minute and take them with it.

Michael hauled Claire against him and, with a powerful lunge, surged up and through the open door.

She felt herself cradled in his arms as they hurtled through the air. They hit the snow-covered pavement with a painful thud. He rolled, his big body protecting her.

A few minutes later, chilled and wet, Michael sagged with relief when he was able to raise Cruz on the phone. He briefly stated their plight. "I tried to contact you twice earlier. What happened to you, man?"

"Sorry," Cruz replied. "The guy stopped his truck and ran into the woods. When I chased him, the phone must have fallen from my pocket. By the time I found it, he'd circled back around and driven away."

"Bad luck. Any idea who it was?"

"I feel like a damn amateur, but at least I got the license. I think it's our target."

At those words, Michael's nerves screamed, and a stony ache tightened in his gut. So Santerre had been at the funeral, had taken the monumental risk of being recognized. And for what? To spy on Claire? To meet her? To protect her from the gang? The possibilities battered his tired brain.

"I'll be there as soon as I can," Cruz said.

Before he disconnected, Michael asked him to call a wrecker. Without their body weight, the guardrail was strong enough to hold them on the cliff edge for a while longer. If the sickening slide continued into the bay, it might be next summer before it got fished out.

He turned to Claire. Disheveled, wet, and hatless, she'd pulled up her hood. She huddled beside him at the roadside and massaged her right shoulder with her left hand. Once again, her courage and spirit touched him. She'd been scared but hadn't allowed panic to rule. And she'd trusted him to save them.

Warmth and tenderness mingled with a leap of desire and the need to hold her. But she wasn't his. Couldn't be his, especially with Santerre alive. He pounded back twin surges of protectiveness and jealousy. Nothing to be gained by examining that too closely.

She was safe for the time being. In spite of his stupidity in driving a lonely country road with no backup, he'd managed to pull it off. Barely.

But he hadn't managed to convince her that her husband was still alive. That issue was crucial to her safety. And that of others. Santerre being the damn stalker had a hell of a lot of implications. After they traced the tan car, he'd have more evidence.

Half an hour later, he heard a familiar vehicle approaching.

Claire lifted her head, her face ashen inside her black hood. "Have they come back to finish us?"

"It's Cruz," he said. "That government sedan has a distinctive engine ping." He let himself relax a fraction, but his nerves still jangled.

A tow truck sporting the painted logo Reggie's Reck 'n' Rescue followed Cruz. Police sirens whooped in the distance. The more the merrier.

After that, he had no privacy with Claire. The Weymouth cop's extracting the details of the chase and crash occupied them both. After the police photographed and examined the SUV, Reggie hooked his winch onto the rear bumper and towed the vehicle to safety. Clucking his tongue, he pronounced it a goner. The undercarriage was crimped like a paper fan.

Michael retrieved his belongings and stowed them in the sedan. Reggie drove away with what was left of his vehicle. Calling his insurance company would have to wait. Claire was his priority. But as the cops prepared to leave, she slid into a cruiser.

"Claire," he said, "we're ready to take you home. You don't need to go with them."

Her lips spread in a facsimile of a smile. "That's all

right, Quinn. These officers have offered me a ride."

All he could do was stand and watch them drive her away. He'd failed again.

"I can get some guys to watch her house," Cruz offered.

Michael nodded. "Keeping that woman safe is harder than climbing Mount Washington in the winter. She won't cooperate."

Cruz clapped him on the back. "You got both of you out of that carnival ride, didn't you?"

"Olívas clipped us a good one, then zoomed out of sight. Thank God he didn't wait around to see whether we went over or not."

"His employer must question his ability to finish a job." Cruz shook his head and brushed snow from a parka lapel. "Now that you've saved her life, maybe she'll listen to you. Give her a chance to rest and think about it. Then go see her later. I'll even lend you a little of my natural charm."

"It's worth a try. She hasn't accepted my warnings so far."

"Come on, Quinn. Let's get that dig on your forehead patched up. You'll have matching scars front and back."

**\*\*\*\***

That evening when Michael parked the government sedan in Claire's driveway, the only vehicle he saw was Elisha Fogg's ancient truck. In the house, lights illuminated the living room window and one upstairs bedroom, Claire's.

At the memory of their last night together, the familiar flash of desire streaked through him. Claire had needed him. In her distress, she'd wanted his support.

Then later, she'd craved the release of making love with him.

Even after what they had survived together today, he doubted she'd let him through the door. That concern revived the pain centered in his forehead. He raised a hand to the bandage. This time only three stitches.

Fogg emerged from the house. He closed the door and stood in the circle of the porch light. Squinting at the vehicle in the darkened drive, he waved a hand.

*What the hell's he doing here this time of night?* Heart racing, Michael leaped from the sedan and jogged up the walk.

"Evenin', Mr. Quinn," the old man said. "You get a new car? Not good wheels in the snow, I expect."

"No, I, uh, had a slight accident, but—"

"Surprised to see you. Miz Claire said you left." The old man settled a threadbare cap on his grizzled head.

"I, uh, came back. Elisha, what are you doing here?"

"Oh, I come to set up timers on some of the lights, so's the house'd look lived in." He winked at Michael. "For safety's sake, ayuh."

Apprehension prickled up Michael's spine. "Where the hell is Claire?"

"Gone, didn't you know? She packed up and left town late this afternoon."

Chapter Twenty-Six

CLAIRE WOKE THE next morning to a soft, rumbling murmur in her left ear. Opening one eye, she spied her alarm.

"Spooky, you climbed out of your box!" She scooped up the black furball and propped him on her chest.

At the sound of her voice, Alley left her dog bed and jumped up. Claire thought that because of the strange setting, they'd all be happier in the same room. It comforted her to have their companionship and love. Theirs might be the only love permitted her.

A few moments later, she rose and pulled on a bathrobe. She hadn't expected to rest, but after arriving so late at the Caribou Peak cabin, she tumbled into a dreamless sleep immediately upon hitting the mattress.

She'd objected to Paul's buying the cabin, another of his status symbols, but being in its rustic isolation now soothed her jangled nerves. After a stop in the bathroom, she shuffled in her slippers along the balcony that formed a loft above the living and kitchen areas.

She opened the other bedroom door to air out the room, closed since last winter. Odd that the place didn't smell musty. The caretaker must have opened windows occasionally and done some cleaning. As she descended the stairs she made a mental note to check on that.

The animals scampered down with her.

"After that big, formal house, this place is cozy, isn't it, little ones?"

Promising Alley a long walk later, she let the little dog out to the fenced-in run behind the cabin. While the coffee brewed, she prepared both animals' food.

Sipping her coffee, she reflected on the warm ambience of the log walls and the fieldstone fireplace. The sofas and chairs, faithful to the rustic setting, had wooden arms and green plaid upholstery. A smattering of colorful braided rugs completed the decor.

"Perhaps I'll keep this place. Move here after I sell the big house. This suits me better. For now, I think we'll stay a few days to clear our heads." She wrinkled her nose at the attentive faces, waiting for their breakfasts. "*My* head."

Ah, but clearing Michael from her head might take longer than she had. A lifetime. Unlike the old Broadway musical song, she couldn't wash that man out of her hair. Or her heart. If she had one left.

Learning of his deception had ripped her heart from her body, leaving her a hollow, brittle shell. Yesterday she'd had to depend on his skills and quick thinking to save them from certain death on Suicide Curve. Many people would have thought it a fitting end if she died exactly like Jonathan.

She'd begun to buy into Michael's insistence that the curse was only superstition, not reality. *Mon Dieu*, she wanted it not to be real. But did their near-death experience prove she needed to flee far away from him? Again, death menaced him because of her.

In spite of his duplicity and his odd assertions about Paul's being alive, she couldn't stop loving Michael. Too much to endanger him any further. She could face existence alone if it cost no more lives. Curse or not.

She would survive, as she'd survived before. Amazing how many blows a person could absorb and keep going. The fresh air in these mountains and exercise would surely help.

After a breakfast of croissants and jam, she prepared for a cross-country ski. The clock read seven-thirty, barely daylight. Cross-country trails wove like French braids through the woods and fields on both sides of the ski slopes. This early before the ski lifts started and downhill skiers filled the slopes, she could easily cross the downhill slopes to the cross-country trails.

She glanced at her cell phone in its charger, then at the wall phone by the back door. Cell phone coverage was spotty here in the mountains, nearly nonexistent now that a recent storm had disabled the closest cell tower. At least she had the land line. Maybe she should let someone know where she was. Not Michael. Maybe she'd telephone Pratt. Give him a shock. After a ski, she'd decide.

Outside, brilliant sunlight glistening on pristine snowfields greeted her. The heavy snow had continued overnight, leaving the world new and clean, the way she wished she felt. The crisp air brought the fragrances of pine and wood smoke to her nostrils.

She locked the door behind her. Then she collected her skis from the outdoor storage locker.

"I won't be long," she called to her pets. "Be good." A little stiffness remained in her shoulder from slamming against the car door and tumbling onto the pavement, but skiing would work it out. She slipped her headband over her braid, set her ski poles, and glided away.

Not a hundred feet from the cabin towered one of the pylons holding up the chair lift for the Cougar trail and a few others that departed from the same point. Nearing the groomed edge of the Cougar, the site of Alan's death, Claire angled her skis to stop. A shiver of gruesome memory chilled her. Or was it foreboding?

Shaking off the eerie sensation, she set out in the other direction, to the nearer cross-country trails.

****

"Can't you drive any faster?" Michael jerked and twisted in the passenger seat as he peered at the two-lane, tree-lined road ahead.

Cruz slanted him an indulgent look. "No, man, this agency-approved sedan won't take these hilly curves like my sports car."

"Could your wheels handle the snow?"

He shook his head and laughed. "Like a duck on skates, *mano*, but the sedan will get us there in one piece."

Informing their boss about the loss of the company vehicle hadn't loosened his purse strings for a four-wheel-drive vehicle. He couldn't even call Claire. Most of this mountain had no cell-phone service. Worse, he couldn't call the land line on the off chance Santerre was already there. His gut clenched.

He could do nothing but focus on the mission. He coached himself to relax. "Who knows how much of a head start the gang has?"

"They couldn't have found out any sooner than we did that the lady left town. With the old handyman under wraps, they might not figure out where she went."

"I hope you're right. But Santerre would." Michael laid his head against the headrest. "If only it hadn't taken so damn long to switch the team rendezvous to the ski resort. It's a three-hour drive. Nearly nine-thirty now. Shouldn't we be there soon?"

"No sweat. There it is." Cruz pointed ahead. He turned left at an engraved wooden sign that read Caribou Peak, Skiing for Everyone. "We'll reach the cabin in a few minutes."

All the GPS could do was point them onto this road. After this they could only watch for Claire's car. "If we can figure out where the hell it is." Dammit, he should've known that already.

****

At nine-thirty, Claire whooshed onto the hillside near her cabin. A flock of chickadees chattered in a nearby spruce tree. They darted from branch to branch like winter butterflies. Tired but exhilarated, she maneuvered a snow-plow stop to enjoy the view.

Caribou Peak, in truth a ridge of connected peaks, formed a semi-bowl called a cirque. Claire, at its edge, had an excellent vantage point. Brightly clad skiers swished down the slopes, Otter and Moose and Bobcat and Cougar. Except at that moment, no one skied down Cougar.

Snow conditions resembled those of last year. Then, fluffy snows alternating with ice or wet snows had created weak snow layers. Was this slope as dangerous as then? She hadn't stopped at the lodge to check. Until she did she'd avoid Cougar.

Not allowing the steep slope's proximity to intimidate her, she set off in an easy stride toward the cabin. Laughter and snatches of conversation from the chairlift wafted to her on the light breeze. Ski-bound legs dangled with carefree abandon, but their owners held on tightly to the lift when they bumped over the pylon's pulley.

*Thump-thump.*

Claire froze.

Another chair neared the pylon. Its occupants were oblivious to her gaping at them as she strove to maintain her balance and stop. She stared at the pylon and to the cabin and back.

*Thump-thump.*

The background noise on the phone.

Light-headed, Claire gulped in air and blinked away dizziness. No mistaking that sound. At least some of the time, the anonymous caller telephoned from her own cabin. Whoever it was must have a key. Locking her door would be no protection. No security. But if it was a cell phone, they could've been outside.

Either way, how could it be?

*Who* could it be?

Did Quinn—for emotional distance, she forced herself to call him that—ever interview the caretaker here?

Behind her a branch snapped with a loud report. Heart crashing against her ribs, Claire looked around. She let her gaze the snowfield and the scattered trees leading to the wooded trail. Only her tracks and those of small animals marred the snow's virgin surface.

Branches and twigs did crack of their own volition. Especially in cold weather.

The thump-thump's significance frightened her more than anything that had happened. Since the day of

Martine's death, she'd received no more phone calls. Perhaps the stalker had gone away. Given up. She was a crazy woman if she believed that. The truth was that someone had visited the cabin more than once to threaten her, and that person might return.

She couldn't stay at Caribou Peak any longer.

She bent to release her ski-boot catches, but her clumsy fingers kept slipping. *Come on, come on.* There, finally on the third try. Without cleaning off snow and ice, she slammed her gear into the outdoor locker. She fished her key from her zipped parka pocket and jammed it in the door lock. A false turn or two and at last she stumbled into the house.

Alley set up a racket, but she'd be fine outside in the sun for a while longer. She might not get that promised walk.

Spooky pounced at her ankles as she strode to the kitchen. Picking him up, she cuddled him and buried her nose in his soft fur. She would pack the animals and her stuff into the car faster than a squirrel stowing nuts. When she released the kitten, he scampered up the stairs.

First she had to telephone someone. But not Pratt. Not for this.

She had no choice but to call Quinn on the land line. She scrolled through the listings on her smart phone and copied his personal number on a pad of paper. Yanking the wall-phone handset from its cradle, she tapped in the number. While she waited, she straightened the canisters arrayed before her on the counter and fiddled with the pencil and pad of paper.

*Voice mail?* No, no, no, she needed him to answer and *now*. She sighed and drew a deep breath. "Quinn, he's been here and—"

A hand covered her mouth. Another snatched away the phone.

## Chapter Twenty-Seven

"WE'LL HAVE TO approach the cabin through the woods." Michael handed Cruz a pair of snowshoes. Of lightweight plastic with metal cleats on the bottom, they made for easier going through the woods than skis. The men stood beside the car at an empty house downhill from Claire's cabin. "Everything takes so damn long."

"If we hadn't waited, we wouldn't have seen Santerre's truck. He must have followed her here last night after he ditched me," Cruz said.

Michael made a noncommittal grunt. He didn't want to think about Claire with her so-called dead husband. Dammit, he couldn't stop thinking about it. Too many possibilities. If he meant her harm. If he meant to kidnap her.

If she welcomed him. If she kissed him. If she slept with him. He shook his head, dismissing the questions as irrational. That didn't stop the worry.

Failing to detour his brain, he snatched the rifle case from the trunk and opened it. Action would force him into professional mode. With the automatic, detailed care of long practice, he checked over the weapon and its laser scope. Then he loaded the twenty-round magazine.

Cruz loaded his sidearm, the standard nine mil. He nodded toward Michael's high-tech rifle. "I didn't want to mention this before now, buddy, but have you practiced with that on the firing range since last year?"

Michael slung the gun over his shoulder. "I didn't for a while, but I missed it. I'm up to speed. If it comes down to it, it's something I have to do." For himself as much as for Claire.

"Understood. You can count on me." Cruz slammed down the trunk lid. He pulled on a polypropylene stocking cap and lined leather gloves. "Ready?"

Michael too donned cap and gloves. His guts were wound tighter than guitar strings, and sweat beaded his back, even in the twenty-degree temp. Cruz wasn't the only one who had doubts. Could he pull the trigger this time? If necessary, he would. To save Claire. Maybe it wouldn't come to that. Yeah, right. "Check."

Covered in warm layers topped with mottled white camouflage ski pants and hooded jackets, they trekked up the wooded hill.

\*\*\*\*

*Who?*

Heart racketing loudly in her chest, Claire pivoted away from her assailant. When she saw his grinning face, her heart stuttered. The blood drained so quickly from her head, she nearly fainted. Backing against the kitchen counter, she gripped it for support.

*"Paul!"*

"In the flesh, darling." A wide smirk on his thin mouth, he replaced the phone handset. Taller than his father and strongly built, Paul Santerre had aged noticeably during the last five years. White peppered his dark hair, and grooves lined his mouth and eyes. Like her he wore cross-country ski gear, his in dark green.

Rushing noises in Claire's ears prompted her to breathe, and she finally dragged in enough air to clear her head. *Michael, you were right! Why didn't I believe you?*

*Mon Dieu,* what did he want? Did he mean her harm? What should she do? The lack of answers made her dizzy again. But to her first question she knew the answer. This was Paul. Her... husband. She knew him, knew how to handle him. And she'd have to do some fast thinking.

Outside, Alley barked and howled. Unsure how Paul might treat the dog, Claire decided to leave her outside for now. Spooky had fled upstairs. *Please stay there, baby.*

A life in hiding hadn't dimmed the gleam in Paul's keen blue eyes. Eyes that scanned up and down her body.

With an effort, she quelled a shudder. She didn't want him to touch her. Whatever he wanted from her, she had to find a way to notify the DEA or the police. There was much she understood only dimly. Though clarity might be painful, she had to know everything.

"You! It was you—the anonymous phone calls. The threats." She rubbed her eyes as if she could erase the sight of him. "But why...?" At his upraised hands, she let her question trail off.

"Whoa there. Aren't you happy to see me? Why aren't you rushing into your husband's loving arms?" His grin held no humor.

She had to keep secret that the DEA believed Paul to be alive. If he thought himself safe from the authorities, he might be careless. "I mourned you, Paul.

I'm still in mourning."

"I suppose rainbow colors are the newest trend in funereal garb." He gestured at her ski suit.

"This is the only bright color in my wardrobe," she insisted. "I—everyone—thought you were dead. What happened? Where have you been? Why the phone calls?"

"Because you're still my wife, darling. It was the only way to ensure your safety, your faithfulness. Besides, I needed to hear your sweet voice." He held out an arm, curling his fingers slowly in a beckoning motion. "Now, come here and show me how glad you are to see me."

"Since you're not dead, that means you left me, deserted me. Why should I be glad to see you?"

He shrugged. "Leaving couldn't be helped. The DEA and Customs were closing in on me." His gaze browsed her features. "You must know all about that now."

"The DEA questioned me about your smuggling. As much as I appreciate your not involving me in your dirty business, I abhor all the things you've done, including desertion." An understatement. If Quinn and the DEA were correct, he'd committed murder and engaged in drug smuggling and blackmail. Her stomach roiled, and blood thundered in her ears.

Suddenly Alley ceased her barking. At the silence, Paul relaxed visibly.

Claire forced herself erect. No cowering before him, criminal or not.

The kitchen was a small U-shaped extension off the living room. She remained at the counter beside the sink, and Paul maintained his stance beside the door, blocking her exit, with his back to the table and the window behind it.

A shadowy flicker at that window caught her attention.

*Michael!*

Quickly, she swerved her gaze to Paul. Which of them had Michael followed? That didn't matter, but his arrival explained why Alley had stopped barking. Another glance and she saw Michael place a device against the windowpane. A microphone? That sealed what she had to do.

Paul drew himself up to his full six foot three. Still lanky and lean, his demeanor had more of an edge than before. "Everything I did was for you, my dear."

"For me. That's a crock! You had grand ambitions long before you met me."

"For us, then. I did what I had to do. Cozying up to the Farnsworths earned me scholarships and, later, loans to start my business." He unfolded his arms and beckoned to her. "But true confessions can wait, darling. We have to be going."

"Why should I go anywhere with you, Paul?" She had to keep him there, talking, coax him to spill everything. "You deserted me, left me alone."

His eyes darkened, narrowed. "I may have left, but you sure as hell reaped the benefits. And I ensured that Worcester added to the pot with the rest of us before he bit the dust—or the snow, in his case."

"Alan? You?" The noises whirled inside her head with increased force. Like a reverse tornado, the spinning linked the pieces together instead of ripping them apart. She understood what he had done. The agony of it twisted inside her, clawed at her heart. But she couldn't yield yet to regret or rage.

"Of course, me." He folded his arms and threw out his chest, as always when he gloated over a triumph. "I met him in a bar in Boston. I had a beard then, so he wouldn't recognize me from a photograph. He poured out some sob story about how this wonderful widow wouldn't marry him. I convinced him to show his good faith by changing his will. The fool."

"And you're the one who started the avalanche. Who fired the shots. You're the one who killed Alan." The police had found no signs of a break-in when the Beretta came up missing because there'd been no break-in. Paul had used his own keys. They hadn't sunk to the ocean bottom. "But why, Paul?"

"For you, darling, for you. I couldn't have my goddess be a bigamist, now could I?" She'd always considered the narrow line of his mouth determined, but it now seemed nothing but cruel.

Hands fisted at her sides, she longed to pummel him, to scream and rail at him for killing Alan. "No, instead of a bigamist, I became a murder suspect."

"That I didn't intend. Forgive me, my love." He returned to his braggadocio stance. "I planned each death to the last detail, my own disappearance included, so they all appeared accidental."

Her heart fluttered and then hammered. "*All*. Jonathan. You killed Jonathan too." She struggled with memories, but no longer could picture Jonathan's features, recall his smile. But no fury at his cruel murder would restore him. "He was your friend, your best friend."

"As I said before, I did what I had to do." He spoke matter-of-factly, his manner cool, contained. "At first, I couldn't support you. He could. In matters of money, there was no way for me to compete. I needed time."

"You… you stepped aside, retreated from me. I always wondered why." Her gaze swept the kitchen, absorbed the homey normalcy. She still smelled the aroma of her breakfast coffee. So she hadn't tumbled into a nightmare from which she'd soon awaken.

"I allowed him to have you for as long as I could tolerate," Paul said. "Until I convinced him to write that will, and until I arranged my business dealings with my foreign partners."

Everything he said exploded mini-bombshells in her brain. She ached from the blows. "How did you do it, whatever happened on the Cliff Road that night?"

"It was so simple. He wanted to time his car, see how fast it would take the curves. Of course, I put the idea in his head, encouraged him. Then I merely filled his brake lines with baking soda and vinegar. Amazing what you can learn on the Internet."

"Afterward you hurried home so when I telephoned, you pretended to be asleep."

"Clever, don't you think, darling? Clever as a fox. What is it you French say?"

"*Malin comme un singe*, clever as a monkey." Diabolically clever. He'd plotted everything from the start, as the police had insisted *she* had done. They merely chose the wrong master criminal.

"Come to me, Claire." When she retreated, he continued, "The DEA and Customs pushed me until I lost everything I'd worked so hard for. I had to give up everything, but in these past five years I've built up another fortune. We can go away together, live like royalty. The Mediterranean or perhaps the Caribbean."

In one long-legged stride, he approached her and clasped her arm. "We have to go."

"No. I won't go with you. Why should I?"

"Foolish darling." His voice purring at her like that of a jungle cat, he stroked her braid from her shoulder and trailed a finger along her hairline. "Raoul Olívas and his thugs haven't given up yet. They're on their way here now."

Claire wrested her arm from his grip and stumbled to the table. "Why? Why are they after me? The ledger?"

"El Águila doesn't give a damn about the ledger. My records can't touch him." He curled his lip in a contemptuous sneer as he stalked toward her. "No, they're trying to get to me through you. They want me to involve my old man in their operation. That's where I draw the line. Besides, it's time I got out. With you."

She risked a glimpse at the window where she'd seen Quinn. Nothing. Was he still recording? Did he have Cruz with him? Other agents?

Ignoring Paul's demand that she join him, she forged on. "They've attempted to kill me at least three times. The bomb that destroyed the *Rêve*, was that you or the Mexicans?"

He yanked a chair from under the table and sat, pulling her between his knees. His fingers dug painfully into her hips. "You have me to thank for that, intended for your P.I. boyfriend. Except my man got a little carried away with the explosives and the timer." He made a clucking sound with his tongue. "A real shame about the *Rêve*. A great boat. Better than the one I have now. Ah, well."

He stood with her firmly in his grasp. "My skis are

out in the other locker. You'll have to leave everything here. There's no more time."

"But my animals—"

"Think, Claire," he said impatiently, pulling gloves from a pocket. "We're on skis. They remain here."

If she could open the back door, Quinn might have a chance at Paul. "At least allow me to let Alley inside. She'll freeze."

"No." His voice was firm, unwavering. "That damn dog tried to take a chunk out of me once before. It stays outside."

So Alley had done her guard duty, after all. *Good girl, Alley!* "You were the one who snooped around the house."

His smile chilled her. "I had to check on my sweet goddess, didn't I? Had to see if you were still faithful. I saw him kissing you, holding you. Don't think I didn't know. Lucky for that muscle-bound guy you ditched him. A second time I wouldn't have missed."

Squeezing her jaw with his right hand, he pulled her close and lowered his mouth to hers. He ground himself against her with such force she whimpered in pain. He tasted bitter and cold, like his ambition and his life. She willed away tears.

Abruptly, he dropped a gentler kiss on her stinging lips, and then shoved her ahead of him. "Enough delay. Let's go. I don't want to hurt you, but I will if that's what it takes to persuade you to accompany me."

Claire opened her mouth to protest further, but closed it again when she saw what he held in one gloved hand.

The pistol.

The black muzzle of the automatic pointed directly at her.

## Chapter Twenty-Eight

MICHAEL CLICKED OFF the digital recorder and stashed it in his pocket. He edged along the cabin wall away from the window, and then slipped downhill into the woods. From there, he had a clear view of the door.

True to his reputation as the Invisible Man, Cruz was nowhere to be seen. No cell coverage, and no police radios to connect them. But trusting his partner, Michael gave the hand signal indicating that Claire and Santerre were coming out before he crouched in the shrubbery. The snow-draped evergreens provided cover.

If Santerre behaved as expected, he'd take Claire across the ski runs to his pickup at the lodge. Michael and Cruz would follow by an access road beyond the Cougar trail where more DEA agents waited. Surrounded, Santerre would have to give up.

But what if he went another way? What if something had happened to Cruz? What if— Hell, This second-guessing would make him crazy. He was soaked with sweat and ready to chew nails. He had to block his emotions, do his job. The plan would work. It had to. Claire would be safe. He willed his shoulders to relax and his gut to unknot. When the cabin door opened, the knots cramped tighter.

From cover, Michael watched as first Claire and

then Santerre left the cabin. His nostrils picked up the scent of wood smoke from nearby cabins, and his ears the chatter of chickadees. All his senses kicked into hyper, but his nerves scraped sandpaper raw.

Damn, if he could just march out and plow his fist into the slimeball's pretty face.

Claire wore her sexy sunset-colored ski suit. A bright splash that would be easy to trail. Head high and mouth defiantly taut, she fumbled with the ski locker. Delay tactics to give Michael an opening.

*Way to go. Hang in there. Rescue will come.*

He clenched and unclenched his fists. He'd have to wait, as would she.

Donning her skis, Claire glanced around as if searching for rescue.

*Hold on, babe. Don't make the son of a bitch suspicious.*

Smiling like a crocodile at its next meal, Santerre kept a close eye on his captive. He slipped the ski fastenings onto his boots and then motioned to Claire to move out.

"Wait, Paul. Why skis? Why don't we take my car?" Claire's voice was high-pitched with desperation.

"Raoul and his pals, darling. They might spot us driving down the mountain. Going across the slopes is safer. I doubt El Águila's goons know one end of a ski from the other." He snorted a bitter laugh. "Now, get moving."

The two skiers glided across the Cougar run, Claire in front. The lift continued to ferry other more upbeat skiers up the mountain, but no one swished down Cougar to block their way. Santerre seemed oblivious to the watchers in the adjacent woods.

"Quinn."

Cruz stood no more than an arm's length behind him. Exhaling a white-plumed breath, Michael marveled at his partner's stealth, even with the cumbersome complication of snowshoes. He lowered his gun and gestured that they should leave their wooded cover.

Weapons in hand, the two agents ran to the corner of the cabin nearest the slope. Michael peered around, Cruz behind him.

The ski resort's terrain map was imprinted on his brain. Cougar, a double-black-diamond trail, pitched downward at, in some parts, a sheer fifty-degree angle. Trees and boulders lined both sides, and scattered hillocks heightened the challenge. To a downhill skier, it appeared a nearly vertical obstacle course. Even with the eight feet of snow cover, a parachute might come in handy.

Squinting in the sunlight reflecting on the snow, Michael focused on their quarry ahead. Using an uphill-climbing stride, Claire and Santerre trekked across the slope, which was the width of a football field. Claire appeared to be having difficulty with the short push-and-glide technique.

Michael knew her expertise. Another delaying tactic. At her guts, his heart gave an extra thump. He swallowed past the constriction in his throat.

"Wait until they're halfway before we follow," Cruz advised.

Michael jerked a nod. On snowshoes they might have difficulty keeping up. That worry gnawed at him with sharp teeth. Santerre wouldn't get away, couldn't get away. The other agents were waiting to apprehend him. Still, Michael didn't want Claire out of his sight.

When Santerre and Claire neared the crest, he said, "Let's go."

They rushed onto the slope as Paul urged Claire down the other side. Snowshoes crunching into the icy surface, Michael and Cruz strode quickly across.

"Hold it right there." On the crown of the slope, Paul Santerre turned and faced them.

Michael dropped to his belly. He pointed his rifle at Santerre's chest. Damn, even though they'd waited, the bastard heard them and turned around.

At the same time, Cruz hit the snow and, kicking off his snowshoes, rolled away to the side into a similar position. He cocked and aimed his nine-millimeter.

With a tight grip on Claire's upper arm, Santerre pulled her to his left side. She fought to escape, but he maneuvered them both sideways.

Michael's heart plummeted. The slime placed Claire between them. He would sacrifice her to save himself. Michael watched him through his scope. Saw the fever in his cold blue eyes, the desperation. Was the son of a bitch greedy and obsessive, or was he crazy? How far would he go?

Michael would take no chances with Claire's life.

"Federal agents, Santerre," he called out. "You can't get away. Let the woman go, and you won't get hurt."

"How gullible do you think I am?" Santerre spread his lips in a cold smile. "Quite the opposite. If I keep my beautiful wife with me, I won't get hurt. Now drop your guns and get out of here."

"Don't do it, Michael," Claire shouted. "He has a pistol."

Michael hadn't seen it earlier, but no surprise. The pistol was how Santerre forced Claire to accompany him. The gun created little danger for the agents. But to Claire…

"So the P.I. lover is really DEA," Santerre said. "How convenient. She's mine, and don't forget it." From an inside parka pocket, he withdrew the pistol. The missing Beretta. He pointed it at the snowy ground.

Maintaining his position and his aim, Michael said, "You might as well give up, Santerre. Federal agents are waiting wherever you turn on this mountain. Take the weapon slowly by the barrel and toss it away. Don't make your situation any worse. Let the woman come to me."

"Never." He yanked her closer and planted a smacking kiss on her temple. Claire winced and closed her eyes. "She remembers my warning on the phone. Perhaps she told you. You can't have her."

As he'd suspected, Santerre had been the phone stalker. One more nail in his coffin.

Michael forged the burning fury in his chest into the necessary cool calm. He would do what he was trained to do. He raised the gun barrel and squinted into the scope. The crosshairs hovered over Santerre's heart.

*Come on, Claire, move! Six inches to the right, and I'll have him.*

Even though she didn't love the guy, she might hate the one who killed him. To save her, it was a chance he'd take. He would take down the freaking bastard. No qualms. No hesitation. No nerves. And this time he wouldn't miss. Sweat slid like teardrops down his cheeks.

"Quinn, you can't shoot," Cruz said in an urgent

tone. "This is the trail listed as high-avalanche risk at the lodge. The Cougar trail."

"Hah, avalanche danger!" Ski pole swinging wildly, Santerre waved the pistol like a flag. "Freaking fitting!"

Michael choked at his forced impotence. Not knowing what else to do, he lowered his rifle barrel and snicked on the safety. He didn't dare shoot, but he didn't trust that damn son of a bitch not to.

Santerre tucked away the pistol and released Claire. He lifted his right ski and angled it out in the first move of a step turn. "Come, my goddess, these gentlemen won't stop us."

When he lifted his left ski to complete the turn, Claire kicked out her right ski.

In the tangle that ensued, Santerre lost control. Waving his poles like conductor's batons, he staggered and then pitched heavily onto his side. "No!"

Heart thumping, Michael gaped with admiration as Claire regained control of her skis. Wasting no time, she kick-turned to the left and pushed off toward him in a powerful start worthy of an Olympic medalist.

"Hurry, Claire!" he yelled, getting to his feet. He started toward her.

She swished across the snowfield in long, fluid strides. "Michael, get down! The... pistol!"

He plowed on toward her, his snowshoe-clad feet seemingly mired in quicksand, slogging in slow motion. Maybe two targets would confuse the bastard.

She neared a point halfway from the crest, about twenty-five yards, planting her poles and gliding strongly.

Santerre clambered to his knees. He drew out the

9mm and clicked off the safety.

Michael stared helplessly. "You crazy son of a bitch, you can't shoot her. She's your wife. You love her. Avalanche, remember?"

"You fool, you think I used this puny weapon? To start an avalanche, you have to fire heavy rounds directly into the snow." In a two-handed grip, he raised the pistol at his fleeing wife's back.

Safety off, Michael aimed the pistol at Santerre.

Claire skied straight into his line of fire.

"Claire! Get down! Now!"

With a single negative head shake, she pushed on.

Santerre pulled the trigger. The weapon emitted a pop, like a branch snapping from the cold.

Claire recoiled, her arms flopping like a marionette's. She swayed on her skis, but remained erect. She dropped one pole.

On his feet, Santerre snarled a curse. He raised the gun again, aiming it toward his wife.

Michael fired the rifle. The sharp report echoed from tree line to tree line. Without needing to check the outcome, he dropped the weapon and bolted toward Claire.

She lay crumpled in a heap. A crimson streak stained the right shoulder of her bright ski suit.

He revved to a sprint, but the snowshoes slowed it to a waddle. "Claire, I'm coming!"

Right arm dangling uselessly, Claire struggled to her knees. Blood dripped from her finger onto the pristine snow. She leaned heavily on a ski pole. "I can… make it."

Clutching his belly, Santerre pushed off shakily to continue his escape. Ten yards farther, he toppled to the snow. He lay motionless.

"Forget him," Cruz yelled. "Our guys will get him later."

At last, Michael reached her. He looked in horror at Claire's shoulder, where the bloodstain blossomed across the bright fabric. So much blood. Fingers shaking, he fumbled with the parka zipper. How bad was the wound? Finally he got the jacket open. The shot appeared to have gone cleanly through the fleshy part. His heart still raced, but he suppressed the paralyzing fear. It could be worse. Much worse.

He slid one arm around her to support her lolling head. "Take it easy. We'll get you out of here pronto."

"M-Michael, did... you hear... in the cabin?" she murmured, slipping into unconsciousness.

"Hush, babe. Yes, I have him on tape. It's over now. You're safe. You'll be all right." He dragged the scarf from his neck and tied it over the wound. They'd get her to a hospital right away. He had to get her off the mountain before she went into shock.

As for himself, his jinx was broken. He made the crucial shot.

She'd be all right, but would he? He'd fulfilled his mission to flush out the damn drug-dealing swine only to find he'd fallen in love with a courageous widow who wasn't a widow after all. Until now. And how would she feel about that? About him? He still had to explain himself. Would she listen?

A barrage of gunfire exploded above on the mountain. Assault rifles. The DEA team? Olívas and his men?

When the echoes died away, an eerie silence blanketed the mountain.

Icy dread clogged Michael's throat. He unsnapped Claire's skis from her boots and lifted her limp form into his arms.

Uphill a deep rumble shook the mountain, an angry, awakening giant hungry for human flesh.

"Get the hell out of there, Quinn." Rifle on his shoulder, Cruz waved from the slope's wooded edge, twenty yards away. "Avalanche!"

Fate had forced him to fire a gun again to save her, and by heaven, Michael would beat this damn snow monster too.

With every ounce of strength, he powered toward the trees. Above him, a thundering alabaster cloud roared toward them. Surrounded by a chalk-white curtain, ice-and-snow boulders as hard as granite charged downward.

He hit the edge and raced into the heavy tree cover with Claire cradled in his arms.

Behind them, the fifty-foot wall of snow and ice crashed down the steep slope.

Chapter Twenty-Nine

Claire stood in her office and contemplated the contract from the auction company. When the house was sold, she would sell the rest of Paul's ostentatious trinkets. The profits would go into a charity fund she would establish. Living in the mountain cabin, she'd need only her personal belongings, her animals, the computer, and her research materials.

She twisted to drop the contract on her desk. At the movement, sharp pain shot through her injured shoulder. A week since she'd been shot, she was still weak from trauma and loss of blood. She adjusted her sling and sank onto her desk chair. No pain pills for her though.

For a minute, she concentrated on the shoulder pain, analyzed it, savored it. The physical discomfort held at bay the more wrenching emotional agony and sense of loss.

She hadn't seen Michael since he rescued her on the mountain. The other agents who came to question her would say only that he was busy. It was over. He'd moved on with his life, and so would she. Her empty future loomed bleaker than before. Only one small glimmer for the future kept her going. Exhaling slowly, she pressed her left hand to her abdomen.

The doorbell jarred her from her reverie. Fatigued to the bone, she forced herself to slog to the hallway.

From the kitchen, Alley and Spooky dashed to greet the visitor. Alley uttered happy yips, not her usual warning barks.

She peered through the sidelight. *Michael.* She flung wide the door.

Square-shouldered and square-jawed, he stood granite still, filling the doorway. A new red scar, from their Cliff Road misadventure, marred his broad forehead. His eyes surveyed her painstakingly from head to toe.

Her heart thrummed under his heated gaze. Chin up, she struggled not to glance down at herself to see if she'd spilled soup on herself or left open a zipper. "What are you doing here?"

"Out of mourning at last, I see. Now that he's truly dead. I like the dark red pants." Without invitation, he strolled inside.

She closed the door behind him. "Is that why you've come? To assure me he's dead?"

"Partly." He removed his parka and draped it on the hall tree. In his black pants and gray pullover he looked dangerous and very, very sexy. "A crew reached the body yesterday. He's dead, all right."

A sigh escaped her lips. "I'll admit it's a relief. I imagined he would return to torment me again."

He knelt, responding to the insistent yipping and mewing at his feet. Alley wriggled ecstatically at his gentle ministrations, and Spooky rubbed against his ankle. Michael hoisted the kitten in one hand and stood. "I'll explain the rest, if you like."

Why not? What harm could it do to listen? She'd learned only bits and pieces of the story from the agents who questioned her. "Let's go to the kitchen. If you want coffee, you'll have to make it." She hitched up her bandaged arm and winced at the movement.

He nodded, his gray eyes lambent with sympathy. "That looks damn tender. You relax. I think I know my way around this kitchen by now. But it's been a long day. I'd prefer a beer, if you have any." He deposited the purring kitten on the floor.

Spooky frolicked away to pounce on a feather toy in the corner. With a contented sigh, Alley collapsed on her bed.

Claire cradled her right arm with her left. "Help yourself. I think I have one or two." The beers were ones he'd left. She couldn't bring herself to discard them. She lowered herself gingerly onto a wooden chair at the small table.

Once he'd twisted off the bottle cap, he said casually, "Join me? Should I open a bottle of wine?" He tugged out the chair to her right and sat.

She shook her head. "I'm still on painkillers and antibiotics. I'll pass." Besides, if she had any alcohol, she might slide onto the floor like a leaking balloon.

"I've listened over and over to the recording of your conversation with Santerre in the cabin. He was shrewd and obsessed from the beginning. He plotted everything, including his boyhood friendship with Jonathan Farnsworth."

"He must have been what psychologists call a sociopath," she said.

"Totally amoral and self-absorbed, but clever and charming."

"When it suited him."

"There was one more thing on the recording that might offset his crimes a fraction. The reason the gang

261

went after you. He refused to involve his father in the smuggling operation."

She put on a shaky smile. That Michael searched for some redeeming feature in Paul in order to ease her pain stung her eyes with tears. "I told Russ about that. I thought it might help him cope with the new burden of his son being a murderer."

"You talked to him? When?"

"He came to see me in the hospital. Actually apologized for the way he'd treated me."

"Any overtures from Farnsworth?"

"Sort of. He allowed Robert to telephone me. Eventually Newcomb will relent." She adjusted her position. Every movement seemed to aggravate her shoulder. "Please tell me what happened after the ambulance took me away."

"We managed to capture two of the Mexicans. Just henchmen, not Raoul Olívas. The shots that started the avalanche came from them. They rented snowmobiles and beat our DEA team up the access road so they could ambush Santerre."

"Ambush Paul? They weren't after me anymore?"

"Apparently the drug lord, El Águila, found out Santerre was skimming profits and decided he was a liability. If you hadn't swung your ski around and Santerre had dragged you along much farther, they'd have killed you both."

A shudder rippled through Claire. "What will happen now?"

"They'll be tried, but they'll get off easy. Those two gorillas are singing like South American quetzals. Among other things, they gave us the name of the guy that stepped in for some of the smuggling after Santerre so conveniently *died*."

He set his beer bottle on the table and grasped her hand, folded his big one around it. "I wanted to come see you at the hospital, but the DEA sent Cruz and me after the other smuggler."

"Did you get him?" His warmth seeped into her cold hand and threaded spirals of heat down her spine. She forced herself to listen to his words, not just revel in the sound of his deep voice.

"No. The guy split. Cruz is still on the case, but I'm out. My resignation came through."

"Congratulations." Before she lost courage, before she weakened and professed her love, she had to do something she'd neglected. "Michael, I know you couldn't tell me you were a DEA agent. You were caught between two loyalties. I was hurt at first, but now I understand. I'm sorry that I overreacted."

When he opened his mouth to reply, she stopped him with a shake of her head. "Let me finish, please. I need to say this. You were so full of doubt that you could protect me, but you saved my life more than once."

"You were so brave, foolishly brave to escape from him the way you did. Having the chance to pull you out of the way of that mountain of snow saved me as much as you. Made me feel worthy again." Lifting her hand to his lips, he gently kissed the palm. "I'll understand if you hate me for shooting Paul. In spite of everything, he was your husband."

That he'd even think that had her shaking her head. "No. Paul was never my husband. Not really. He killed Jonathan, remember. And the avalanche would have buried him, anyway. I could never hate you, Michael. I owe you for saving me. In more ways than one." She stopped there before she said too much.

Releasing her, he slid his chair closer to hers and draped his left arm on her chair back, a move that effectively caged her. His gray eyes, as soft as a summer cloud, caressed her face. "Claire, I don't want your thanks. I want you."

Dragging her eyes from his heated gaze, she licked her dry lips. It would be the hardest thing she ever had to do, but she must turn him away. She forced a nonchalant tone and a cool expression. "Michael, it's over. We had a nice fling, but it's time to move on."

He flinched, his jaw clenching. As if searching for dissemblance, his gunmetal gaze drilled into her. "A fling. What the hell? You're saying that what we had together meant nothing to you?"

Managing to scoot her chair back, Claire pushed to her feet and stepped away. If she remained close to him, he'd perceive her true emotions because she'd fall apart. Fatigue and anguish weighed her down, threatened to smother her like the avalanche they'd escaped.

"Of course it means something, just not what you want it to." Every word, every lie sliced away a chunk of her heart. Edging to the oven, she straightened the salt and pepper on its back shelf. Then she reached toward the spice rack, pulled back her hand when she saw how much it shook. She smiled. "You were wonderful. You helped me through a very difficult time. And you showed me that sex didn't have to be passive and boring but could be transcendent and glorious."

"But?"

She chanced a glimpse at his fierce brow and tight mouth. She'd hurt him more than she'd expected. Shaken again, she turned to her spice rack. What else could she say? There was something else she ought to tell him, but not now. Not yet. "It's... over. I think you should go."

Puzzled and pain stabbing his chest like razor wire, Michael stared at Claire's hunched shoulders. He knew she loved him. The way she moaned his name when they made love. The little touches and caresses at other times. The desperation not to put him in jeopardy when Santerre drew his pistol. Her concern about his estrangement from his family. Her fear for him that sent her searching for him before the boat exploded. So many little things together meant love.

He studied her stiff posture, her trembling shoulders. Rebuffing him was tormenting her. That business of realigning the little bottles was a dead giveaway.

No reason to reject him now. She was a widow after all. No threats from anonymous callers or dead husbands or drug gangs. No charges hanging over her head. Free. Except for... the curse. That damn curse.

In two strides, he stood close behind her. Close enough to inhale her scent and see the rainbow in her mahogany hair—brown, russet, gold, black—as sensual as that wood itself. As beautiful as the woman herself.

"Claire, I love you, more than I ever thought it possible to love anyone. And I think you love me. You can't get rid of me this easy." Tenderly, he placed one hand on her uninjured shoulder and turned her to face him. "Paul was behind all the deaths. Don't tell me you still believe in the curse."

Her eyes grew as wide and round as a frightened doe's and as dark as bittersweet chocolate. "I want to believe all of that was Paul and only Paul. After all this, I do have doubts the curse is real, but how can I take the chance? *With your life,* Michael? Paul's culpability solves nothing. He's dead too. Tears glistened in her eyes. "I've always believed the curse to be real. To be true. It's difficult…"

He gathered her loosely in his arms, taking care with her injury. She was so brave, so strong, but no one should have to bear such a burden alone. "Santerre bragged he plotted his ambitious future long before he met you. You were only one means to an end. His obsession extended way beyond possessing a lady for a wife, a goddess as he said. You don't have to atone, to be perfect with a perfect house or good deeds."

Her chin shot up. "That's not why I—"

He silenced her with his lips and tongue. His caress tender and coaxing, he drank in her delicate taste, the softness and heat he'd longed for. At first she stiffened, and then with a sigh, she leaned into the kiss to return his passion with the same sharp-edged need. Blood thundering in his veins, he hardened to a painful ache. Beyond lust, he poured his love and his soul into her with his tender kisses.

"Claire, I need you. I love you. I want to go to bed every night and wake up every day with you next to me."

With her free hand, she touched his cheek, his lips.

He placed a whisper of a kiss on her forehead. Grief had blinded him, but Claire's insight helped him begin to deal with his past. In the midst of her own crises, she had a big enough heart to care about his problems. He'd fought against caring, against the possibility of more grief, but she didn't allow him his isolation. Her passion for life, her gentleness and courage led him to love her. Now he had to help her apply that insight to herself.

"I believe what you taught me. We're not responsible for what other people do. That truth freed me. Let it free you. Amy's death was not my fault. Her recklessness and the actions of her killers own the blame. The death of little Kathy sits squarely on the shoulders of her captor. And, like you said, my boss should never have allowed me to be the shooter that day."

Fear shadowed her gaze, but behind the fear a glimmer of hope. The glimmer disappeared behind a veil of tears. " 'We're not responsible for what other people do.' Oh, I want to believe that and let go of the old fear. *Je t'adore*, I do love you, so much. Don't you see? That's why I'm so afraid still."

He guided her back to a chair and positioned her on his lap, her left arm around his neck. "There is no curse. There never was. Santerre's greed was the cause. Not a curse. Not your beauty. Not this face I love. That's the real, tangible truth."

"I want to believe you. I do." She kissed him.

"Marry me and leave Weymouth. We'll make a new life together. You have to trust me. I'll keep us both safe."

Her tortured gaze showed the war raging in her head and in her heart. She loved him, he knew it, but to be with him she had to let go of a lifelong mistaken belief. With his own steady gaze, he willed her the strength to choose freedom. And him.

His heart seemed to stop, and he held his breath until he saw her expression soften. Her shoulders straightened with the lifting of her burden. And her brilliant smile started his heart with such force it nearly leaped from his chest.

"Yes, Michael. I do trust you. If you can let go of your misplaced guilt, I can banish mine along with the curse that's hung over me since childhood. I love you. I never thought I'd ever say that. Wherever you want to go, it doesn't matter as long as I'm with you."

"How about New Hampshire, the White Mountains? I drove here today from buying the camp where I went as a kid on those wilderness survival hikes."

"I see I won't have to worry about what to do with Paul's ill-gotten gains. It sounds wonderful." Her gaze clouded with concern. "What about your family?"

"I was in Boston yesterday. Mom would love to give us a wedding. They want some more grandkids." At her enigmatic expression, he paused and recalled an earlier conversation about her difficulty in getting pregnant before. No, it would be all right. With love, they would cope.

"About children, Michael—"

He brushed a curl off her shoulder as if sweeping away the problem. "If you can't get pregnant, if we can't have children, we can adopt or we can help someone else's kids learn to rely on themselves."

A gleam brightened her gaze, and a slow smile curved her mouth. She took his hand and pressed his palm to her belly. "Um, that problem I had with not getting pregnant, it doesn't seem to be a problem anymore. I think we should get married right away."

## A word about the author...

Occasional bouts of insomnia led to Susan Vaughan's writing career. When she couldn't sleep, she made up stories to fill the long, dark nights. Her favorite books have always been mysteries and romances, so the mix in romantic suspense was a natural. Her stories throw the hero and heroine together under extraordinary circumstances and pit them against a clever villain. Besides curling up with a good book, Susan enjoys walking her dog, boating, traveling, and gardening. A former teacher, she is a West Virginia native, but she and her husband have lived in Maine for many years. Find her at www.susanvaughan.com or on Facebook at www.facebook.com/SusanVaughanBooks or on Twitter @SHVaughan.

Thank you for purchasing
this publication of The Wild Rose Press, Inc.

For questions or more information
contact us at
info@thewildrosepress.com.

The Wild Rose Press, Inc.
www.thewildrosepress.com

www.ingramcontent.com/pod-product-compliance
Lightning Source LLC
Chambersburg PA
CBHW051539260626
47170CB00003B/1011